EX LIBRIS

VINTAGE CLASSICS

SO DISDAINED

Nevil Shute Norway was born on 17 January 1899 in Ealing, London. After attending the Dragon School and Shrewsbury School, he studied Engineering Science at Balliol College, Oxford. He worked as an aeronautical engineer and published his first novel, *Marazan*, in 1926. In 1931 he married Frances Mary Heaton and they went on to have two daughters. During the Second World War he joined the Royal Navy Volunteer Reserve where he worked on developing secret weapons. After the war he continued to write and settled in Australia where he lived until his death on 12 January 1960. His most celebrated novels include *Pied Piper* (1942), *No Highway* (1948), *A Town Like Alice* (1950) and *On the Beach* (1957).

OTHER WORKS BY NEVIL SHUTE

Novels

Marazan

Lonely Road

Ruined City

What Happened to the Corbetts

An Old Captivity

Landfall

Pied Piper

Pastoral

Most Secret

The Chequer Board

No Highway

A Town Like Alice

Round the Bend

The Far Country

In the Wet

Requiem for a Wren

Beyond the Black Stump

On the Beach

The Rainbow and the Rose

Trustee from the Toolroom

Stephen Morris and *Pilotage*

Autobiography

Slide Rule

NEVIL SHUTE

So Disdained

VINTAGE BOOKS
London

Published by Vintage 2009

Copyright © The Trustees of the Estate of Nevil Shute Norway

Nevil Shute has asserted his right under the Copyright, Designs
and Patents Act 1988 to be identified as the author of this work

First published by Cassell & Co in 1928
This edition first published by William Heinemann in 1951

Vintage
Random House, 20 Vauxhall Bridge Road,
London SW1V 2SA

www.vintage-classics.info

Addresses for companies within The Random House Group Limited
can be found at: www.randomhouse.co.uk/offices.htm

The Random House Group Limited Reg. No. 954009

A CIP catalogue record for this book
is available from the British Library

ISBN 9780099530183

The Random House Group Limited supports The Forest
Stewardship Council (FSC), the leading international forest
certification organisation. All our titles that are printed on
Greenpeace approved FSC certified paper carry the FSC logo.
Our paper procurement policy can be found at:
www.rbooks.co.uk/environment

Mixed Sources
Product group from well-managed
forests and other controlled sources
www.fsc.org Cert no. TT-COC-2139
© 1996 Forest Stewardship Council
FSC

Printed and bound in Great Britain by

AUTHOR'S NOTE

THIS WAS THE SECOND of my books to be published, twenty-three years ago. It took me nearly three years to write, because I was working as an engineer on the construction of an airship and I wrote only in the evenings in the intervals of more important technical work. It was written through from start to finish twice, and some of it three times.

Clearly, I was still obsessed with standard subjects as a source of drama—spying, detection, and murder, so seldom encountered by real people in real life. Perhaps I was beginning to break loose from these constraints: the reader must judge that for himself.

In revising the book for re-issue I have altered half a dozen outmoded pieces of slang, but I have made no other changes. The book achieved publication in the United States under the somewhat uninspiring title *The Mysterious Aviator*.

NEVIL SHUTE

1951

PREFACE

THE GREATER PART of this book is based upon my written state-ment to the Foreign Secretary, dated April 6th, 1927. Reference has also been made to the official notes of my evidence before the Italian Secret Police given through the British Vice-Consul at San Remo on March 26th, 1927, and to the deposition sworn before the Italian civil authorities by Captain Philip Stenning, D.S.O., M.C., upon the same day. I am indebted to the Foreign Office for permission to re-draft the less confidential portions of these documents, and to Lord Arner for permission to detail certain personal events without which this account would hardly be complete.

These are the dry bones of my story, and it may well be urged that the time has not yet come when they can be brought to life unbiased. But memory is short; in this book—and before my recollections have grown dim—with the great assistance of my wife, I have tried to set down something of the history of that great pilot and most involuntary adventurer who came to me in the night, stayed with me for five days, and went.

PETER L. MORAN

THE OLD HALL
UNDER
SUSSEX

And then none shall be unto them so odious and disdained as the traitours . . . who have solde their countrie to a straunger and forsaken their faith and obedience contrarie to nature or religion; and contrarie to that humane and generall honour not onely of Christians but of heathen and irreligious nations, who have always sustained what labour soever and embraced even death itself for their countrie, prince, and commonwealth.

—Sir Walter Raleigh

CHAPTER ONE

As I HAVE SAID, this matter started in the night. I was agent to Lord Arner at that time; steward and agent, for most of the family affairs passed through my hands, and I ran the outdoor business of the house itself. I lived by myself in the Steward's House at Under Hall, about a couple of miles from the little town of Under, in West Sussex. I live there still.

Very late, on the night of which I am writing, I was driving home over the South Downs, after a dinner in Winchester. I forget for the moment what that dinner was about; I do not think it can have been connected with my old school; because I was driving home in a very bad temper, and so I think it must have been the Corn Association. They tell me that I am reactionary. Very likely they are right, but they should give a man a better dinner than that before they tell him so.

In any case, all that is beside the point. I started home to drive the forty odd miles from Winchester to Under at about half-past eleven that night. It was March; a fine night with a pack of loose cloud in front of the moon that gradually turned to rain. I was in a dinner-jacket, but the hood of my old Morris is pretty watertight. I could take the rain phlegmatically, and so I set the wiper going, jammed my foot down a bit harder, and wished I was in bed with a fire in my bedroom instead of bucketing along at forty miles an hour over the black country roads.

Now, on that run from Winchester to Under, you pass over give-and-take sort of country for most of the way, but about ten miles from Under the road gets up on to the high ground by Leventer, and runs along the top for a couple of miles. That two miles runs with a fairly good surface straight over the unfenced down. You can let a car out there in the daytime, but at night you have to be careful, because of the cattle.

It was about half-past twelve when I came swinging up over that bit of down that night, doing about forty and keeping a sharp look-out for sheep. The night was as black as the pit. By that time the rain was coming down pretty hard. There was no traffic on the road at that time of night; I sat there sucking my dead pipe and thinking no evil, watched the rain beat against the windscreen, watching the wiper flick it off again, and thanked my lucky stars that I wasn't out in it.

About half-way along that stretch of down I passed a man on the road.

He was walking along in the direction of Under. I didn't see very much of him as I passed, because the rain blurred the windscreen except just where the wiper caught it, and I was going at a fair pace. He seemed to be a tallish well-set-up fellow in a leather coat, but without a hat. The water was fairly streaming and glistening off him in my headlights. I drove past. Then it struck me that it was a pretty rotten trick to drive by and leave a man out on the road in a night like that. I jammed both feet hard down, and we stopped with a squeal about twenty yards beyond him.

I stuck my pipe in my pocket, switched on the dashboard light, leaned over, and opened the door.

"Want a lift into Under?" I called.

On a night like that I should have expected to hear his footsteps squelching along at the side of the road. When I didn't, I turned and looked out of the little window at the back. He seemed to have stopped dead. I fancied that I could see him dimly in the rain, standing by the side of the road in the red light of my tail lamp.

The rain came beating steadily against the car, with little patterings. To put it frankly, I thought it was our local idiot. In a job like mine one gets to know the look of those chaps and the way they wander about the country in the worst weather, often with no hat on. We have a good few naturals about my part of the world, and they don't come to much harm. Their people seem to like to have them about the place, and they're good with animals.

2

In any case, it was a rotten night for an idiot to be out. It didn't much matter to me what time I got to bed now, and I had a fancy to collect this chap and see him safely home. His people live at a farm about five miles off that road, more or less on the way to Under.

I thought that he was frightened at the sudden stopping of the car, and so I slid along the seat and stuck my head out of the door to reassure him.

"All right, Ben," I said. They call him Ben. "I'm Mr. Moran from Under Hall. I'll take you back home in the car if you'll come with me. It's a rotten wet night for walking. That's right. Stay where you are, and I'll bring the car back to you. Then you can come in out of the wet."

I slipped the gear into reverse and ran the car back along the road to him. He was still standing motionless by the grass; I could see him in the gleam of the tail lamp through the little window. I stopped the car when he was opposite the door.

"Come on in," I said. "It's all wet out there. You know me —Mr. Moran."

He moved at last, and stooped towards the door. "It's very good of you," he said. "It's not much of a night for walking."

I knew he wasn't an idiot as soon as I heard his voice, of course. And while I was wondering why he had held back from accepting a lift upon a night like that, he stuck his head in under the hood and followed it with his body.

He settled himself into his seat and turned to face me. "I'm going as far as Under," he said quietly. "If you could put me down at the station I'd be very grateful."

He had a lean, tanned face, which he was wiping with a khaki handkerchief; his hair was straight and black, and fell down wetly over his forehead towards his eyes. In the road the rain dripped monotonously from the car in little liquid notes that mingled with the purring of the engine. I stared at him for a minute. He returned my stare unmoved.

"My name is Moran," I said at last. "Aren't you Maurice Lenden? We met in the Flying Corps. In Ninety-two Squadron, in 1917. About June or July. I remember you quite

3

well now." I paused, and eyed him curiously. "It's funny how one runs across people."

He avoided my eyes. "You must be mixing me up with someone else," he said uncertainly. "My name is James."

From the way he spoke I knew that he was lying. But apart from that, I never forget a face. If I wasn't pretty good that way I shouldn't have been agent to Lord Arner. I knew as certainly as I was sitting there that he was Lenden. I remembered that I had met him since the war at a reunion dinner—in 1922 or '23. I remembered that somebody had told me that he was still flying, as a civilian aeroplane pilot. And there was something else that I had heard about him in gossip with some old Flying Corps men in Town, quite recently—divorce, or something of the sort. At the moment I couldn't bring that to mind.

I wrinkled my brows and glanced at him again, and for the first time I noticed his clothes. It was probably the clothes which brought him to my mind so readily at first. Damn it, the man was dressed for flying. He had no hat, but he wore a long, heavy leather coat with pockets at the knee. There was a map sticking out of one of these, all sodden with the rain. He had altered very little; in those clothes he might have come walking into the Mess, in 1917, when I used to play that game myself. Below the coat he was wearing sheepskin thigh-boots reaching high above the knee, with the fur inside.

I was so positive that I smiled. "James or Lenden," I said, "I'm damn glad to see you again. Been flying?"

I suppose I was a bit riled at his refusal to know me. I was watching him as I spoke, and I saw his lips tighten irritably. But all he said was:

"I should be very grateful for a lift into Under, if you're going that way."

The rain streamed down into the headlights, and the wiper flicked uneasily upon the windscreen. "You won't get a train from Under tonight," I said, "and you'll have your work cut out to wake them at the pub. It's a rotten hole. If you're Lenden, you'd better come along back with me. There's a

4

spare room in my place that you can have. Dare say I can fix you up with a pair of pyjamas, too."

He was about to say something, but hesitated. And then: "It's very good of you," he muttered. "But I'd rather go on."

I sat there staring at him in perplexity. He was hugging a little square, black case in the crook of his arm, but at the moment it didn't strike me what that was. I couldn't understand why he had given me a false name. And then it struck me that he'd made a damn poor show of it if he wanted to get away unnoticed, and that I could have done it very much better myself. But that was in keeping with the man as I remembered him. He was a simple soul, and quite incapable of any sustained deception.

"Look here," I said at last. "Purely as a matter of general interest—where have you come from? You've been flying, haven't you? I see you're in flying kit."

He didn't answer for a minute, but then: "I had a forced landing," he said.

"Here?"

He jerked his head towards the down. "Just over there."

I wrinkled my brows. "How long ago?"

"About an hour. Hour and a half perhaps. Just before the rain came."

I leaned forward on the wheel and stared at him. I couldn't make out for the moment whether to believe a word of what he said. There was something wrong about him, and I didn't know what it was. He wasn't drunk. I thought it might be drugs. He didn't sound natural. His talk about a forced landing seemed to me to be all nonsense. I've been a pilot myself, and I know. When one is in sole charge of a machine worth several thousand pounds, and one has just put it down very suddenly and unexpectedly and hard—one doesn't just go off and leave it. Especially on a night like that.

The rain drummed steadily upon the fabric of the hood.

"You are Lenden, aren't you?" I inquired.

He laughed shortly, and a little self-consciously. "Yes, I'm Lenden," he said. "Just my infernal luck, running up against

5

a man like you. I've been a regular Jonah lately." And he laughed again.

"Thanks," I said dryly.

He stirred uneasily in his seat. "Let's get on," he muttered.

"Right you are," I said, and slipped in the gear. I didn't want to go ferreting about in his affairs if he wanted to keep them to himself. "You weren't speaking the truth, by any chance, when you said you'd had a forced landing?"

That stung him up a bit.

"You'll know in the morning, I suppose," he replied. "They'll find the machine."

I slipped it out again. "Damn it," I said. "Do you mean you've got an aeroplane out there?"

He nodded.

"Did you crash her?"

"No, she's all right, but for the oil pressure. It was that that brought me down."

I could make nothing of his way of treating the affair.

"What have you done with her?" I asked. "There's a barn about half a mile down the hill over there. Did you get her under the lee of that?"

He looked embarrassed. "I just left her where she was."

I gazed at him blankly, hardly able to believe my ears. It was the sort of thing a novice might have said—not a pilot of his experience. After all, one expects a man to do his best for the machine.

"Do you mean she isn't pegged down, or anything?"

He shook his head. "I just left her."

I leaned forward and switched off the engine of the car. "But damn it all," I said, "she'll blow away!"

He didn't stir.

"Let her," he said.

I knew then that it must be drugs.

"We can't do that," I said irritably. "She'll be blowing about all over the country, on a night like this." It riled me that I should have to get out of the car into the rain in my dinner-jacket to go and tie up this man's aeroplane, but there seemed

6

to be nothing for it. I reached out and took an electric torch from the dashboard pocket, and nudged him.

"Come on," I said. "Get out. We're going to peg her down. Get on with it."

He didn't move. I paused for a moment.

He seemed to make something of an effort. "Look here, Moran," he said. "Let's get going to Under. That machine's all right where she is."

"Leaving her loose?" I asked.

He nodded. "That's right. Leave her loose. Look here, I don't want to bother about her. Just take me along to Under and drop me at the station."

Well, drugs are the devil.

"Can't do that, old boy," I said cheerfully. "She's on our land—Lord Arner's land. It might cost us a couple of pounds if she blew through a hedge, leaving her loose like that. More, perhaps."

I shoved him towards the door. "Come on. Let's go and have a look at her."

He shrugged his shoulders. "If you like."

I had a couple of garden forks and a hank of cord in the back of the car, as luck would have it, that I'd got in Winchester for the house. There was a strap in the dickey, too. I took the lot out, wrapped my raincoat closely round me, swore a little, and set out with Lenden across the down.

It was infernally dark. The lights of the car behind us gave us a direction and prevented us from wandering in circles on the slopes. Lenden didn't know where he had left the machine, but thought that he had walked for ten minutes or a quarter of an hour before it hit the road. We went stumbling on into the darkness for a bit, flashing my torch in every direction.

Presently I stopped. It was pretty hopeless to go on groping for her that way on a night like that.

"Did you land into wind?" I asked.

He nodded. "It was pure guesswork, of course. The wind must have been a bit under the starboard wing, because she went down to port as I touched. Still, I got her up again, so she can't have been far wrong."

"Right," said I. "Now, did you land uphill or down?"

He considered for a moment. "Uphill, by the feel of it," he said vaguely. "She pulled up pretty quickly. Yes, I'm sure it was uphill. Not much of a slope, though."

"You had lights to land by?"

"Wing-tip flares. They burnt out as soon as I was on the ground, so I couldn't see much." He hesitated. "I say, let's leave the ruddy thing."

I disregarded that, and stood thinking about it for a minute. If he had landed uphill and into wind it localised the machine pretty well, especially as it was only ten minutes' walk from the road. I bore round to the right, and began to traverse the only uphill slope that faced into the wind.

We found her at the top of the down, where the slope was gentle. I heard her before we got the light on her, a series of drumming crashes as the loose rudder flicked over from hard-a-port to hard-a-starboard, and then to port again. I switched the light in that direction, and there she was, facing more or less into wind with the controls slamming free. He hadn't even troubled to drop the belt around the stick.

"Damn fine way to leave a machine," I muttered. If he heard, Lenden did not reply.

That was a very big aeroplane. I hadn't flown myself since 1917, when I went down with a bullet through my chest to spend the remainder of the war in Germany. I thought that I had forgotten all about that game. But now I am inclined to regard it as one of those things that no man ever really forgets; an old pilot will always linger a little over the photographs of aeroplanes on the back page of the *Daily Mail*. That is the only way in which I can account for the fact that I knew that machine by sight. The French had been doing a number of record-breaking long-distance flights upon the type; I stood there in the rain for a minute playing the torch upon the wings and fuselage, and wondered what on earth Lenden was doing with a French high-speed bomber.

"Where d'you get the Breguet from, Lenden?" I asked.

8

He hesitated for a moment. "I've been doing a job on her," he said vaguely.

There was no point in standing there in the rain questioning a man who didn't want to talk. The first thing was to stop those controls slamming about; I made him get up into the cockpit and tighten the belt around the stick. He obeyed me quietly. Then we set about pegging her down for the night.

In a quarter of an hour it was done. We'd buried the garden forks beneath each wing-tip and stamped the sods down over them, lashing the wing loosely to them with the cord. That was the best that we could do in the circumstances. It was a pretty rotten job when it was done, but it only had to hold till daylight. I didn't think it was going to blow hard.

I went all round before we left to have a final look that everything was shipshape. The wind went sighing through the wires in the darkness, and the rain beat and drummed most desolately upon the fabric of the wings. Flashing my light under the fuselage I saw a sort of blunt snout four or five inches in diameter sticking out down below the clean lines of the body. I stooped curiously, and ran my fingers over the bottom of it. There was a lens.

"All right," said Lenden from the darkness behind me. "It's a camera."

I straightened up and thought of the black packet that he had left in the car. But I had had enough of asking questions.

"Let's get along back to Under," I said, and turned towards the lights of the car. "Unless you're staying here?"

He shook his head, and we went stumbling through the rain over the down towards the car. I was thoroughly wet by the time we got there, and not in the best of tempers. I'd done my best to help the man for the sake of old times, but I couldn't help feeling a bit hurt at the way that he had received the assistance I had given him. And it was a funny business, too. I didn't see what he was doing with a Breguet XIX in England, and I didn't see what had brought him to make a forced landing with it in the middle of the night. And it was very evident that he didn't want to tell me.

9

We reached the car in silence, and bundled in out of the wet. I paused for a moment before pressing the starter.

"You'd better come along back with me to my place," I suggested.

He seemed embarrassed at that. "It's very good of you," he said diffidently. "But I'd rather go straight to the station. I'm . . . in a hurry."

"You won't do much good at the station at this time of night," I remarked. "There isn't a train till twenty past seven."

I considered for a moment, and added: "You'd better come along with me and sleep on the sofa if you want to catch that train. There'll be a fire to sleep by, which is more than you'll find at the station." I eyed him thoughtfully. "There's nobody else in the house. I'm a bachelor." I don't quite know why I added that.

He hesitated again, and gave in. "All right," he said at last. "I'd like to very much."

We were about five miles from Under Hall. I lived there, in the Steward's House, just across the stable-yard from the mansion. It had been the most convenient arrangement in every way. Arner himself was over seventy years old, and too busy a man to occupy himself with the management of his estate; his only son was in Persia.

It was no great shakes as a job, but—it suited me. The screw wasn't much to boast about, but I had a small income of my own that was getting gradually larger with judicious nursing, and the family treated me as an equal. It's the sort of job that I'm cut out for. I was articled to a solicitor some years before the war, though I was country-bred. I tried it again for a year after the Armistice, and then I gave it up. I should have made a rotten lawyer.

I drove into the stable-yard at about a quarter-past two that night, left the car in the coach-house, and walked across to my own place with Lenden. The Steward's House at Under is built into the grey stone wall that separates the gardens from the stable-yard, and the one big living-room has rather a pleasant outlook on the right side of the wall. There are three little bedrooms and a kitchen. It suited me to live there.

They had banked up the fire for me, and left a cold meal on the table with a jug of beer standing in the grate. There was a cold pie, I remember, and a potato salad. I threw off my coat, kicked the fire into a blaze, gave Lenden the use of my room for a wash, and settled down with him for a late supper.

I didn't eat much at that time in the morning, but Lenden seemed hungry and made quite a heavy meal. I lit my pipe and sat there lazily with my back to the fire, waiting and smoking till he had finished. Between the mouthfuls he talked in a desultory manner about the war. The Squadron was re-equipped late in 1917, after I was shot down. With Bristol Fighters. I had heard that. Later they got moved to a place near Abbeville. He got shot through the thigh soon after that, and his observer was killed in the same fight, and he crashed in our support trenches. He became an instructor at Stamford when he came out of hospital. And afterwards at Netheravon. Yes, he supposed he'd been luckier than most.

"Damn sight better off than if you'd been in Germany," I said shortly. "You didn't stay on at all after the war?" I paused. "Someone told me that Standish had gone back," I said, and watched the smoke curl into the darkness above the lamp. "Short-service commission, or something. I forget who it was."

He nodded. "He did. But I came straight out at Armistice." He glanced at me darkly across the table. "I was married. Got married in August, 1918, an' I wanted to be out of it. Make a home for my girl, an' all that sort of thing." He grinned without laughing. "Like hell."

I nodded absently.

Lenden had finished eating. "Went joy-riding with a fellow from Twenty-one Squadron that summer," he said. "Early summer of 1919, just after the war. We had an Avro sea-plane." He mused over it for a minute. "My God, we'd got a lot to learn in those days. We took our wives with us, for one thing. . . ."

He leaned his head upon his hands and began to tell me

about this joy-riding concern. They spent practically the whole of their savings and gratuity upon this seaplane, and they started in with it to tour the South Coast towns, giving joy-rides at a guinea a head. In the prevailing optimism of those days they thought that they could make it pay.

Perhaps, if they had had a land machine they might have got away with it, in spite of their total lack of business experience. Lenden, with the knowledge that he had gained in later years, had no illusions on that point. But he himself put down their failure to the difficulty of operating the machine from the beach of a crowded seaside resort, and he talked for a long time about that.

"Handling the machine on to the beach. That's what did us in—properly. Damn it, it took the hell of a time. Days when there was a sea breeze I'd come in to land over the town, side-slipping down over the houses and the promenade. We were always getting pulled up for flying too low over the promenade. They didn't think about our having a living to get out of their ruddy town."

He stared morosely at the table-cloth. "The sea breeze was hell. I'd land a couple of hundred yards out, and then turn to taxi in to the beach. Then the fun began, and we'd come taxi-ing in to the beach with a twenty-mile wind behind, blowing us straight on to the sand. We hit the beach like that once or twice when we were new to the game, an' stove in a float each time. When we got sick of patching floats I used to try and swing her round into the wind again at the last moment, to check her way. Often as not I'd get outside the stretch of shore the Council had roped off for us in doing that, and go driving in among the bathers. That meant stopping the prop for fear of hitting them, and blowing ashore on to the beach. And there was always a row about it afterwards.

"We never got more than three ten-minute joy-rides done in the hour," he said. "And the engine running the whole time. It meant that we had to make the charge thirty shillings a flight."

And so it came to an end. They began operations in May at Brighton; by July they were in difficulties, and in September they gave up. They were lucky in that they were able to sell the machine, and in that way they realised sufficient of their capital to pay off most of the bills and to leave them with about fifty pounds each in hand.

"I sent my wife back to her people for a bit," said Lenden. "That was the first time."

He relapsed into silence, and sat there brooding over the table. And when he spoke again, I was suddenly sorry for the man. "It's ruddy good fun having to do that," he said quietly. "Especially when it's the first time."

He went on to tell me that he had been out of a job then for about two months, hanging about the aerodromes and living on what he could pick up. He bought and sold one or two old cars at a profit; in those days there was ready money to be made that way. And so he eked out his little means until he got a job at Hounslow with A.T. and T.

I raised my head inquiringly.

"Aircraft Transport and Travel," he replied. "On the Paris route. We used to fly Nines and Sixteens from Hounslow to Le Bourget, and get through as best you could. Later on we moved to Croydon."

I nodded. "I crossed that way once. They gave us paper bags to be sick into."

"Dare say. It was all right while the fine weather lasted, but in the winter . . . it was rotten. Rotten. No ground organisation to help you—no wireless or weather reports in those days. Days when it was too thick to see the trees beyond the aerodrome we used to ring up the harbour-master at Folkestone and get a weather report from him. But we didn't do that much.

"And people used to pay to come with us," he said slowly. "On days like that."

He rested his chin upon one hand and stared across the white table into the shadows of the room. "I've taken a Sixteen off from Hounslow with a full load of passengers when the clouds were right down to the ground," he said, "and flown all the way to the coast without ever getting more than two hundred feet up. Time and again. Jerking her nose up into a zoom when you came to a tree or a church, and letting her down again the other side so's you could see the ground again. At over a hundred miles an hour. Crossing the Channel like that—ten minutes in a cold sweat, praying to God that your compass was right, and your engine would stick it out, and you'd see the cliffs the other side before you hit. And then, at the end of it all, to have to land in a field half-way between the coast and Le Bourget because it was getting too thick for safety." He paused. "It was wicked," he said.

They used to carry the much advertised Air Mails. That meant that the machines had to fly whether there were passengers to be carried or not. It was left to the discretion of the pilot whether or not the flight should be cancelled in bad weather; the pilots were dead keen and went on flying in the most impossible conditions.

"Sanderson got killed that way," he said. "At Douinville. An' all he had in the machine was a couple of picture postcards from trippers in Paris, sent to their families in England as a curiosity. That was the Air Mail. No passengers or anything—just the Mail." He thought for a little. "Now that was a funny thing," he said quietly. "Sanderson hit a tree on top of a little cliff, and he died about a week later. An' all the time in the hospital he was explaining to the nurse how he'd put his machine in through the roof of the Coliseum and what a pity it was, because there was a damn good show going on at the time and he'd gone and spoilt it all. And presently he died.

"We got a bit more careful after that," he said.

For Lenden that had been a good job. He told me that he had been making about nine hundred a year while it lasted. He took a little flat in Croydon and lived there with his wife for twelve months or so.

"That was a fine time," he said. "The best I've ever had. We'd got plenty of money for the first time since we were married. An' Mollie liked the flat all right, and she made it simply great. We thought we was going on for ever, an' we were beginning to make plans to get into a house with a bit of garden where we could have fruit trees and things. And we were going to have a pack o' kids—two or three of them, as soon as we got settled."

There was silence in the room for a minute. "You can't run a show like that without a subsidy," he said at last. "Or you couldn't in those days, with the equipment we had. It lasted on into the winter of 1920. Then Aircraft Transport and Travel—it was a damn good name, that—they packed up. And that was the end of that."

He was staring into the shadows at the far end of the room, and speaking in a very quiet voice. I had heard something of that early failure in the heroic period of aviation, but this was the first time that I had heard a personal account.

This time he was longer out of a job. The flat in Croydon was broken up and his wife went back again to her people, while Lenden went wandering around the south of England in his search for flying work. The time had gone by when motor-cars could be bought and sold at a profit by those outside the trade, and I gathered that by the end of four months his wife's parents were financing him. In the end he found a job again in his own line of business, as pilot for an aerial survey to be made in Honduras.

"D'you ever meet Sam Robertson?" he inquired. "He was an observer in the war, and he got this contract for a survey for the Development Trust. Raked round in the city and got it all off his own bat. And he got me in on it to do the flying for him.

"In Honduras. They'd taken over a concession up the Patuca —there's lashings of copper up there if only you could get it out. Lashings of it. This survey was one of the first shows of that sort to be done. It was a seaplane job. Sam bought a Fairey with a Rolls Eagle in her from the Disposals crowd, and we left for Belize in March, 1921.

"It meant leaving Mollie with her people," he said. "I could make her a pretty fair allowance, of course. I'd got the money then—for as long as the job lasted."

I stirred in my chair. "Was this a photographic survey, then?" I asked.

He nodded. "In a way. The contract didn't run to a proper mosaic of photographs. There wasn't any need for it for what they wanted, and, anyway, we'd have had a job to line it up because there's never been any sort of ground work done there to give you a grid. No. We picked up one of their people at Trujillo, a fellow called Wilson who was their resident out there, and he came on up the Patuca with us. We did most of the work with oblique photographs, and each evening he made up a rough map of the country we'd flown over."

He paused. "It was the copper he was mostly interested in. You can tell it by the colour of the trees, you know. They look all dusty and dried up from the air, different to the rest of the jungle. You can see the copper areas quite clearly that way."

He said it was the devil of a country. From Belize they had gone by a little coastal steamer, Brazilian-owned, to Trujillo. There they erected the machine, on the beach, in the sun. The inhabitants were a sort of Indian, very quiet and mostly diseased.

"They used to come and sit round staring at us, without saying anything at all," he said. "And then when we'd sweated a bucket we'd go in to the pub and drink with the Dagoes. It was a rotten place, that. Rotten."

When the machine was ready they sent a launch full of stores round by sea to the mouth of the Patuca; he told me that the concession was about a hundred miles up the river. Wilson went with the launch; Lenden and Robertson gave them three days' start and went after them in the seaplane. In a couple of hours' flight they had passed the launch, and then they carried on up the river to the agreed meeting place—Jutigalpa.

He told me that that was a glorified mud village, with a Spanish-speaking half-caste to collect a few taxes from the Indians. They lived in a native hut, picketing the machine in the shade of the trees on the beach. That was to be their home for the next six months.

They started flying operations as soon as the launch arrived. They had a very fat mechanic, Meyer by name; within the first three days he was down with fever and some form of heat apoplexy, and had to be sent back to Trujillo in the launch. That delayed them for a week. Then they carried on with the flying, and had surveyed about a third of the area when they crashed a float. Lenden, in taxi-ing the machine on the water, ran her over a submerged snag which ripped their port float from bow to stern; he was fortunate in being able to run the machine ashore before she sank.

"And there we were," he said, "for the next three months, till we got a new float out from England. Wilson went back with Robertson to Trujillo to send the order, and then Robertson came back to Jutigalpa, and we built a sort of palm-leaf hut over the machine with the Indians. And then we just sat on our backsides in that rotten little hole and waited for the float."

When the float came they repaired the machine and carried on, finishing the survey in about six weeks. From the point of view of the Development Trust it was a success; they had found out what they wanted to know about their land cheaply and accurately.

"We finished the job, and came back to Trujillo," said Lenden.

The coals fell together with a little crash. It was about half-past three in the morning. I had lost all desire to go to bed; now that Lenden was talking freely I wanted to hear the end of his story. I knew what was coming. Gradually, and in his own way, he was working up to the point of telling me what he had been doing with that Breguet on the down. I wanted to know about that.

I swung round, pitched one or two more lumps of coal into the grate, and poked them up. Lenden got up absently from the table and came and threw himself down into a chair before the fire.

17

"No," he said at last. "You wouldn't have heard about it here. But there was a tornado out there that year. Sam Robertson and I settled down at Trujillo for a few weeks while he got in touch with some of the mines in Nicaragua. We thought that while we were there we might get one or two more jobs of the same sort in that district, and Wilson gave us a whole lot of help in getting them. We'd just about fixed to go down to the Santa Vanua—it was a sort of forestry survey that they wanted there—when the storm came."

He was staring into the fire, and speaking very quietly. "It came one evening, quite suddenly. We had the Fairey pegged down upon the beach in the lee of a cliff—it was the only place we had to put her. But no pickets could have stood against that wind. We got the whole town out to hold her down. I dare say there were fifty of us hanging on to her in the dusk, and she blew clean out of our hands and away up the beach."

He glanced at me. "She was all we had, you know—the whole capital. Sam and I hung on to her after she took charge —and she chucked us off like a horse. Robertson fell soft, but I broke an arm as I went down." He passed his hand absently up his left forearm. "Yes—she was all we had, and she went flying up the beach till she cartwheeled into a little corrugated-iron hut and knocked it flat, and then on—what was left of her—till she fetched up against the forest. We lay on the beach all that night because we could hear the houses crashing in the town, and Robertson made splints for my arm. And when the morning came and it blew itself out, half the houses in the place were down and Sam was as rich as me."

"That's rotten luck," I muttered.

He nodded. "Yes, it was bad luck, because there was all the makings of a survey business out there. But that finished us, and we came home Third Class."

And so he gave up aviation. He had been bitten three times, and he'd enough of it. He wanted to settle down, he said, and live with his wife. He told me that he had come to the conclusion out in Trujillo that flying was no good for a married man, and that he must look for more stable employment in the future. He realised that he would have to start at the bottom. Wilson stepped in there and gave him an introduction to a cousin who ran a firm of wholesale clothiers in St. Paul's Churchyard, and Lenden came home to England to start work in the city on four pounds ten a week. With Robertson he had been getting seven hundred a year.

"I took Mollie out of pawn again," he said, a little bitterly, "and we got furnished rooms between Eltham and Lewisham, not very far from her people. And that year it went all right."

He stared into the fire. "I was the proper city gent. Mr. Everyman. I wore a bowler hat and a morning coat like all the other stiffs, and carried a pair of gloves, and read the *Daily Mail* going up and the *Evening News* coming down."

It seemed to have been a poor sort of job. From the first there was little chance that he could make a success of it; the clerks with whom he worked had forgotten more about business than he had ever known. He was unsuited for it temperamentally, and he was getting fifteen shillings a week more than the others, which didn't make things any easier for him. And he was desperately hard up. He couldn't live on his pay; his wife's parents had to come forward again and make him a substantial allowance, and that got him on the raw. He told me all this that night.

He stuck it out for two years.

"I chucked it in the early summer of 1924," he said, and shot the ash from his cigarette into the fire. "It's the spring that gets you, in a job like that; when the days begin to get a bit warm and sunny, an' you know you could make better money out in the clean country on an aerodrome."

He was quiet for a little after that, and then he said: "We were right on the rocks by then, and not a chance of things getting any better. I was still on four pounds ten a week. The way I put it to the old man—I said I simply had to go where I stood a chance of earning a bit more money. It wasn't good enough to stick on like that. He cut up pretty rough about it, but I was through with the City. Mollie went home again for a bit, and I went back to the old game."

It was joy-riding again this time, as a paid pilot to a concern called the Atalanta Flying Services. The Atalanta Flying Services was a three-seater Avro, painted a bright scarlet all over. The pilot who had been flying her before had just cut off with all the loose cash in the kitty, and while they tracked him down Lenden got the job to carry on. This time, however, the directors put a secretary into the concern to keep him company.

"We picked up the machine at Gloucester," he said, "where the other fellow left her when he vanished. There were four of us in the game. There was the secretary—a chap called Carpenter—and a ground engineer, and an odd-job man, and myself. We had the Avro, and a Ford lorry that was all covered-in with tarpaulins and fitted up for sleeping and living in, and a Cowley two-seater. Carpenter used to drive the Cowley on in front and get to the next town a day or so ahead of us, and fix up the landing-ground with the farmer, and get out the posters."

He thought for a minute. "I dare say you've seen the posters," he said. "We came all round this part of the country. We had 'em printed in red, very big and staring. Like this:

WATCH

FOR THE RED AEROPLANE!

You've seen people walking on the wings at the cinema, but have you ever seen it with your own eyes? Have you ever flown in an aeroplane at a dizzy height above the ground while a man walked coolly to the extreme tips of the wings?

NO!

BUT YOU CAN NEXT WEEK!

The Atalanta Flying Services are coming, with Captain Lenden, M.C., who shot down fourteen enemy machines in the war and is one of Britain's most experienced airmen. The Air Ministry have certified that Captain Lenden is

ABSOLUTELY SAFE!

Flying daily from Shotover Farm, by kind permission of Mr. Joshua Phillips.

"And a lot more of the same sort of thing," he said. "You know."

Two very happy years followed. The job was one that suited Lenden; it was a country life with few business worries. The pay worked out at about four hundred and fifty, and that enabled him to make a respectable allowance to his wife, though he seldom had an opportunity of seeing her. With the Avro, the Ford lorry, and the Morris-Cowley, the Atalanta Flying Services went wandering, and for the first eighteen months wherever they wandered they made money. They were entirely self-contained.

"We did it this way," he said. "We'd pick our field, and put up a fence of sackcloth round as much of it as we could. We charged sixpence for admission to see the flying. Just by the entrance we had the lorry, and we used it as a sort of office in the day. At night we used to picket the machine as close to the van as we could get her, and then turn in, all snug for the night."

They went all over the country in the next two years, staying ten days at each little town. From Gloucester they worked down through Devon into Cornwall; then back along the whole length of the south coast, till in the winter of 1924 they found themselves in Kent. At Croydon they overhauled the machine and went north into Essex, and up the coast to Sheringham and Cromer. In 1925 they went right up the east coast as far as Edinburgh, and back through the Midlands; till in the spring of 1926 they found themselves again in Gloucester.

He glanced at me. "I don't know that I've ever enjoyed a job so much as that, taking it all round. It was damn hard work. But it suited me—the life did."

He stopped talking, and remained staring moodily into the fire. I realised that the next episode had proved less prosperous and left him to himself for a bit. The fire was dying down; I got up and threw a few more lumps on, and raked the ashes from the hearth. I settled down into my chair again and lit a pipe. It was about four o'clock in the morning.

"What happened next?" I asked. I wanted to hear the end of this story if it meant sitting up all night.

He roused himself, and smiled a little. "What happened next," he said quietly, "was that Mollie left me."

I wasn't prepared for that, though on his own showing nothing was more probable. I said something or other, but he went on again without listening.

"It was my fault, of course. We'd never been able to have a proper home, or the kids we wanted. And one way or another I'd given her a rotten time of it. We hadn't lived together for two years when that happened. There was a cousin of hers, a chap in the Navy . . . She was still a girl, you know—a good bit younger than me. I went down to see her at her people's place."

He was quiet for a minute, and then he laughed. "I came away out of it as soon as I could. There was a girl at Gloucester who got me out of that mess. Worked in an office there. She was a damn good sort, an' her name was Mollie, too. I took her to the Regent at Cheltenham, and we spent a night there, and I sent my wife the bill. And presently I got a notice that she was suing for divorce. . . ."

He sat brooding in his chair for a bit then, staring into the fire, immersed in memories. But presently he roused himself again.

"That killed my luck," he said. "After that happened everything went wrong. We started off again from Gloucester to do the south coast, and at every place we went we showed a loss. At every ruddy place. Places like Taunton and Honiton, where we'd been really busy a couple of years before—if we got a dozen of them into the air it was all we did. People seemed to have got tired of it. We carried on that way for a couple of months, and then the directors got tired of it too. I brought the machine up to Croydon to be sold, and that was the end of that."

He lit another cigarette. "I hadn't got a home to go to then," he said.

He said no more than that, but something in the way he said it revealed to me something of what that meant to him. I know now that he was a man of little stamina. In all his roving and uncertain life since the war he had always had a base, somewhere to retire to, to be alone with his wife and to regain his self-respect. I think his wife must have been a great backbone to him. He wasn't the sort of man ever to make a name for himself alone, and in the loss of his wife he had suffered a grave injury.

"I had about fifty pounds in hand, and while that lasted I hung about Croydon touting for a job. But there wasn't much doing there. Stavanger gave me a few odd taxi trips to do for him, but nothing regular. And then I went and did my Reserve training, and that carried me on for a few weeks.

"By the end of the summer I was on the street," he said. "It was either earn something or starve then. I got a job in a garage, as a fitter. In Acton. Two pounds ten a week."

He grinned unpleasantly at me. "Temporary, of course. Just till something else turned up. I suppose that's how everyone looks at it when they go down the drain."

He told me about his life in the garage in little short, cynical sentences. From something that he said I gained a very clear impression that he had been drinking heavily ever since his wife left him, a circumstance which probably accounted for his failure to get a flying job. Unlike the other failures to which he likened himself, however, he hated the garage enough to rouse himself to get out of it. Possibly he gave up drinking—I don't know about that. At all events, he told me that he began to look about for a chance to get out of the country. He thought that if he could get out to Australia he might be able to pick up a job in aviation again. He said he wanted to get out of England.

He could have got a free passage to Australia, but he didn't know that.

And then a queer thing happened to him. He used to take

a packet of lunch to work with him from his fifth-rate lodgings in Harlesden, and every other day he bought a copy of the *Daily Mail* to read in the lunch hour. And there, one day, he read an article about the Red Menace.

He lit another cigarette. "Bit of luck I got the paper that day," he said. "I might have missed it. God knows what would have happened then—I was about through with fitter's work. It said in the article that the Russians were building up the hell of an air service that was getting to be a menace to the whole of the rest of Europe. I'd heard somewhere or other that they were enlarging their service, but I'd no idea till I read that bit in the paper that it was anything like that. And then it went on to say how they were getting hold of British ex-officers and sending them out to Russia to train the Red Army in the latest tricks of aerial warfare, and what a sin and a shame it was that Englishmen should go and do that, and how the Government ought to stop it. It went on like that for a couple of columns. It said that they were paying as much as a thousand a year to these chaps."

He lifted his eyes from the fire and stared across at me. In the firelight and the shadows of the room there was a momentary pause. "Well," he said at last, "so they were."

I stirred in my chair, a little uneasily. "You went after it, then?"

"Like a knife. So would you have done."

He read that at lunch time, and he abandoned the garage and went straight off to the Public Baths in the High Street and had a sixpenny hot bath. Then he went back to his room and got out the most respectable of his old suits, and found he had a visiting card left, and he went straight off to the Soviet Embassy in Chesham Place.

He sat there in my armchair, staring into the fire for a minute and fingering the matchbox on his knee. "And it was all quite true," he said. "I'd got away from all that muck, just when I was beginning to think I never would."

The tone of relief in which he said that silenced me abruptly. It silenced me then, and it has done so ever since. For him, service with the Soviet meant a deliverance from hell, and a chance to get away and make a fresh start. That was a great injury that his wife did him when she went.

It was a sort of Polish Jew who interviewed him. He took Lenden through it pretty thoroughly, asking him the most searching questions about his war service. He was particularly anxious to know whether he had had any experience on post-war single-seater fighting machines. Lenden had done half an hour on one of the earlier Siskins, and made some capital out of that; for the rest he judged it better to speak the truth.

They sent him away with instructions to come back next day. In the interval they must have looked up his record at the Air Ministry in some occult manner, for they told him quite a lot about himself that he hadn't mentioned before. Then they gave him a pretty stiff medical examination, and then they photographed him. And finally they presented him with a contract, drawn up and ready for him to sign; eight hundred a year for a two years' engagement, with repatriation at the end of it. He signed it on the spot, and they gave him thirty pounds salary in advance.

"You could have knocked me down with a feather," he said. "But they've treated me damn well all through. I know they're dirty dogs in other ways, of course. I've seen it—a damn sight too much of it, out there. But they've always given me a square deal, and I don't mind saying so. Jews mostly—all that I've had anything to do with. And you mostly get a square deal in business from the Jews."

In three days' time they sent him his passport and some tickets. He went out to Russia indirectly, travelling under an assumed name. There was a place up on the hills behind Ventimiglia, he said, the villa of an Italian profiteer, that seemed to serve as a centre for their activities in that part of Europe, and it was to this place that he was told to go. He reported there in due course, and the next day he was sent on through Austria and Poland into Russia. He had a fair command of languages that he had picked up through flying about the continent, and the travelling didn't present many difficulties. From San Remo he travelled on a forged American passport.

25

They sent him first to Moscow. He did a little flying there, and in about ten days' time he was sent on down to Kieff, where they were forming a squadron for instruction in advanced fighting.

"We're a pretty mixed crowd," he said. "Most of the instructors out there are Germans, but there were a couple of English there before me, and one or two French and Italians." He shifted in his chair. "Never hit it off very well with the other two English out there—not my sort. The Germans aren't a bad crowd, though. There's one chap there that I got to know pretty well—a fellow called Keumer, who comes from Noremburg. Married, with two or three children. Like the rest of us —couldn't get anything to do in his own place. Used to fly a Halberstadt in the war—in our part of the line, to. He's a damn stout lad. We live in pairs out there, in little three-roomed huts, and after a bit I went and shared his place."

He stared reflectively into the fire. "Kieff's a good town," he said. "It must have been better before the Revolution, but it's a good spot still. They put us out beyond Pechersk, with the aerodrome about a mile from the river. Not much to do away from the aerodrome. You can go into the town—they lend us a car whenever we want it—and eat a heavy meal with the Germans. Or you can go toying with Amaryllis—there's any amount of that to be had for the asking. Or you can go to the cinema and see Douglas Fairbanks and Norma Talmadge and Mack Sennett pretty well as soon as you can see 'em in London, with Russian sub-titles. And eat crystallised fruits. I tell you, there's a glut of crystallised fruits in that town. You can't get a proper cigarette for love or money, but you can get those damn things pretty well chucked at you. It's a local industry, or something."

He went on to talk for a long time about the type of machine that they had out there, and the ability of the Russian pilots. He was of the opinion that the best pilots were the Cossacks, and he said that the Russians were concentrating on trying to turn the best of their cavalry into fighting pilots. He thought that that was sound, and he had a very high opinion of their ability. The trouble was that they were so illiterate. Everyone coming to that course was supposed to be able to read and write; in actual fact their best pilots could do neither with any accuracy. Many of them had their horses with them; there were horse-lines along one side of the aerodrome.

"They fly into a fight . . . like riding a horse. No theory about it; but they're good. They've got a feel for the machine from the very first. It's a natural genius for the game. And they've got any amount of guts."

There was a very long silence then. He sat there in that chair before the fire, staring at the coals, his hands outstretched upon the bolstered arms, his long black hair falling down over his forehead in the half-light. I thought that he was shivering a little as I watched him.

"That went on till about six weeks ago," he said at last. "I had a pretty good time of it out there, taking it all round. My pay comes regularly, and I send a good bit of it back to England. I arranged that before I signed the contract, and they stuck to their side of it. The money gets through all right. And I like the work. I'd have been there still, but for this job."

I leaned forward and knocked my pipe out slowly against the palm of my hand over the grate. I knew that we were coming to the root of it now.

"This is for them?" I asked.

He didn't answer that at once. "They've grown to trust me pretty well out there," he said. "More than the others. They came along one day about the middle of last month, and made me an offer. They wanted a long night flight, or rather a series of night flights, done outside Russia. They offered me a thousand pounds sterling, with all expenses, as a fee for doing it."

He paused, irresolute.

"Where'd you got to fly to?" I asked.

"Portsmouth," he said laconically.

I had guessed something of the sort, I suppose. At all events, it didn't come as much of a surprise.

He went on without looking at me. "I'm getting to the end of my time out there. I've saved a bit, of course—about a couple of hundred pounds. But that's not capital. It wouldn't go any way if I was out of a job. I tell you, half a dozen times in the last three years I'd have been on my feet if I could have raked up a thousand or so. Dawson wanted me to go in with him in that show of his in Penang, you know." I didn't know, but I was silent. "And I couldn't, and he sold out to the Dutch as a going concern at three hundred per cent. And then Sam Robertson gave me a chance of going in with him on the Argentine Survey, and he's doing damn well, I hear. And I'd have liked to have been with Sam again. . . ."

I cut him short. "Why did they choose an Englishman?"

He laughed. "Bar the English and the Germans, I don't suppose there's a pilot in Russia that can lay a course properly, night flying. Not to call a pilot.

"They wanted a set of flashlight photographs taken from the air," he said. "Of Portsmouth."

The scheme, as they put it to him, was worth the thousand as a pilot's fee alone. There was the devil of a lot of risk about it. He was to take a machine from Kieff and fly by night across Poland and Germany to a place near Hamburg, where he was to land and wait during the day. On the next night he was to fly to Portsmouth, do his job, and return to Hamburg before dawn. The following night he was to return to Kieff.

If anything went wrong he was to land and burn the machine, and get away back to Russia with the plates by land.

I stared at him incredulously. "I never heard of night flying like that," I said. "It's absolutely crazy. Do you mean to say you took it on?"

He smiled a little bitterly. "I wanted that thousand. You see, I'm getting towards the end of my time out there. Yes, I took it on. I made damn sure about the money, though. I had it paid into my bank at Croydon by the Trade Delegation, and I wouldn't stir a finger till I had a letter from the manager about it in his own handwriting. That made it as certain as it could be—and when I got that I carried on with the preparations."

He began upon a long, technical description of the machine and its equipment for this flight. It was many years since I had

had to do with aeroplanes, and much of what he told me passed over my head. I was afraid to put him off his tale by asking questions. He said that they had several of those Breguets in the school at Kieff, and he chose one of them for the job. And he told me, in a mass of technicalities, that they had a propeller for that machine which at slow speeds was very quiet.

Now half the noise of an aeroplane comes from the propeller. Virtually they had washed that out; they set to work then and built a silencer for the exhaust of the engine. They made the machine into a single-seater, and fitted her with fuel tanks for about fifteen hours' flight. By the time they'd finished with her they had a machine which would fly from Hamburg to Portsmouth and back in a night, and would keep in the air without losing height . . . silently.'

"We did two machines like that," he said. "One for a reserve, in case anything happened to mine. We fixed it that old Keumer should fly the reserve one if it was necessary. By the time we'd done with mine she'd fly at about eighty so quietly that you could hear the rustle of a map as you unfolded it in the cockpit. It gave me a queer start the first time I heard that. And they couldn't hear her on the ground at all when she was a couple of hundred metres up."

They had one or two rehearsals of the photography, using a parachute flare, and then they were ready.

"What day's this?" he asked suddenly.

"Thursday," I said. "Or I suppose it's Friday by this time."

He thought for a little. "We were all ready last week. I started for Germany on Sunday night."

The landing-place in Germany was between Lubeck and Elmshorn, a little to the north of Hamburg. The flight, by the route he took, was about seven hundred and fifty miles; he took about six and three-quarter hours to do it. He left Kieff with a full load of fuel at about five o'clock in the afternoon, mid-Europe time, and set a compass course for the Baltic. It was a very dark night, and the ground was covered with snow. He said that it was very cold.

He flew most of the way at about five thousand feet. The

Breguet wasn't a silent machine at her cruising speed by any means, and he didn't want to wake the Poles up down below. Between Kieff and Danzig he didn't check his course at all. He just sat there watching his compass and trying to fight the miseries of cold, and when he had been in the air for four hours he came down to about a couple of hundred feet to see where he was.

He saw the lights of a village on the snow, and he nearly hit a hill in trying to get down lower to see the sort of country he was over. Upon that he went up again and carried on for another twenty minutes. At the end of that time he found that he was over sea.

He thought it out, and came to the conclusion that he must be to the east of his course, since there was a westerly wind blowing and he had seen no sign of Danzig on the coast. Accordingly he swung round and set a course south-west by south to hit the coast again, and in a few minutes he had picked up the lighthouse at Putzig.

That gave him his position, and he set to flying along the coast towards Rügen, about a hundred and twenty miles farther on. There was a stiffish wind against him, and that leg of the course took him an hour and a quarter. The darkness and the intense cold, together with the strain, were making him sleepy. He had several drinks out of his flask, he said, and presently he picked up a lighthouse on Rügen.

After that he was pretty well home. He passed over Rostock and Lubeck, and then set about looking for his landing-ground. The Russians had secured a great country house that stood in the middle of that marshy land; he said that it was all shut up except for three rooms that they lived in. He said he didn't ask many questions about the place.

"Anyway," he said, "they'd done their part of it all right. The arrangement was that they'd have the devil of a great bon-fire lighted half-way between Elmshorn and Lubeck, and three miles south of that I'd find the landing lights laid out on the ground for me to land by, inconspicuous-like. Well, I picked up the bonfire all right. They'd given a beano to some village there, and supplied the wood and the drink and everything. It was a good fire, that. The flames must have been getting on for fifty feet high at times. I saw it twenty miles away, and gave it a pretty good berth. It was easy then. I circled round a bit and found the landing, and put the Breguet down on to the grass along the line of lights."

He said that it had been a very cold flight. "Living in England, you don't know what it's like. I was all sort of cramped and stiffened in the one position. I tried to get out of the machine when she stopped, but I had to sit there till they came and climbed up on to the fuselage to help me out. I've never been like that before. The usual crowd of Jew Boys, but they were damn good to me that night. They had hot soup all ready, and a fire, and as soon as I was thawed out a bit and had a quart or so of soup inside me, I fell asleep where I was, pretty well standing up."

He slept till noon the next day, and spent the afternoon with a mechanic, overhauling the machine for the flight to Portsmouth.

"That was Monday afternoon," he said. "I started at about six in the evening, with fifteen hours' fuel on board. That flight should take about eleven hours for the return journey, allowing a bit for head winds and for about a quarter of an hour over Portsmouth."

He took a compass course over Holland, passing pretty well inland. He said he was afraid of getting mixed up with the Zuyder Zee. He came out on the coast near Ostend, and took a departure from there for Dover, flying at about three thousand feet. Finally he came to the Island at about half-past eleven. He picked up the Nab lighthouse first, and from there he followed straight along in through Spithead.

He took up the poker absently, and scraped a little of the ash from the bars of the grate. The fire was glowing very red into his face.

"I throttled down at the Nab," he said, "and then we went creeping in, doing about eighty, and so quiet that I might have heard my watch ticking if I'd put it to my ear. I had the parachute flare all ready, with a little stick to poke it down the tube with. It was the entrance to the harbour that I had to take—the narrow part."

My pipe was out, but I was afraid to interrupt his narrative by stirring to relight it.

"It was easy enough. The lights from the town—the street-lamps—showed on both sides of the water, so that the entrance looked like a great streak of black between the lights. I cruised round a bit before I set off the flare and dropped off a little height, so that I finished up at about two thousand five hundred feet. Eight hundred metres was the height that we'd fixed for the focus of the camera, you see."

He paused. "I could see that there was something funny going on before I set off the flare," he said. "There was a string of green lights stretching right across the entrance from side to side, near the mouth. Like a barrier to stop vessels coming in. And about half a mile inside from that there was a sort of faint glow in the middle of the harbour. Like a couple of floodlights running a bit dim. You couldn't see anything from the air but just that there was light there—in the middle of the water. Not like the lights of a ship, either. More like a quay."

He laid down the poker and glanced across at me. "Well, I was all ready. I went over to the Gosport side to start the fun. It was a westerly wind, you see, and I wanted to place the flare so that it would drift over the target. I turned her beyond the town and came back again down wind towards the entrance. And when the target bore about thirty degrees from the vertical with me, I made contact and shoved the flare down through the tube. It burst about thirty feet below me, and I had time for a quick glance round before the sights came on."

He relapsed into a long silence. I knew that having got so far he would finish the story in his own time, and I left him to think it over. Looking back upon it now, I think he may have been reluctant to tell what he had seen to any living person. I think that may have been one of the reasons for his pause.

"Was there much going on?" I asked at last.

He raised his head and eyed me steadily. "I don't know what

it was," he said, "and that's the truth. I've never seen anything like it before. There was some damn great thing out there in the middle of the harbour—it wasn't a ship, and it wasn't a barge. I don't know what it was. There were three or four vessels standing by it, and there was a sort of thick black line of something running from it to the Gosport shore. That's what I saw—it's all I had time to see, because the sights began to bear and I got busy. It stood out pretty well as clear as daylight, the shadows all black and sharp. That flare was a corker of a thing."

He flung his half-smoked cigarette into the fire, and lit another.

"It burnt for about thirty seconds. I flew straight over the target and got in three good shots one after the other, that would join up to make a long strip photograph, you see. When the sights ceased to bear, I chucked her round in a quick turn and made another run over the target. I went slower over the ground that time because I was flying against the wind. I got in five shots on that run and I passed the flare about half-way, a little below me and to starboard. I swung her round again at the end of that run and got in two more shots as I headed east over the thing. In the middle of the second one the light went out. I tell you, it was a fine flare, that. There wasn't even a red glow to show where it had been and make them smell a rat. It just flicked clean out into the darkness."

He was heading east when that happened. He didn't linger over Portsmouth, but went straight on ahead and back the way he came. He kept his machine flying slowly and quietly till he was well out at sea past the Nab, then opened up his engine and made straight along the coast for Dover.

I got up from my chair and crossed to the back of the room. The daily papers generally lie about there for a week or so before they disappear, and I had no difficulty in finding the one I wanted. That passage was there as I remembered it.

FIREBALL AT PORTSMOUTH

Meteorologists to-day are eagerly discussing the appearance of a large fireball, or meteor, over Portsmouth on Monday night. According to eyewitnesses the phenomenon made its appearance at about half-past eleven, and lasted for a period variously estimated as from forty seconds to a minute. The body materialised at a comparatively low height, and according to one statement was accompanied by a low rumbling noise. The streets of the city and the harbour were brilliantly illuminated for a few moments during the passage of the phenomenon, which moved slowly in an easterly direction. No damage is reported.

I showed it to Lenden. He read it through, and smiled.

"You got back all right, then?" I asked.

He was staring into the fire, and shivering a little. "Yes, I got back," he said slowly. "I landed at about four o'clock. It was twice as long a flight as the one from Kieff, but I didn't feel it half so much. I was tired, of course, but nothing beyond the ordinary. It hadn't been so cold, for one thing."

As soon as he landed they set about pegging down the machine for the night, and draining the radiator. Then they went to get the plates from the camera. He said that the plates for that camera were held in two chargers; they were all in one box to start with, and as you exposed each plate it slid over to the other box automatically leaving a fresh plate all ready over the lens. They went to take off the box of exposed plates. It didn't come away freely, and when they finally got it off there was a crack and a tinkle of glass.

He glanced at me. "The first plate had jammed," he said quietly. "It was the tripping gear. They hadn't been passing the lens at all. I'd taken all the ten exposures on the one plate. I'd done it all, and flown all that way—for nothing."

It was bad luck, that, from his point of view. It meant that the flight all had to be done again. He told me that he was forced to leave it for a day or two. He'd done two long night flights on two successive nights, and he wasn't fit to do another one straight off. He had to have some rest; he said that he was getting jumpy and feverish with the exposure. He talked it over with the Jews, and they made it Thursday night for the second shot; the interval he spent mostly in bed.

"There was another thing," he said. "I knew there'd be some

risk about the second trip. I mean to say, whatever it is that's going on there, it's pretty secret. One can't go on letting off fire-balls over Portsmouth indefinitely, and think they won't tumble to the game. And it's a protected area, you know. They've got every right to shoot you down if you go monkeying about over that sort of place. It had been all right the first time; I'd taken them by surprise. But I knew it wasn't going to be so easy the second time."

He paused. "And, by God, it wasn't!"

He shivered violently, and drew up closer to the fire. He flew over in exactly the same way. He found the same subdued light in the middle of the entrance, but the thing had moved nearer to the Gosport shore. And as he drew closer, he saw one thing that scared him stiff and put the wind up him properly. They had the landing-lights out on Gosport aero-drome.

He sat there very still, staring at the glowing embers of the fire. "I could see that I was in for it then," he said very quietly. "And from our own people. I knew that as soon as I let off my flare it'd be like poking a stick into a wasps' nest. I knew there'd be machines coming up from the aerodrome after me, and that in a few minutes I might have something like a Gamecock hang-ing on behind me, and then I'd have to land or be shot down."

He was silent for a minute.

"The worst part of it—what put the wind up me most"—he was speaking so quietly that I could hardly hear what he said— "was that they'd be our own people. Somebody like Dick Scott or Poddy Armstrong, that I'd played pills with at the Royal Aero Club, sitting there in the Gamecock pooping off tracer bullets at me, and thinking he was doing a damn good job. . . ."

He pulled himself together and lit another cigarette. He was still shivering a bit; I wondered if he had taken cold.

He said that the job went through almost exactly as it had before. He set his flare off on the Gosport side of the harbour and began taking photographs as he went east. As he turned the machine at the end of that run he saw the first of the green lights come up.

They were setting off green rockets from Gosport, in groups of three at a time. It was the signal to land at once. The things rose to a height of about a thousand feet and burst in a cluster of green stars. They were shooting them up in groups of three at intervals of about ten seconds. Lenden paid no attention to them, but he got in five photographs on his way west over the target. He took nine exposures in all, and then swung the machine round and went straight out to sea.

"I didn't dare to open out my engine. The Breguet can do about a hundred and sixty miles an hour, but to do that you've got to make a noise. I kept her throttled down and silent, and went drifting out towards the Island, doing about eighty. I turned in my seat as I went, and had a good look at the aerodrome behind me. They had stopped sending up the rockets, and as I watched I distinctly saw a machine sweep across the aerodrome in front of the landing-lights as she took off. I knew then that they were after me."

He sat playing with the poker for a bit. "Well," he said. "They didn't find me."

They didn't get their searchlights going fast enough. By the time the first of those came up he was miles away, right out to sea above Spithead. He carried on like that till he was somewhere off St. Helen's; then he thought that his best course was to put on speed and get clear. So he switched on the little shaded light over his instruments and, with an eye wandering over the dials, thrust forward the throttle. He saw the needle of the oil gauge go leaping up till it jammed at the limit of the dial.

He glanced at me. I had barely appreciated the significance of that; it was so long since I had flown. "It's rotten when a thing like that happens," he said quietly, "at night, and over strange country. And I was right out to sea, mind you—about five miles from land. I didn't see the fun in coming down in the water if my engine was going to pack up, and so I turned towards the coast, somewhere by Selsey. And then, quite suddenly, the gauge flicked down to zero, and oil began to come spraying down the fuselage from the engine, coating the windscreen and blowing in my face. Warm oil, all black and sticky in the darkness. . . .

"I knew that I was in for it then," he said. "And it was all dark below. Pitch dark, with only a little white surf to show the line of the beaches. No hope of being able to pick out a field to land in. And I knew that very soon the engine would pack up."

He was shivering again. I threw a lump or two of coal on the fire, and he crouched a little closer towards it. He said he made for the downs. He knew that part of the country fairly well from flying over it, and he knew that he could pull off a forced landing on the top of the downs without hurting himself. He didn't care a damn what happened to the machine so long as he could get down uninjured with the plates. His orders were that in such a case the machine was to be burnt.

"I went up between Chichester and Arundel. And as I went," he said, "I was climbing, climbing for all I was fit to get a bit of height while the engine lasted. I got her up to five thousand feet or so, a few miles inland from the coast. I knew it was all open grass land in front of me then, and every chance of a decent landing. I thought I might want the engine again at the last minute to pull me clear of a tree or a house, so I shut off before she seized up for good, and put the machine on the glide down to land. And then, as luck would have it, the moon came out for a couple of minutes and showed me the lie of the country. The only time I've seen the moon since I left Kieff. It was easy then. I set off a wing-tip flare at about fifty feet, and landed where you saw."

His voice died into the silence. He had come to the end of his story, it seemed, and now he was waiting for me to say something. I glanced uneasily about the room in search of inspiration, and saw the black tin case he had brought from the machine lying beside his chair. I would have picked it up, but he was before me.

"These are the photographs?" I asked.

He nodded, turning the box over and over in his hands.

I thought about it for a minute. "Why didn't you burn the machine?"

Crouching towards the fire, he glanced up at me and grinned. "I hadn't got a match."

I suppose I looked doubtful.

He said that he had made a little pile of papers in the cockpit and soaked them with petrol. And then he went through his pockets and found he had one match—just the one. He hadn't thought about bringing proper incendiary materials with him. He struck the head off that match at the first go, and there he was. He tried to get a spark out of the lighting system for a time, but failed to ignite his papers. Then he tried to get one of the flares off the wing, and presently he had to give that up for lack of tools.

"Then it came on to rain in buckets," he said. "I was fed up with it by then. And left her."

That explained why he had not picketed the machine. Lenden crouched a little closer to the fire, and began shivering again. That drew my attention.

"You've got a chill," I said.

He sat back from the fire a little, and stopped shivering. "It's nothing," he replied. "I've had it for some days."

I eyed him thoughtfully for a minute, and wondered if he was going to be ill. He had flushed up in the last hour or so.

"Fever?"

He nodded. "Got it when I was out with Sam Robertson on the Patuca," he said. "I never give it much heed. It was the flight from Kieff that started it this time; I've had it intermittently since then. Off and on, you know. I'll take some quinine, if you've got any."

I went into my bedroom and returned with a bottle of tablets. He read the label, counted out about half the bottle into the palm of his hand, and swallowed them with the help of a glass of water from the table.

It was getting towards dawn. Outside, the lawns of the garden were beginning to show grey; through the uncurtained window I could see the outline of a flower-bed and a shadowy tree. I remained standing on the fender there before the fire, and staring down at him. I didn't know what to do.

He was still handling that flat box of plates. I stood there in perplexity for a bit, and at last:

"What are you going to do with those?" I asked bluntly.

Lenden had begun to shiver again. He seemed not to have heard my question, but sat there crouching down over the fire. He had an odd, flushed look about him, I remember; his hair was ruffled and hanging down over his forehead, giving him a worn and dissipated appearance. I thought for a little.

"Are you on your way back to Russia?" I asked.

Presently I repeated the question.

He didn't take his eyes from the fire. "God knows," he said morosely. "I don't."

It was no use thinking of going to bed now. It was getting on for half-past five, and the daylight was growing fast outside the window. I stood there on the fender studying him for a bit longer, and then I crossed the room and sat down at the piano. It was a Baby Grand that I had bought a year or so before, and I was still paying for it. That piano stands beside me now. It had a pleasant, clean tone, with little volume to it, most suitable to the sort of room that I can afford.

I had done that before, and I have done it since. I've always lived a pretty healthy life. To lose a night's sleep means very little to me, if I may sit quietly at the piano for an hour at the beginning of the new day. I slid on to the stool that morning, dropped my fingers on to the keys, and began upon the overture to my play.

It goes gently, that overture, and in my hands of course it plays itself. I let it ripple on through the various themes, absently polishing it a bit as I went. Now and again I glanced across to Lenden. He was still sitting exactly as I had left him, crouching over the fire, his hair hanging down untidily over his forehead, fingering that infernal box, and shivering. It was pretty evident that he was going to be ill. And that wasn't surprising. He had been soaked to the skin when I met him on the road, and I hadn't thought of offering him a change of clothes. He had dried before the fire.

I finished the overture and began upon the plot. The forest

scenes come first in the play; I don't suppose I shall ever really be satisfied with those forest scenes. I have polished and refined them out of all recognition—continually. I don't know how long I sat over them then, but I was startled by Lenden's voice.

"What's that you're playing?"

I dropped my hands from the piano, and swung round on the stool. He had got up, and was standing on the fender with his back to the fire.

"Sorry," I said. "I'd forgotten about you."

He was staring at me most intently across the room.

"I remember you now," he said slowly. "I'd forgotten all about you, except that there was a man of your name in the Squadron. But I remember you now. Quite well. You used to fly the machine with the three red stars on the fuselage. And you used to play for us in the Mess, when we were tired of the gramophone."

I nodded. "That was my machine. I've got a photograph of her somewhere."

"I remember you now," he repeated. "What's that you were playing, then?"

I turned again to the piano. "It's a play for the cinema," I said. "An opera, if you like. For the films."

I dropped my fingers on to the keys again, and replayed the opening to the forest scene. It goes very pleasantly, that bit. I knew that he was standing there by the fire and watching me as I faced the rosewood of the instrument, and I knew that I was holding his attention. Whether he knew anything about music didn't matter with that thing. I wrote it for the people who didn't.

I came to the end of that theme. I had forgotten all about aeroplanes by then.

"What's it all about?" he asked curiously.

I touched a few chords of the next theme before replying, and then paused. "It's about a King's daughter," I said, "who went walking in the forest and got chased by a bear. By the hell of a bear. You can do that sort of thing on the pictures, you know. You can't go and put on a scene of a bear chasing a girl all round the stage at Covent Garden. Not so that you'd see the Princess all of a muck sweat. But you can do it on the films. . . ."

I began to play the first passages of the next theme, a little absently. "For one thing she wouldn't be able to sing if you chased her properly," I said. "Not for an hour or two, anyway. The story's just that she went into the forest alone . . . Because she wanted to get away from the Court and from her women and to be alone. Spring o' the year, you know. You can do the Court all right on the films. Indicate it. Fourteenth century, with those tall hats with a veil hanging down from them. And a tall, misty castle." Lenden had moved closer to the piano; as I talked my fingers were running automatically through the preliminary forest passages. "She went out after the flowers, and got chased by a bear that came sort of wuffling out of a thicket at her, and frightened her very much."

He had come quite close. I finished that passage, looked up, and grinned at him. "This is the bear."

I thought for a minute, and began upon the bear theme. It starts with the bear rooting and snuffling in the undergrowth, with a second motif of the Princess coming closer among the flowers, because she wanted to be alone. That motif starts faint, and grows. And then there's a bit of blood and thunder when the bear comes out into the open that merges into a regular nightmare bit of music that I take at racing speed. It's quite a simple theme. It starts fairly quietly. She's a good way ahead of the bear. Then as the chase goes on through the trees of the wood that theme gets louder, and faster, more monstrous, more uncouth. On the film one can work that up well, of course. The whole thing lasts for nearly five minutes of tense panic. The trees of the forest get larger, and the bear himself one makes larger . . . and larger, more monstrous, as he gets closer. It's a good bit of writing, that, though I say it myself. I put all I knew into it, and stopped abruptly at the Woodman.

I dropped my hands from the keys and turned to Lenden. "That's the bear," I said.

"By God," he muttered. "I don't wonder she got the wind up."

I think it may have been his simplicity that roused me to a sense of his position, and made me swing round suddenly upon my stool.

"See here," I said. "What about you, Lenden? D'you want to stay here? You can if you like, you know. There's a bedroom in there, and you're welcome to it for as long as you want it. Or are you going on up to Town?"

He shifted his position uneasily, and avoided my eyes. "I don't quite know what to do," he said uncertainly. "I've got these ruddy plates to get rid of. . . ."

His eyes, when I saw them, were half-closed and very bright; he had flushed up, and altogether he looked a pretty sick man. I'm no doctor, but I got up and took his wrist. His pulse seemed to be over-revving badly, and he was very hot. I was morally certain that if he went travelling alone he'd end his journey in a London hospital, and I said as much.

"I know." He pressed both hands to his forehead for a moment, and passed them back over his hair. 'It's this infernal fever . . . and getting wet. I'm in for a searcher this time."

I met his eyes and held them for a moment. "You'd better get to bed," I said. "There's nobody comes to this house but me and the servants. I'll say that I brought you back with me from Winchester."

I doubt if he heard what I said. "It always shakes me when I get a bout like this," he muttered. "It was different when Mollie was there."

He was shivering again. "Lie up here for a day or two, till you're fit," I suggested. "Then you can go on to Town when you like. You can't go travelling like this."

"I'd ha' been all right if I'd got tight last night," he said. "I knew this was coming."

I went through into the spare bedroom. There was a greyness over everything by now; in the sitting-room the lamps were burning yellow in the growing morning light. I found sheets and blankets under the coverlet, and made up the bed for him. When that was done, I went back to the sitting-room. He was still turning that black box over and over in his hands, uncertainly.

I filled a kettle and put it on the fire to boil. "Room's ready when you are," I said. "You'd better go to bed—and stay there. I'll get you a hot-water bottle, soon as this boils."

"It's damn good of you," he muttered. He went through into the bedroom and began to undress.

Presently the kettle boiled. I took the bottle in to him and found him in bed; he was very grateful in an inarticulate sort of way. I cut him short, went out of the room, and left him to go to sleep.

Back in the sitting-room I stood for a minute looking at myself in the glass over the mantelpiece. I can't say it was a pretty sight. I was still in evening kit, but my tie had worked up towards one ear, and my trousers were smeared with mud from the down. The room was littered and squalid in the grey light; the electric lights unwholesome, and the remains of supper on the table an offence. Only the white keys and rosewood of the piano by the window appeared clean in that room.

I went into my bedroom, undressed, and had a bath. That pulled me round a bit. Half an hour later, when I had shaved, dressed, and flung open the window in the sitting-room, I was more or less myself again.

It was a cloudless morning. Over the kitchen garden the sun was rising through the mists left by the rain and in the stable eaves the birds were beginning softly, like a bit of Grieg. I went to the door of my house and looked out over the yard. Nobody was stirring yet, nor would be for half an hour to come, unless some under-housemaid in the mansion.

I had a job of work to do before breakfast, but I needed the help of one or two labourers for it, and I knew that it was no good going out to look for them for a bit. I shut the door and went back to the sitting-room, and kicked the dying fire together, and stood over it for a little. And then, since there was nothing else to do, I sat down again at the piano.

The morning was coming up all sunny and bright. It must have been chilly at the piano, for the window was open beside me, but I didn't seem to notice it. I had arranged that corner of the garden to have a fine show of daffodils that spring; it was a wild part where the family didn't come much. I could see them just beginning to poke up through the grass. There were primroses there—buckets of them—and a few snowdrops. I sat there looking at them for a bit, half-asleep; through the trees in winter you can see the grey whaleback of the down as it sweeps up above the house and the village.

I was sick of my own work. I strummed a bar or two, and played Chopin for a little, till I grew tired of him. I sat there for a bit then, and thought I'd better get out into the yard and start up my car. I had that aeroplane to hide. But I sat there for a little longer before moving, and presently I found myself rippling through the *Spring Song*. It was the cold that started me off on that, I suppose. That, and the flowers.

I must have become engrossed in it again. I know I ran through it several times quite softly, rippling through it and wondering if I should ever write anything myself one-tenth so good. It should be played lightly, that thing. Very lightly, and a little staccato. I don't know for how long I went on playing. It may have been for ten minutes or a quarter of an hour, till some slight sound made me turn my head. Lenden was standing in the doorway in my pyjamas, his hand resting on the jamb to steady him, his face dead white.

I dropped my hands from the keys. "Better get along back to bed," I said. "You've got the hell of a temperature."

He moistened his lips. "For Christ's sake, stop playing that infernal thing. I can't stick it any longer."

I stared at him, puzzled. "Why not? What's the matter?"

He avoided my eyes. "I thought you might be doing it on purpose," he said uncertainly. "If you weren't. . . . The way you went on and on."

I smiled, got up from the piano, and crossed the room to him. "As for you," I said, "you're bats—that's what's the matter with you. You're imagining things. I'm going out now to hide that aeroplane of yours where it won't be seen from the road, before anyone else gets to know about it. You're going to go

44

back to bed and go to sleep, pretty damn quick."

He turned from the door. "All right," he said wearily.

"I'll have some breakfast sent over for you about ten o'clock. Bit of fish, or something."

I paused. "And don't be a ruddy fool."

CHAPTER TWO

I WENT OUT INTO THE YARD to start up the car. It was very fresh and cold outside; I left the engine to run warm while I went back into the house for a coat.

Then I got going on the road for the downs. The wind and the rain of the night had gone completely and left only a thin mist about the hedges in the rising sun. I passed through the main street of Under and let the car rip along the road for Leventer.

I saw the machine when I was a mile away. There she was, stuck right up on top of the down, insecurely tethered and swaying a little in the light wind. She was a landmark for miles around. I stopped the car near to where I had picked up Lenden and began to walk across the down towards her, hoping most earnestly that no one else had passed that way since dawn. It wasn't very likely.

There was a barn in the hollow of the down below the machine, about half a mile distant from her in the opposite direction to the road. I passed her without stopping, and went on down the hill. I thought it might be possible to get her down the slopes and tether her behind the barn. She would be out of sight of the road there, and as secret as it was possible to make her, short of dismantling her altogether. It realised, as I walked, that it might come to that in time. If she was to be disposed of secretly, the only way would be to take her to bits and burn her piecemeal.

The slopes were easy enough on the way down to the barn. There would be no difficulty about getting her down the hill into seclusion. If ever she were needed again, it would even be possible to taxi her up the hill again under her own power till level ground was reached for her to take off. At that time I didn't think that there was the least chance of that ever happening, but there was very little doubt that it could be done if necessary.

I had a bit of luck then. Spadden, the farmer, came out of the barn as I approached; a grizzled, uncommunicative man of fifty-odd. He had a couple of sheep in there with bad feet, he told me. He had had the vet. out to them from Leventer the day before, in a terrible fright that it was foot-and-mouth; the vet., it seemed, had laughed heartily, given him a poultice, drunk a stoup of ale, and departed. Spadden told me all this as he greeted me beside the barn and as he was showing me the beasts. He was a good sort, was Spadden. He'd always given me a square deal, and I knew he wouldn't talk.

I put it to him bluntly. "Been up on the down this morning?" I inquired. He hadn't. "Well, I've got an aeroplane up there."

He nodded slowly. "Nasty dangerous things," he said at last. "You don't want to go messing about with them no more. Thought you'd had your fill in the war."

I laughed. "It's nothing to do with me. I've not been flying it. But I know the pilot. He's an old friend of mine; he landed here late last night. He's had to go to London in a hurry; I said I'd look after it for him, and see that it was picketed down somewhere in shelter from the wind. He said he reckoned to leave it here a week."

It was a thin tale.

"Aye," said Spadden phlegmatically. "Where'll we put it?"

I thanked God for him. "Bring it down into the hollow here," I said, "and picket it under the lee of the barn. It's quiet enough down here."

"Aye," he said again. "It's quiet down here." He stared around. "Never a great wind down here. If you put it here the sheep'll be worrying it."

"They can't hurt it."

"Reckon they'll rub."

"Let 'em," I said. There was very little chance, I thought, that anyone would ever want to fly it again.

He went off and fetched one of his labourers, and then we

47

went trudging up to the top of the down. There we cut loose the lashings that held her, lifted the tail shoulder-high, and began to wheel her down to the barn. It was all downhill, or we'd never have got her there. We must have put her down a dozen times for a spell. She was a big machine, that Breguet, and a heavy one to handle on the ground. I know that by the time we got her down to the barn I—for one—was wishing most heartily that I'd never set eyes on her.

There was everything we needed in that barn, right on the spot. We drove stakes into the ground beneath the wing-tips with a wooden mallet, and lashed her to them loosely to enable her to ride a little in the wind. We lashed sacking down over the engine, the propeller, and the cockpit. I made a proper job of the controls. By the time I'd done with her she was a fixture, and fit to lie out there for a winter without taking any great harm. Apart from the sheep, that is.

I made a rough examination of her before I left. There was an oil pipe broken in the engine mounting; a bit of rubber piping that connected the oil tank to the engine, perhaps an inch in diameter, frayed and burst. There was a great slaver of oil all about that had come from this pipe. That was the trouble that had brought him down. Something must have made the pipe burst, I supposed; some stoppage in the circuit, but what it was I did not know.

I left her then. Spadden said he'd keep an eye on her and see that she didn't suffer too much from the sheep. I took the occasion to urge him not to talk about her. But there was little need for that. He didn't want a lot of sightseers wandering about all over his land.

I went back to Under for breakfast well satisfied with myself. The machine couldn't be seen from the road, and I had left her in as great concealment as could be contrived in England. It is no easy matter to hide an aeroplane. It is a most conspicuous thing, and every village constable seems to have an official interest in it, on all occasions.

I drove back to the Hall, put my car in the coach-house, and went across to my own place. They had made my bed and had begun to lay the table for breakfast. I looked into my spare room. Lenden was asleep in bed, flushed and breathing heavily. I closed the door softly and went out.

Then I crossed the yard and went to the gun-room in the mansion. The morning papers generally tarry a while there on their way to the breakfast table; whenever I want to know any particular item of news in a hurry, I go and look through them there before breakfast. I spread them out upon the gun-room table that morning and glanced quickly through the lot, half-hoping to find a second paragraph about fireballs over Portsmouth. I found nothing at all.

I gave it up at last, rang the bell and sent for Sanders, the butler. He came in due course, grey-headed, lean, and infinitely well bred.

"Morning, Sanders," I said. "I brought a gentleman back with me from Winchester last night, and stuck him in my spare room. I expect the maid told you."

He inclined his head gravely. "She did, sir."

"Well," said I. "I think he's going to be ill."

He looked concerned. "I am very sorry to hear that, sir."

"Yes. So am I. As a matter of fact, I don't think it's anything very bad. Touch of malaria, I should think—he's not long back from the East. Shivering fits, and a temperature. He took enough quinine to kill a dog when we got in last night, and went off to bed. I've just looked in on him now. He's asleep."

I paused, and thought for a minute. "I've got to go to Pithurst for a sale to-day—I can't miss that. I'll be out to lunch. He'll probably stay in bed all day, I should think. Will you see Mrs. Richards about it, and get him some lunch taken over? Something pretty light—bit of fish, or something. I'll see if there's anything he wants before I go. And I'll be back about tea-time."

"Very good, sir. He might fancy a grape-fruit, with the fever."

I nodded. "Good scheme. You might send one over in the middle of the morning, if he's awake."

He went away, and I turned again to the papers. Relations with Russia were more strained than they had been since the time of the General Strike; the *Mail,* in particular, was very insistent on the subject. *The Times* was frankly concerned over the reception of our Note. I spread it out upon the gun-room table and became immersed in the leading article. I don't generally read the leaders in *The Times.* They're not much in my line. I've never taken much stock of politics or legislation or the affairs of state. But that day it was different. I wanted to find out exactly how matters stood, and as I sat there that morning, on the edge of the gun-room table in the sunlight, reading that leading article, I realised that things had gone further in the direction of a breach with Russsia than I had dreamed.

Lenden was awake when I got back to the house. I looked in at the door of his room for a moment before breakfast. He was very hot and restless in bed. He remarked thickly that he had a ruddy mouth like the bottom of the parrot's cage.

He said there wasn't anything that he wanted.

"Better stay where you are for the present, then," I replied, and retired to my bacon and eggs.

I looked in on him again before I went out. He was feeling very thick and rotten, and was evidently in for a pretty sharp bout of fever. I sat chatting with him for a bit, and then rang up the housekeeper and asked her to send over a thermometer. He had a temperature of about a hundred and two.

In ordinary circumstances I'd have sent for a doctor at that point. You can't afford to go messing about with a temperature like that. Lenden wouldn't hear of it. He said he knew what had to be done—lie in bed and take quinine and neat brandy till it went off. That seemed very reasonable to me; in any case, it was the treatment that had cured this thing before. It might have been rather difficult to explain him to the doctor, too; I didn't want his presence in Under advertised more than necessary, until I knew what he was going to do.

He didn't want anything to eat. I made him comfortable and went over and had a chat with Mrs. Richards, the house-keeper. I wasn't very happy about leaving him in a strange house in that condition, and told her to send over someone every couple of hours or so to see that he was all right. More than that I couldn't do; I left him some books and a decanter of brandy, got out my car, and went off to my office in Under.

My office is in the main street of the town, about a hundred yards from the market. I rent a couple of rooms there for the business, in the same building as the Rural District Council and the Waterworks Company. I had a good bit to do that morning, I remember, because it was getting on towards Quarter Day. However, at about half-past eleven I left my clerk to cope with the rest of it, and got going on the road for Pithurst.

I had to go. There was a chap there who'd made a real effort to get a pedigree herd of shorthorns together. Arner was keen on all pedigree stock, and we'd helped him quite a lot. This chap had put every bean he'd got into this herd, and borrowed a lot he hadn't, and then died. It really was rather important that I should be there to watch the sale. I had a long chat with Arner about it a couple of days before. We fixed it that if things began to go badly I was to start running the price up on one or two of the young bulls; if they came to us by the hammer we could ship them out to Las Plantas and get a good bit of our money back that way.

As it happened, that wasn't necessary. There was a fellow there who'd come up from Devon for the sale and really wanted the whole lot, I believe. Or at any rate, the heifers and young bulls. I'm not sure that if I'd gone to him privately he wouldn't have made an offer for the whole issue as it stood; still, we'd arranged an auction, and there were a good many of the local people interested. This Devon chap would have had it all his own way in spite of that, if I hadn't been there. Time after time I ran him up to a decent price for the beast when the locals had dropped out, and then left him to it. As things turned out he paid a pretty fair average price for what he had, and by the time we'd finished he was ready to see me dead. The locals took what was left. Not a bad sale, and I went home at the end feeling that I'd done a pretty good day's work.

It was about five o'clock when I moved off. I went by the

Under road, because I wanted to drop in at the office to sign my letters. I stayed there for a quarter of an hour or so, and then drove back to the Hall.

Now Under Hall lies about two and a half miles from the town, on the other side of the Rother. You come out of the town past the station and go on for about a mile or so, till you come to a humpy stone bridge across the river. Under Hall is about a mile farther on from that. I came swinging along that road in the Morris, thinking no evil, and pulled up with a squeal of brakes as I came upon the bridge. Sheila Darle was there, Arner's niece, sitting on the stone parapet in one of the triangular recesses.

She hadn't got a hat on, and I can remember that the wind was ruffling her short brown hair. That meant that she'd just strolled down from the Hall. She was sitting there on the bridge waiting for someone, and I had a feeling when I saw her that probably she was waiting for me.

I pulled up beside her.

"Good evening, Miss Darle," I remarked.

Well, it was. It had been a fresh, windy sort of day. Now in the evening the wind had dropped, the clouds had turned white and the sky deep blue. The sun was setting behind the down.

She slid down from the parapet and came and leaned her arms upon the hood, on the opposite side of the car to me.

"Good evening, Mr. Moran," she said. Somewhere behind her there was a thrush—the first I'd heard that year.

"Can I give you a lift back?" I asked. "I'm going straight home."

She shook her head absently. "It's a nice evening for walking. I wanted the walk."

She glanced up at me. "Mr. Moran," she said. "Who's that you've got in your house?"

There was no point in wasting petrol. I leaned forward to stop the engine, and took my time over answering that question.

"A chap I used to know in the Flying Corps," I replied, and

stared her down. "I met him in Winchester, and brought him back with me last night. His name's Lenden—Maurice Lenden."

She smiled at me across the car. "Maurice Lenden," she observed. "Now that's about the only thing I didn't know about him."

I eyed her thoughtfully for a minute. "I see," I said at last. "You've been doing a bit of Lady Investigating."

She nodded.

I had known Sheila Darle since first I came to Under. When first I came here she was still at school. She used to spend her summer holidays with her uncle at the Hall. One day that summer she went to London and had her hair bobbed in the Children's Department at Harrod's, and came back looking about ten years older. Fired by that, on the same evening, she took her uncle's little Talbot two-seater—that we kept for running in and out of town—and proclaimed her intention of driving it. Drive it she did, too—very neatly and accurately into the gatepost of the stable-yard and the dog-kennel. That was my first acquaintance with Sheila Darle, when she came to me very nearly in tears about it, and wanted to know what she was to do. I was younger then than I am now, but not so young as to miss the implication that the damaged wing and radiator should be repaired before Lord Arner came back from Town. I got it done in time, but I made her go and tell him about it. That set the keynote to our relations. Since those days I had sent off a couple of men with a horse to bring her car in about once every six months. Sometimes it was too bad for that, and then we had to get the garage to go and fetch it in.

I knew she wouldn't let me down in this.

"You've been talking to him?" I asked.

She shook her head. "He's been talking, but not to me. He's very ill."

I wrinkled my brows. "He's got a touch of fever," I said. "He took a cold a few days ago, and made it worse last night. But he should be all right. D'you mean he's off his head?"

She nodded. "Mm."

I reached out and put my hand to the starter. "I'd better get along back to him."

She didn't move from her position, leaning against the car. "He's all right now," she said. "He was sleeping quite nicely when I came out, and Mrs. Richards is in the sitting-room. But you shouldn't have left him like that. You gave Mrs. Richards a great fright."

"I'm sorry about that," I said. "I didn't think he was going to be off his head. He gets this thing whenever he takes a bad chill. Malaria, or something. He picked it up out in Honduras."

She didn't make any reply to that, so that there was silence for a bit. Then she looked up suddenly.

"Is he an airman?" she inquired.

I nodded. "He was in my squadron in the war. He became a professional pilot after that."

"And now," she said casually, "he's just come back from Russia."

I glanced down at the river. It runs pretty fast over pebbles beneath that bridge, and with a rippling sound. I have heard that there are grayling in it, and I remember wondering then if that were true. And presently I glanced at her again.

"You'd better tell me about it," I said quietly.

She laughed. "There's nothing much to tell. Only it's so funny. Mrs. Richards sent a maid over to him in the middle of the morning with a grape-fruit and some barley water, because she thought he'd like it. And the girl came back and said she couldn't make him understand anything, but he was talking to himself all the time. Mrs. Richards thought you'd got a looney over there, and went over herself. And then she came and fetched me."

"I see," I muttered. "That's how it was. Did you send for Armitage?" The local doctor.

She shook her head. "I didn't think it was necessary unless he got worse. You see, you'd told them that he'd got malaria, and that he'd have to lie up for a bit. You hadn't told them that he was going to be off his head, though. No, we just took it in turns to sit with him."

"That was kind of you," I said.

"Not a bit. He's a nice man."

I knew what she meant by that. There's no better way to get to know a man's character than to get him tight and see how he talks then. And I suppose delirium is much the same.

She leaned both arms upon the hood of the car and looked straight at me. "He was saying such funny things," she remarked.

I nodded ruefully. "I expect he was. What did he say?"

She considered for a minute. "It was all so mixed up," she said. "He seemed to be talking most of the time about a long night flight that he had made in the dark. In the cold." She glanced at me. "Do you know where that was?"

I shook my head.

"It was over snowy country, and it was very cold. He was frozen in his seat so stiff that he couldn't move, and his head kept dropping forward with the sleepiness of it. And to keep himself awake he raised his goggles, and the cold bit his face and made his eyes water, and the tears froze on his cheeks. And he was most terribly frightened."

She paused. "That's one of them. He gets a sort of cold fit every now and again, and whenever he gets that he comes back to talking about that cold flight. He shivers."

"Poor old soul," I remarked. "What else did he say?"

"He was talking a lot about his wife. But I don't want to repeat that, and there wasn't anything that really mattered. Except to them."

"All right. What else?"

It was very quiet by the river. "He was talking about a man called Poddy Armstrong that he used to meet at the Royal Aero Club. It was rather horrid, that. Where's the Royal Aero Club, Mr. Moran?"

"It's a London club," I said. "In Clifford Street." I glanced at her. "I suppose you're going to tell me that Poddy Armstrong was chasing him in another machine, and trying to shoot him down in the dark."

She stared at me. "How did you know?"

"Why," I said simply, "he told me."

"Why was Poddy Armstrong going to shoot at him?"

I took a long time over answering that question. "Perhaps they'd had a quarrel," I suggested in the end.

She was about to say something to that, but checked herself. I knew that I had hurt her. In the end she smiled at me. "I know it's not my business," she said. "But one can't help being curious."

"Neither yours nor mine," I said. "It's his own affair. He's been in a good bit of trouble lately, one way and another. He told me some of it last night, when we didn't go to bed. Did he say any more?"

She considered for a little. "No. Only one funny thing happened. He woke up at about three o'clock, and we gave him a drink of barley water. He was quieter then, and he seemed so hot. We thought it'd be a good thing. He asked for you. And I said that you were away, but you'd be back presently. And then he said a funny thing." She eyed me steadily. "He said you played the *Spring Song* at him."

"Is that all he said?"

"That's all. It didn't seem to make sense. He just rolled over and went to sleep when we'd given him his drink. I think he's sleeping still."

I sat there staring at the last gleams of sunshine upon the radiator thermometer of my car. It wanted polishing.

"Did you?" she inquired.

I turned to her. "I don't play at people," I replied. "I play because I want to. Lenden's a sick man, and sick men have fancies. You mustn't pay any attention to them."

The sun was just disappearing behind the down; in the fading light the soft brown hair clustered about her neck was all streaked and shot with gold. I had loved her for two years, and I had given up being hurt by things like that.

There was silence for a moment. Then I pulled my gauntlets farther on to my hands, leaned over, and slipped the catch of the door. It swung open by its own weight.

"Would you care for a lift home?" I said. "I must get back."

She got in without a word, and I started off for the Hall. That was a silent drive. It wasn't till I had driven into the yard and stopped the engine of the car in the coach-house that we spoke again.

"Of course," I said as the engine came to rest, "he's a man who's had a pretty rough time of it. You can see that for yourself." I paused, and chose my words. "He may even have got himself into trouble. If that were so, it would be a pity to remember anything that he may have said in fever, when he wasn't himself."

She glanced up at me in surprise. "But he didn't say anything that he need be ashamed of. Rather the opposite."

"No. But he may have said things that he'd rather not have talked about.

"In fact," I said, "he did."

There was a long silence after that. Finally she stirred, and got out of the car. "I knew it was something like that, of course," she said, and sighed. "It's a pity, because he's a nice man." She turned away. "All right, Mr. Moran, I'll not give him away. And I'll see Mrs. Richards."

She left the coach-house, and went walking across the yard towards the mansion. I sat there in the car staring after her for a little, wondering how much she knew.

Lenden was asleep when I got back to my house, and a maid was sitting in the adjoining room. I sent her back to the mansion and went in and had a look at him. I stood in the door for a while, staring moodily at him as he lay in bed. He was sleeping fairly quietly, though there was an odd, flushed look about him; his head was tousled and unshaven. There was a glass of barley water on the table by his side, and a few biscuits. Clearly the sleep was doing him a world of good; in view of the life that he had been leading during the last few days, that was hardly a matter for surprise. I stood there in the doorway for a long time staring at him, and wondering what the devil was going to happen about it all.

CHAPTER THREE

LENDEN SLEPT till about nine o'clock that night, and woke up more or less himself. I was working at the rent rolls in the sitting-room when I heard him stirring through the open doors, because it was getting on towards Quarter Day, and I'm always pretty full up about that time. I went in to have a look at what he was up to, and found him sitting up in bed.

"Evening," I said. "How d'you feel now?"

He moistened his lips. "I'm better," he said thickly. He shivered suddenly, and slid down beneath the bedclothes again. "I've had the hell of a go . . . this time. A proper searcher."

I went and sat on the foot of his bed. "Want a drink? There's something there—barley water, or something. Or I'll get you a whisky."

He craned his head to look at the tumbler. "No. Thanks. Not now. I'll go to sleep again in a bit. I don't ever remember being like this. What's the time?"

"About nine o'clock."

He passed one hand heavily across his forehead. "There was a girl here this afternoon," he muttered. "She gave me some stuff to drink."

I nodded. "Miss Darle," I said. "She told me she'd been with you."

"Oh." He was silent for a minute. "I was talking a good bit," he said thickly. "I hope to God I wasn't telling stories."

I laughed. "I don't know what you said," I remarked. "But, anyway, you didn't say anything to shock her."

He smiled faintly. "That's all right, then," he muttered. "Matter of fact, I don't know what I was talking about, but I know I was talking."

I made him comfortable for the night, persuaded him to have

a drink, and he rolled over on his side to go to sleep again. I left him to it.

I went back into the sitting-room and shut up my books. There were a couple of ledgers and the cash-book of the mansion there among the others; I piled these three together and went to put them in the safe. The top of the safe is a sort of repository for all the odds and ends that lie about my rooms and never get tidied up. I was brought up sharply as I approached it by the sight of that box of plates.

There it was, lying on the top of the safe with all the other junk. One of the maids must have put it there when she tidied up the room in the morning. I opened the safe and put away my books, and then picked this thing up and carried it over to the fire. It was a rectangular, flat metal box, roughly half-plate size, made of brass oxidised or blackened in some way, and neatly finished.

I sat down uneasily before the fire, and had a good look at the thing. It wasn't mine. It hadn't anything to do with me, really. It belonged to Lenden, and to him it was worth approximately one thousand pounds—the fee that he had taken. He had that money in his bank.

It was nothing to do with me at all. That was the basic conclusion that I came to, at the end of a quarter of an hour.

I sat there for a long time, turning the thing over uneasily in my hands, wondering what the devil they were up to at Portsmouth, and why the Soviet wanted to know about it. I didn't see what interest it could hold for them; they couldn't possibly be contemplating naval action against us. They hadn't got a navy, for one thing. I didn't see why they should be interested in our dockyards, other than from a purely academic standpoint. It seemed to me that their attitude might very well be: "That's a nice-looking dockyard; let's have one like that at Tkechkrotsz"—but it was hardly likely that they would be interested in the proposition—"That's the place to hit this handsome dockyard a cruel blow when we want to put it out of action next week."

And yet, it must be something like that. The people at

Portsmouth evidently thought it was important, to judge from the precautions they were taking. Sending up aeroplanes to shoot him down . . . It seemed to me that he couldn't possibly have been right about that. His nerves had been running away with him. Three long night flights on end. They must have been.

In any case, it didn't seem to me that I could do anything about it. It was Lenden's business. I've never been a man to go butting into another chap's affairs, and it didn't seem to me that I could go to him and talk about Our Dear Old Country, and what a sin and a shame it was to go and take photographs of it when it wasn't looking. No, I could only leave it to him to do what he thought best, though I knew what that would be. He'd taken their money, and he'd do their work. Still, it was none of my business, and in that resolve I went to bed.

I didn't sleep very well. I was still worried about those photographs. And in the intervals of that I was thinking of the quiet time I had had at Under since the war. I kept sleepily conning over the details of that sale at Pithurst, and the way I'd been able to run up the auction on that stock to make the price. And then I got to thinking of all the other times that Arner had set me on to do that sort of thing, and the way we'd been running the estate since the war. And I thought that really, taking it by and large, we'd made a pretty good show of it. Mind, we've got good land and a good crowd of farmers, and that helps. But we'd made that part of Sussex pretty prosperous. We'd been stuffing back into the land pretty well all that we took out of it. And I knew that Ellersleigh, whose land marched with ours to the north and west, was doing the same.

And then I got to worrying about those photographs again, and to thinking what a corking good county Sussex was. It was about three in the morning before I fell asleep.

Next day was a day of accounts. I spent it entirely at the office with my clerk, deep in the usual Quarter Day rush. I saw Lenden in the morning before I went out. He was looking a bit the worse for wear, but his temperature was practically normal. He didn't seem to be in any hurry to get away. I sat and talked to him for a little after breakfast, but avoided any direct or indirect question as to what he was going to do. I didn't think he knew himself. Till he had made up his mind there was very little to be done; I just encouraged him to stay in bed for another day, and left him to it.

That was Saturday. Arner was in Town that week, living at the house in Curzon Street and oscillating between the Foreign Office and the Athenæum. In the middle of the afternoon I had a trunk call from him.

"Is that Moran?"

"Speaking, sir."

"Moran. I shall be coming down this afternoon by the four-fifty. You'd better send the car to Petersfield, I think."

"Right you are, sir. I'll see to that."

"And, Moran. I am bringing Wing-Commander Dermott, of the Air Ministry, down with me. He will be staying with us over the week-end. Will you ring up the Hall and let them know? We will dine at eight o'clock tonight."

"Right," I said. "I'll ring up at once."

"And, Moran. I should be very glad if you would dine with us this evening. Is Sheila dining in to-night?"

"I think so. I haven't heard that she'll be away."

"Oh. Then we shall be an odd number. Still, I should be very glad if you would dine with us. I want you to meet Dermott."

"I'd like to very much, sir."

"All right. Is there anything else?"

I stirred in my chair, and settled to the more important business of my work. "That sale of Petersen's yesterday, over at Pithurst. It went off very well."

I gave him a short summary of the business done and the prices the beasts went for. We had another three minutes over that, and then he rang off.

I called up the house to give them their instructions, and settled to my accounts again. But my work was spoilt. Arner's sudden introduction of this Wing-Commander worried me and took my mind completely off my business. In all the years I had been at Under we had never entertained any officer of His Majesty's Royal Air Force. This was something quite new. Lord Arner was over seventy at that time, and a Civil Servant of the old type. We had Admirals and Generals at Under frequently, because these were old friends of his—men that he known at school and at Oxford and at the Athenæum. The Air Force was since his time—something new, and possibly not quite nice. I don't think he had any definite bias against it, but . . . it was since his time. He didn't know any of their Group-Captains, or Air Vice-Marshals, or whatever their peculiar titles were. They were all twenty years or so younger than he. And so it happened that Wing-Commander Dermott would be the first officer of that distinguished service who had ever been to Under, unless it was myself.

I wondered irritably who he was, and what the devil he was doing here. I couldn't repress a most uneasy feeling that he was after me.

There was a book that I wanted to consult, and I gave up the pretence of work at the office early in its favour. I left the town at about tea-time, and walked back to the Hall. I crossed the stable-yard, entered the mansion by the back door, went through into the Hall, and so to the library. The volume that I wanted lives on the writing-table there, together with Whitaker and Bradshaw. I crossed the room and opened it upon the blotting pad.

"D for Dermott," said Miss Darle reflectively.

It was a dull evening and that room faces north, as all libraries should; in the dim light I hadn't noticed her sitting in a deep chair before the fire. She couldn't have been reading because it was too dark; if I had thought about it at all, I had assumed that she was in the drawing-room. Now that's a queer thing. Looking back upon those days now, it seems very strange that I shouldn't have known that she was with me in the room. But I didn't.

I glanced towards her chair. "Exactly," I replied. "I always have to do this, I'm afraid. I'm not sufficiently acquainted with the *beau monde*."

I turned the pages to the Ds.

"His name's John Hilary Dermott," she said quietly, without stirring from where she sat. "He went to school at Uppingham. And then he went to Sandhurst. And then he went into the Shropshires, and then he got transferred to the balloon service of the Sappers, before they made it into the Flying Corps."

I had found the place by now. She was quite right, except that he was attached and not transferred. He had served with the flying branch of the Army from 1912 till it became the Royal Air Force, and so had attained the rank of Wing-Commander (Int.) at the age of thirty-eight.

"What does Int. after his name mean?" she asked.

I shrugged my shoulders casually. "I don't know," I replied. But I did. It meant Intelligence, and the sight of it gave me a nasty turn.

I stood there blankly for a minute, wondering if I ought to get Lenden out of the place before he came.

Sheila Darle got up from beside the fire and came over towards that writing-table by the window. I was still staring at that brief account.

"Mr. Moran," she said gently.

I raised my head to meet her eyes.

"Is this bloke coming on any sticky business?"

There was no point in beating about the bush. She knew too much already.

"I don't know," I muttered. "I hope to God he's not. I don't see how he could possibly be. But . . . I don't know."

She stood there eyeing me for a moment, silent. And then at the last she said:

"Can I do anything? Anything at all?"

I turned to face her. "I don't think there's anything you could do," I replied. "It's just that he's got himself into the dickens of a mess. And I suppose I'm in it too. It's a rotten business to be mixed up in, and I'd rather that you kept out of it."

"It's with Russia?" she inquired.

I nodded. "Yes."

She thought about it for a minute. "I'm so frightfully sorry," she said quietly. "If I can do anything at all to help, you must let me know."

And went.

I put that book back in its place between Whitaker and Bradshaw, left the library, and went over to my own house. Lenden was still in bed, but sitting up and reading a novel; he was looking very much more himself. He said that he was getting up next day. He said that it had been damn good of me to let him lie up like that.

I cut him short, and went and sat on the end of his bed. "D'you know anything about a fellow called Dermott?" I inquired. "Wing-Commander Dermott?"

He wrinkled his brows, and shook his head slowly. "No. I've heard the name somewhere."

"Well," I said, "he's coming down here to-night. Lord Arner's bringing him down to spend the week-end." I paused. "The only thing I know about him is that he's in the R.A.F. Intelligence."

There was a little silence, and then Lenden smiled. "I thought this was too good to be true," he said quietly. "I'd better get along out of it."

I shook my head. "I wouldn't do that. He may not be coming about you at all. I don't see how he can be. And anyway, you can't cut off now. Everyone knows you're here. You'll have to stay and bluff it out."

He stared at me wonderingly. "I don't see how they could know I'm here," he said. "Unless they've found the Breguet."

I thought that over for a minute. It was certainly a possibility. "I haven't seen it since yesterday morning," I said. "But I should have heard if it had been found. I hear everything that goes on here."

"Does this chap come down here often?" asked Lenden.

I laughed shortly. "No," I said, "he doesn't. We've not had an R.A.F. officer in the place since the war."

There was a little silence at that. "I'd better go," he said.

"It's been damn good of you to put me up like this, and I don't want to get you into trouble."

"Frankly," I replied. "I think you're more likely to get me into trouble if you go than if you stay."

"Do you think so?"

"I do. If this bloke's really after you and he gets to hear that you've shot off the minute you heard he was coming, I don't see how he could help putting two and two together. Even if he is in the Intelligence."

He considered the position for a bit.

"I suppose you're right," he said uncertainly. "I'd better stay —for to-night, anyway." He paused, gloomily. "I've got those photographs to get rid of—somehow. . . ."

He flared up suddenly. "I wish to hell I'd never touched the ruddy job," he said irritably.

I left him soon after that, and went into my room to dress for dinner. It was early, but I was tired and worried, and I wanted a bath. I stayed in it for a considerable time that evening, I remember. I was wondering what was going to happen to me. I had about a couple of hundred a year of my own at that time, and I was wondering how far that would go if I had to find another job over this business. I was wondering what I could turn my hand to if I had to leave Under. I was wondering why I had been such a fool as to take in Lenden, and why I didn't give him up. I had only to ring up the police, and the thing would be done. I was wondering whether it would be much of a blow to Arner when he found out the game that I'd been playing in his house. I was wondering how the next agent would run the estate when he took over from me, and if he'd grow to care about it all as I had done. I was wondering if the game was worth the candle.

I got out of my bath as it began to cool off, and dressed very slowly for dinner. In the end I was ready, and I went into the sitting-room to my piano.

It was dark in there. I lit the reading-lamp by the fireplace, sat down absently, and began polishing the second period of my play. That is the part where the Princess goes to live with the

Woodman in his hut; from that point I begin upon the change in values under the harsher conditions of the rustic life that in the end turn the Peasant into a Prince within the hut, and the Princess to a Peasant girl. Those are effects that one can work up rather subtly upon the screen, but it's a difficult bit of music. I became immersed in the thing, and sat there in the half-light before dinner for the better part of an hour, polishing those passages. Till in the end, by the time I got up from the piano, I was ready for what I could see was going to be rather a trying evening.

At about half-past seven I went over to the house.

There was nobody about downstairs. I passed the open door of the dining-room on my way through the hall, and paused for a minute. The table was laid for five. That room would seat fifty without inconvenience, I suppose; the house is Georgian. But Arner entertained very little; in all the years that I had been at Under I don't suppose that I had seen that table laid for more than ten people. It was his fancy always to dine by candle-light; I remember that the white and silver table in the shaded light from the candelabra made a little gleaming oasis in the darkness of that great room.

Sanders was there, wandering reverently around the table. Now and again he would pause to shift a salt-cellar an inch or two, or to pick up a spoon, breathe on it, and polish it. He told me that Commander Dermott had arrived. He was dressing.

I passed on to the deserted drawing-room. There was a bright fire in the grate; I switched on a light and went and stood before it. I had had great kindness from the Arners during the seevn years that I had been at Under. One of my uncles married a second-cousin of Lady Arner. They had chosen to regard that as a close tie, and had treated me more as a member of the family than as a salaried official of the estate. I remember thinking about those things as I stood there before the fire that evening, waiting for the family to come down. I was wondering what sort of a show I was going to put up.

That quarter of an hour came to an end before I had decided in the least what I was going to do. Lady Arner came down first, followed by Sheila Darle in a little green filmy dress that made her look a child. Lady Arner was frankly curious about this Wing-Commander that her husband had brought down. She wanted to know what he had come for; I wanted to know that, too, but with the best will in the world I couldn't tell her. She said that Arner had had a very heavy day in Town, from which I inferred that things were none too bright at the Foreign Office.

And then, till the others came, we talked about her garden—the one subject of which she never tired. She was a great gardener. She used to spend all the summer grubbing about in an old skirt, and an old straw hat, and a pair of gloves, with Watson, our head gardener, in attendance. I can remember winter evenings when she would sit from half-past eight till eleven before the fire in the drawing-room, pencil in hand, with catalogues from Carter, Sutton, and Bunyard on her knee. Dreaming and, as often as not, falling asleep. She didn't go to London much.

Arner came down at last, with Dermott, and we went in to dinner. Dermott was a younger-looking man than I had expected; he must have been about six foot two in height, and thin. He was clean-shaven, with thin fair hair, blue eyes, and long, young face. He looked very little over thirty. I was introduced to him.

He greeted me frankly. "Good evening, Mr. Moran," he said. "I've been hearing about you from Lord Arner. He tells me that you were in the R.F.C. in the war." He had a pleasant, quiet voice.

"That's a good long time ago," I replied. "I've pretty well forgotten all about it."

He smiled, a little anxiously. "You haven't kept up with flying?"

I laughed. "Lord, no," I said. "Give me pigs." And we sat down to table.

Dinner was a constrained meal. Arner sat at the head of the table, a sombre little figure with rather untidy thin grey hair, and a monocle on the end of a black silk ribbon. This evening he was evidently tired, and seemed in some way to have grown smaller and older. Things must have been going very badly up in Town that day. He spoke very little. There was some understanding between him and his guest; both were pre-occupied, though Dermott was talking rather at random to Lady Arner. Clearly there was business to be done, and both of them were only waiting till the ladies had left the room.

That happened at last. I got up to open the door for them to pass out, and closed it softly behind them. Sanders placed the port convenient to Lord Arner, and disappeared into the gloom. I came back to the table and sat down.

Arner motioned us to the cigars, but did not take one him-self immediately. Instead he leaned a little forward with his elbows on the table and put both hands to his forehead, raising his head and drawing his hands down his face till he was staring straight ahead of him again. I knew that motion.

I took a cigar. "Things bad in Town, sir?"

He dropped his hands on to the table. "Middling," he said rustically. "Middling. Remind me to order the *Studio* for Curzon Street, Moran."

I nodded. "I'll see about it to-morrow," I replied.

I knew what he meant by that. He had in the library at Under all the bound volumes of the *Studio* since the begin-ning. When he was worried or upset over anything he used to go in there and sit down beside the fire, and turn these volumes over slowly. When he came to a picture that he liked he would sit staring at it for a long time without moving. He liked water-colour reproductions best, I think, and especially garden sketches, water-colours of herbaceous borders, and paintings with delicate, bright colours. Sometimes he would pass the heavy volume across to me when he had found a drawing that he particularly admired.

He roused himself. "Look here, Moran," he said. "I've brought Wing-Commander Dermott down from London to have a talk with you. He's in the Intelligence Service of the Royal Air Force."

He dropped his head into his hands again. "You know the

trouble with Russia," he said wearily. "It's been going on for years now—been brewing for the last eighteen months. I had a long talk with Faulkner to-day. Well, it's come to a head at last, I think. When we must force the issue. There was a Cabinet all yesterday afternoon, and again this morning. There's been an espionage at Portsmouth. That's what Dermott's come down about. And we think it's them. . . ."

He stared at the decanter. "If that should be established, it might prove to be the deciding factor. The least thing can swing the balance now. This thing has been done by an aeroplane. Dermott will tell you about that. I was sent for this afternoon to the Air Ministry. They are of the opinion that one of the aeroplanes engaged in this espionage was brought down on Thursday night. They think it landed in this part of the country. They've named an area. In the square formed by Pithurst, Leventer, Courton Down, and Under."

"That's all our land," I said quietly.

He turned to me. "I know. That's what I want you to consult with Dermott about. This thing's too delicate to be handled by the local constable. But you know the country and the people better than I do myself. Much better than the police. You know every hedge and field on the estate, and you know the tenants. I told them at the Ministry that if an aeroplane had landed on my ground and they wanted to find out about it quietly, you were the man to see. I told them I'd bring Dermott down with me, and he could have a talk with you."

He turned to Dermott. "You'll want to go over the ground to-morrow, I suppose?"

"I shall be able to say more about that when I've had a talk with Mr. Moran, Lord Arner."

Arner nodded wearily. "You'd better carry on straight ahead. Moran is completely in my confidence. You can speak plainly to him."

I shifted uneasily in my chair.

Arner reached out slowly for a cigar, and lit it. Dermott turned to me. "I understand that you were a pilot in the war, Mr. Moran," he said.

69

"Of a sort," I replied. "I was never anything to write home about."

He smiled. "Still, with that experience you'll probably be able to give me a lot of help. First of all, I think I'd better give you the outlines of this—this espionage. You'll see better then what we want to know."

He paused. "There's something going on at Portsmouth," he said at last, and seemed to consider for a minute. "A certain operation. At the Ministry—the Air Ministry—we do not consider this operation to be our concern at all. We regard it as purely an Admiralty matter. You'll appreciate the position. There's very little to be gained by discussing this—operation."

I nodded. "I can take that for granted."

"Right. Now, a part of the work necessary in the carrying out of this scheme is maritime, and is so placed as to be in full view of the shore. Generally speaking, all operations that concern harbour defences and matters of that sort are regarded as secret, but usually that secrecy is only relative. You see what I mean. If a fort is to be built, the Admiralty can go on saying it's secret till they're blue in the face—but there it is, and any passer-by can see the muzzles of the guns sticking out."

He blew a long cloud of smoke. "In this instance—which is in no way connected with the defences of the port—secrecy really is most urgent. It's vital. For that reason, since a part of the operation can be seen from the shore, it was arranged to carry out the necessary maritime work at night."

He paused, and eyed me steadily. "Twice in the last week this work has been overlooked, and possibly photographed. Each time an aeroplane, the nature of which we don't yet know, has flown over and dropped a large magnesium flare."

I nodded slowly, without taking my eyes from his face.

"The first time it happened was on Monday night. The flare appeared suddenly at a height of about two thousand feet, and burnt for perhaps a minute. It came as a complete surprise. There was a tendency at first to put it down to a natural phenomenon—a meteor of some sort. That's all nonsense, of course."

I wrinkled my brows. "If it was an aeroplane, surely you'd have heard it," I remarked. "They make the devil of a noise."

"Unless they are silenced. There's been a lot of progress made in that direction—in this country."

"I hadn't heard of that," I said. "I've been away from flying for so long."

He knocked the ash from the end of his cigar on to a plate. "The same thing happened last Thursday night," he said. "This time the machine was seen. It got too close to the light, and was seen clearly for a few seconds in the light of its own flare. We were fully alive to the situation then, and certain anti-aircraft measures had been put in hand. Well, they didn't come off. The machine got away without being identified."

I blew a long cloud of smoke. "I imagine you'll make it pretty hot for him if he comes again," I remarked.

"If he comes again," repeated Dermott. "He may not. We're by no means sure that he got away on Thursday. In fact, we think he landed. Here."

I paused for a moment before replying. "I see," I said at last. "What makes you think that?"

"Two bits of evidence. The lighthouse-keepers at the Nab Tower report that they heard the engine of an aeroplane come on suddenly, not so very far away. They've got an acoustic apparatus there that tells them roughly the direction of any sound. It's a simple thing; they use it for ships in fog. They turned it on to this aeroplane."

He smiled. "Now, their evidence is rather interesting. They say that the sound was steady for half a minute or so—just the normal noise of an aeroplane. It seemed to be coming straight towards them. Then they heard the engine shut off, and opened out again. That happened three times. Then the machine seemed to stop coming towards them and apparently turned towards the coast, travelling in a northerly direction till they lost it. None of our own aircraft were in the vicinity at the time.

"Apart from that," he said, "we have definite evidence that the machine turned inland."

I raised my eyebrows.

"We had a bit of real good luck. A sergeant fitter from the Gosport squadron was on leave that night, and was cycling with his girl between Chichester and Arundel. He's a Chichester man. He heard this aeroplane come over him, and he saw it. There was a moon behind some clouds—thin clouds, so that there was a light patch in the sky. He got off his bicycle when he heard the machine, and as he was looking round he saw it cross this patch of light."

I moistened my lips. "That's a bit of luck," I said.

He nodded. "Just one chance in a hundred—but he saw it. The machine was flying due north, and by his account it was climbing to gain height rapidly. He says it was a large single-engined biplane, possibly with extensions to the upper wing. As an Air Force sergeant, he could tell a good deal from the noise of the machine. He was of the opinion that the engine was a twelve-cylinder, water-cooled, broad-arrow type—three banks of four—of about four or five hundred horse-power, fitted with a large, slow-running propeller, driven through an epicyclic gear with a reduction of at least two to one, and with a double exhaust-manifold that carried the gases well down the fuselage."

Lord Arner laid down his cigar and drew one hand across his eyes. "Now that, to me," he said, "is one of the most curious features of Commander Dermott's story. I find it most remarkable that this man should be able to give full details of the engine in an aeroplane merely from the sound as it flew over him. Most remarkable, and most extraordinary."

He relapsed into silence.

Dermott paused for a minute, and then continued: "He only saw the machine for a few seconds, but he continued to hear it for several minutes. When it crossed the moon from him he judged it to be at a height of about three thousand feet, and climbing rapidly. He heard its engine for two or three minutes longer, by which time it was a considerable distance to the north of him. The engine was then shut off, and he heard nothing more."

I nodded slowly. "The machine landed?"

"Apparently."

"Did the sergeant make any effort to find the machine?"

"No. When he heard the engine shut off he judged the machine to be four or five miles to the north of him. It was a quiet night, you see. To look for the machine in those circumstances was hopeless for one man—and besides, he was on leave and he'd got a girl with him. He thought he'd seen a forced landing by one of our own night-flying aircraft on a practice flight. So he cycled on to Chichester and parked his girl, and rang up his commanding officer at Gosport to give him the information."

He was silent.

"That is all the evidence?" I asked.

"That's all."

I laid down my cigar and leaned forward on the table. "And from a study of the map you think he put down in the area Lord Arner mentioned? Pithurst, Leventer, Courton Down, and Under?"

"We think so."

I thought about it for a minute. "There are a great number of places in that area where an aeroplane could land, even at night," I said. "But surely, it's a bit premature to assume that she landed at all. She may only have started to fly silently. If she could do that once she could do it again."

He shook his head. "That has been suggested. But against that we've got what happened at the Nab. You know what happens when a pilot finds his engine flagging—a stoppage in the petrol supply, perhaps. He throttles his engine down, and then opens out again to try and clear it. You do it on a car, just the same. And if he can't get it right, he turns towards the best country for a forced landing and climbs to gain height before it peters out altogether, so that he can have time to look about for a safe landing-ground while he's gliding down."

There was a long silence. At last:

"That all fits in," I said. "I must say, it looks as if something of the sort had happened. Still, that's two days ago. I can hardly believe that the aeroplane can still be here. I must have heard of it before this."

I paused for a moment. "You see," I said quietly, "I hear everything that goes on here."

He inclined his head. "Quite so. Frankly, I don't expect to find the aeroplane. That would be too much to hope for. Too good to be true. I think it most likely that the pilot landed, contrived to rectify the trouble, and got away again. Very likely I've come down here on a wild-goose chase. But the least evidence about this thing will be of value to us now."

"You've named a mighty big area of country," I muttered.

The candles were flickering in some draught about the table, throwing great dancing shadows in the corners of the room, and glinting on the silver. I dropped my head into my hands, and sat staring at my plate for a minute or two. I was thinking of Lenden. I'm not a strong man myself, nor a clever one. I had to make my decision in that moment; I'm damned if I know now whether I did right or not.

I raised my head. "The funny thing is that I was out that night myself," I said. "I was driving back from Winchester with a friend. We didn't get in till about two in the morning. But I saw nothing of all this."

Now that, to me, sums up the whole essence of that evening— the earlier part of it, at any rate. Looking back upon it now, after all these months, I don't know that I regret it.

"A further point," said Dermott. "Do you know of anyone disaffected in the neighbourhood? Anyone who might be expected to give assistance in such a case?"

"You mean, anyone with Russian sympathies?"

He nodded.

I shook my head slowly. "We're an agricultural county, you see. I don't know of any red-hot Bolsheviks here. We've got a few cranks, of course. There's a chap here in Under, a hairdresser, who talks Communism in the market on Saturdays. He doesn't count. No, there's nobody that I know of."

Lord Arner nodded gravely. "That is also my opinion."

"You don't see much chance of a conspiracy?"

74

"No," I replied, "I don't. Quite frankly, from what you've said, I think that if that machine had trouble that forced her to land she must have put it right and got away again without anyone being any the wiser. Otherwise, I think I must have heard of it."

There was a long silence, and then:

"It doesn't look very promising," said Dermott ruefully. "It was an off-chance from the first, of course."

I began to describe to him the various possible landing-grounds in that part of the country. They were innumerable on the downs, and very many in the farming land. For the better part of an hour I led him in a random, detailed discussion of the neighbourhood. I told him everything that I could think of about the area that he was interested in, and I told him nothing that was of any value to him at all.

We gave it up at last, and went through into the drawing-room. It must have been about ten o'clock by then. We had settled that in the morning I should take Dermot for a run over the area in a car, and point out to him what I considered to be the most favourable landing-grounds. But I had done my work pretty well. By the time we left the dining-room I could see that he regarded the whole matter as a useless quest, and that he was already wondering whether it would not be better for him to get back to London straight away. Lord Arner said roundly that he thought we should find nothing at all.

I didn't think that I should have much difficulty in concealing the Breguet from an investigation conducted in that spirit.

In the drawing-room we all had to brace ourselves a little to be entertaining for an hour before bed. As the easiest way out of a difficult position—for we were all preoccupied that night—Arner picked on me. I wasn't sorry to sit down and play to them; it saved the necessity for talking. Lady Arner has a great attachment to light opera. I remember playing Saint-Saëns for her that evening, with a considerable effort to take the treacle out of *Mon cœur se lève à ta voix,* and a little Verdi. Then I went wandering for a bit, and I remember playing *One Fine Day*. Now that was a funny thing. She liked that best of all, but would never ask for it. She used to ask for *Mon cœur* and for bits of *La Traviata,* and she liked Schubert; but I cannot remember that she has ever asked for *Butterfly,* although she likes it best of all.

The evening came to an end at last—that part of it, at any rate. Lady Arner gathered her things together presently and went up to bed, taking Sheila with her; I think our acting must have been pretty poor. Arner rang the bell and we had a whisky and soda together, rather a silent one, and then I said good night and went back to my house across the still, moonlit stable-yard.

Lenden was up when I got back, and sitting in a chair before the fire in my pyjamas and dressing-gown. He told me that he was much better, and had got up while they made his bed. And had stayed up. I could see that he was better; he had shaved and looked altogether more himself.

I mooned uncertainly about the room for a bit, and then lit a cigarette and sat down. "This fellow Dermott," I said.

Lenden looked up quickly. "What about him?"

"He's after you, all right. They've got quite a good idea of what you did and where you came from. They know you landed somewhere near here." I paused. "Dermott came to get me to help try and find you."

"Oh." He stared at me darkly. "Did you?"

I chucked the match into the fire. "No," I said after a minute. "As a matter of fact, I didn't."

"Why not?"

I shrugged my shoulders. "I don't know."

"What did he want you to do?"

I leaned back in my chair. "Just to help him get any information there was to be had. They know the machine landed in this part and they came to me—as a sort of private detective, I suppose. Because I hear all the gossip. Because if anyone knew anything, it would be me. That's why they came. We had a long talk about it. They don't know you by name, and they're not sure where the machine came from. They know you had engine trouble and had to land. That's all. They think now that you must have put it right and got away again."

He stared morosely into the fire. "So I would have done if I'd had a bit of pipe. It's only a little thing. But I'd got nothing. Not a tool of any sort. One never thinks of carrying tools in an aeroplane."

He sat there brooding in his chair for a long time after that. It must have been a long time, because I remember that his cigarette went out between his fingers. Till at last:

"I don't know why you went and did that," he said slowly. "Why didn't you tell them that I was here?"

I turned to him in blank amazement.

"It'd have meant about ten years in quod for you if I had," I replied curtly.

Apparently that was quite a new idea to him. He looked across at me vaguely. "Would it?"

I laughed shortly. "It ruddy well would. I used to be a lawyer."

He was silent then for a minute, staring into the shadows of the room beyond me. "Even so," he said quietly, "it might have been the best thing to have done."

I got up irritably and stood with my back to the fire. "I'm damned if I see that," I said. "You're out of the wood now— practically. This chap Dermott will go away to-morrow. I've just about finished with him. I've only got to run him round a bit in the car and keep him away from the Breguet, and then he'll go. You'll have nothing to worry about then. We'll burn the Breguet, and then you'll be free to do what you like."

He took me up at once. "What do you suppose that's going to be?"

That point hadn't occurred to me before. I stood there eyeing him for a minute. And then I made a sudden movement. "It's no business of mine," I said impatiently. "*I* don't know what you're going to do."

He laughed, not very pleasantly. "Neither do I."

After that there was a long silence in the room. Presently I went over to the piano and sat down absently, but I didn't play. I sat there fingering the keys, polishing them with my handkerchief, and wondering what the devil was going to happen to him. It hadn't struck me before that that might be a bit of a problem.

"Does anyone in England know you went to Russia?" I inquired.

He shrugged his shoulders. "I didn't tell anyone. And I went out on a forged passport."

I dropped my hands from the keyboard. "Then I don't see that it matters. You can stay in England if you want to."

He turned on me. "England's no damn good without a job. It's all very well for you to talk, in a place like this. But for me —the last job I had was in the garage. Ruddy good fun, that."

I was silent.

And presently he began to talk. "You see, it's not as if I had a home in England now," he said. "I've got nowhere to go to . . . or anything. It's been damn good of you to let me lie up here like this, and it's given me a chance to think things out, lying in bed all the time. And I think I'd better go back to Russia."

I moved over to the sideboard, a little ashamed of myself. "Have a drink," I said.

He took a whisky and sat down again before the fire. "I know what you're thinking," he muttered. "You think I ought to go to Scotland Yard like a Briton and give up these ruddy photographs. Well, I'm not going to. I'm going back to Russia with them."

I set down my glass. "Do whatever you like," I said phlegmatically. "Do what you think'll do you most good."

He disregarded that. "I've thought it all out. I'm going back to Russia. There's good jobs to be had out there, and I'm in one of them. It's a good country if you can learn to hold your tongue. It's good pay, and you can live decently. More than you can in this damn country. I'll take on again with them and stay out there for another five years or so, and then maybe I'll come back and put what I've saved into a business."

"You could do that now," I said.

He turned and stared at me. "What about these plates?"

I fingered my tumbler for a minute. "Forget about them. You don't want to go mucking about with that sort of thing if you're going to stay in England."

He shook his head slowly. "That's not the way I do business," he said. "I've always played what I thought was the straight game, and I'm damned if I'll chuck it now."

I nodded. I had a feeling that perhaps he might be looking at it like that. Business is business.

"Send back the thousand, then," I suggested. "To Arcos."

He stared at me blankly. "I don't see the point of that. That means I'd have no money and no job." He paused. "I'd be a damn sight better off in Russia. I'm getting eight hundred a year there, you know. Sterling."

I eyed him thoughtfully. "There's one other way," I said. "What's that?"

"Send the plates by post to the Soviet Embassy to send back to Russia, but stay in England yourself. With the thousand."

There was a bit of cork in his tumbler. He sat there for a long time studying this thing, swishing it round and round the edge of the glass. Till at last:

"I don't think that would work," he said slowly. "You can't run with the hare and hunt with the hounds like that. It's what every bloody little pimp and dago does. You can stick to the service and be a hundred per cent Englishman—or you can go into business with the other side. It's got to be one thing or the other. You can't have it both ways. And I'm free to choose. If I'd got a wife, and a home to go to, and a chance of kids . . . it might be different. Maybe I'd chuck it up then, and stay in England and hope something would turn up—like I used to. But . . . I don't want to do that now.

"I want to get away from the whole bloody issue," he said, a little plaintively. "I thought all this out before I went to Russia first of all, and I've been thinking about it again now. And I don't see any reason to change."

He drained his glass and set it down upon the table. "It's the kids," he muttered. "If there was any chance of a home and kids . . . it'd be different."

I got up from my chair and put my glass upon the mantel-piece. "Do what you like," I said absently. "I expect you're right."

And with that we went to bed. I undressed slowly that night, wondering what I ought to do about it. I didn't much care for the thought of Lenden getting away with those photographs and taking them back to Russia. And I had an idea, too, that he didn't want to go himself. I thought then, and I still think, that it would have been a relief to him if I had gone over to the mansion there and then and given him up to Dermott. I wish to God I had.

I got into bed, and pretty soon I fell asleep.

I was roused by Sanders in the middle of the night. I sleep pretty heavily, and I woke up slowly to find him shaking me by the shoulder. "Mr. Moran. Mr. Moran, sir."

I opened one eye and leaned up on one elbow. "What's the trouble?" I muttered.

It was still quite dark outside. The old man was inadequately dressed in a shirt and trousers covered by an overcoat, but dignified withal. "Lord Arner would be glad if you would go over to the library, sir. He sent me to wake you."

"Good God!" said I. "What's the time?"

"About four o'clock, sir."

I rubbed my eyes and sat up in bed. It was very cold. "Right you are," I said. "I'll be over in about ten minutes. D'you know what's happening?"

"There was a telephone call came through at about two o'clock, sir. A trunk call. You know, sir, the extension to the bell rings in my bedroom."

I nodded sleepily. "Who was it for?"

"For Commander Dermott. I went to his bedroom, sir, and called him to answer it because they said it was urgent. It was a call from Gosport. Official business, I imagine, sir."

I was suddenly awake. "What's been happening since then?"

"There have been several other calls. The Commander went to see Lord Arner in his dressing-room after the first one, sir.

Lord Arner came downstairs about an hour ago. Commander Dermott is with him in the library now. I think the gentlemen have been speaking to London on the telephone."

I slipped out of bed on to the floor. "Right you are," I said. "I'll be over in a minute or two."

I dressed hurriedly when he had gone, and went across the stable-yard to the mansion. It was very cold outside. In the yard the moon was bright, a brilliant night with patches of loose cloud swinging across the moon in a strong westerly breeze. I paused for a minute, and looked around at the hurrying clouds and at the stars between. That was no night for espionage. There was no cover in the sky.

I found Dermott with Arner in the library. Both were fully dressed in morning clothes. They had made up the fire into a great blaze, and Dermott had drawn up a little table before it. He was sitting at this table when I went in, and he had it all littered with papers and a map. Arner was in his usual chair before the fire, the little table at his elbow.

"Morning, sir," I said as I went in. "Nothing wrong, I hope?"

Dermott raised his head and turned towards me. "There has been a development of this spying," he said. "My information is very brief. The machine has been over Portsmouth this evening for the third time, and dropped the usual flare. Exactly as before. They were ready for it this time. The machine was shot down by one of our own night fighters, and crashed in a field near Hamble."

I didn't speak.

Lord Arner turned to me. "Sit down, Moran," he said. "It will not be long now before we hear the whole of this affair."

Dermott turned again to his papers. "I'm expecting a report in a few minutes," he remarked. "Jackson and the pilot are on their way here now—by road. They started about an hour ago."

In the library it was very still. Arner was sitting huddled up in his great leather armchair before the fire, slowly filling a pipe. Dermott was silent and immersed in his papers at the table; I could not see what he was doing. I drew up a chair upon the other side of the table, and sat down before the fire; for a long time the little roaring of the flames and the little crashes of the embers were the only noises that I heard in that great room. Presently Arner lit his pipe and threw the match into the grate and, reaching down, dragged out a heavy volume from the bookcase by his chair. He snapped on the reading-light beside him, opened the book upon his knees, and began turning the pages slowly, with long pauses, the blue smoke coiling thinly above his head into the darkness.

For over half an hour we must have sat like that, a silence broken only by the fire, by the rustle of Dermott's papers as he made his notes, or by the occasional rippling as Arner turned a page. At last Dermott pushed back his chair, glancing from his watch to the clock.

"They should have been here by now," he muttered.

Arner raised his head. "It is a very long way."

"Forty-five miles," said Dermott incisively. "Say an hour and a quarter." He glanced down at his host as he stood before the fire, and his eyes rested curiously on the volume. For a minute he looked puzzled; perhaps that book didn't quite fit in with his conception of a diplomat. But Arner had a picture of a Devon lane there, and he never stirred or looked up. In the last few days it seemed to me that he had aged very rapidly.

I listened for a moment in the stillness, and stood up. "There's a car coming now," I said.

They must have made pretty good time from Gosport. I went through the hall to the door and opened it as the car drew up—a big American five-seater, perhaps a Stutz or Chrysler. Two men in uniform greatcoats got out of it; in the light that streamed from the door I could see that one of them was very young. As young as I was when I used to play that game.

The elder of the two came up the steps first, and stood peering at me for a moment. "Wing-Commander Dermott?" he inquired.

"He's inside, waiting for you," I replied. "Come in."

I showed them through the hall into the library. Dermott and Arner were standing there together before the fire.

"Evening, Jackson," said Dermott. "Squadron-Leader Jackson—Lord Arner." He turned to Jackson again. "And . . ."

Jackson motioned to his companion. "Flying-Officer Mackenzie, sir," he said. This was a sandy-haired, pale-faced young man. I don't think he can have been more than twenty-one or twenty-two years old. He was a well set-up, athletic-looking young fellow, but he was curiously white; as he stood there his eyes were wandering uneasily around the room. It seemed to me that he was nervous, and more than a little shaken.

"What about the letters?" said Dermott briskly. "You've brought them with you?"

Jackson nodded. "There are three or four, sir," he replied. "So far as I have been able to make out, this pilot was a German subject, operating from Kieff. There is an addressed envelope."

He laid down a large official envelope, and opened it on the table. From it he took two crumpled letters and a little flat packet wrapped in some coarse cloth. "These are the letters," he said.

Dermott opened them one by one, and skimmed rapidly through the spidery writing on the pages. "These are in German," he said to Arner, and dropped his eyes to the paper again. "From his wife." He muttered a sentence or two in German, half to himself, and flicked over the page. "They are addressed to Leutnant Friedrich Keumer, at an address in Kieff. They contain nothing but local gossip and news of his children. What one would expect. . . ."

He smiled at the paper, a little cynically. " 'Elsa has with Franz to the Steiner this afternoon gone,' " he read. " 'So I am alone.' "

He laid down the letter.

Arner inclined his head. "A German pilot flying for the Soviet?" he inquired.

"I think so," replied Dermott. He reached for the cloth packet. "What's in this?"

Jackson was before him, and took it up. "More letters, sir.

Those that you have were found in one of the side pockets on the right-hand side. These are from the breast pocket on the left. I'm afraid you'll find them in rather a mess."

Dermott took the packet and unwrapped it carefully. Inside there was a sodden pulp of paper, reddish black in colour, and very sticky. He turned the mass over curiously with his forefinger, stared at it for a moment, and then wrapped it up again in the fabric.

"Can't do much with these, I'm afraid," he remarked coolly. "They'll have to be treated."

Arner nodded gravely. "Make that boy sit down," he said. "He's looking quite ill."

I saw Mackenzie stiffen. "I'm quite all right sir," he said.

Dermott and Jackson turned and stared at him. He was certainly very white.

I turned to Jackson. "You've had a long drive," I said, "and it's cold outside. What about a whisky?"

"That's right," said Arner. "Give him a whisky." And while I was fiddling with the siphon and the glasses, Dermott turned again to Jackson.

"What was the machine?"

"A Breguet XIX with the Lorraine engine. She's very badly crashed, and it's dark. There was a camera, but the engine is on top of it at the moment. I left instructions that nothing was to be moved till dawn, on account of destroying any evidence. Till we can get a sheer-legs and lift the engine, we shan't be able to get at the camera. The machine seems to be a single-seater, and fitted with an adjustable propeller. But that again—we haven't examined."

They began upon rather a lengthy technical discussion about the best means of salving any evidence in the wrecked machine. They congratulated each other on the fact that it had not caught fire.

"A German pilot," said Dermott at last, "living in Russia, and flying a French machine." He mused over it for a little. "We shall want to know more than that."

He turned to Jackson again. "Did you have much difficulty in getting him down?"

"Mr. Mackenzie had better give you his report, sir."

Mackenzie pulled himself up and set down his glass. There was more colour about him now; I'd made that whisky a good one.

"No, sir," he said. "It went all right this time."

Dermott eyed him for a moment. "How long did you take to get away?"

Jackson interposed. "The machines—three of them—were off the ground thirty-five seconds after the first alarm," he said. "We have been practising that in the last few days. With Hucks starters."

"That's very good indeed," said Dermott. "What happened then?"

"Mr. Mackenzie," said Jackson.

The boy came forward. "There was a bright moon," he said, "and the searchlights were holding the machine. I didn't have to go and look for it."

He paused.

"The searchlights picked up the machine almost at once," said Jackson. "From Gosport, and from a destroyer off Southsea. As soon as the flare appeared."

Dermott interposed. "The pilot first, Major Jackson."

Mackenzie drew himself up nervously. "I took off as soon as the starter was clear," he said. "Before the landing lights came on. Flight-Lieutenant Armstrong was next off the ground, I think. And then Hesketh."

"On what machines?"

"I was flying the Nightjar, sir. Armstrong and Hesketh were on Doves."

He paused to collect his story. "I came up with the Breguet about a minute and a half later, at about two thousand feet," he said. "That was over Southsea. I think Armstrong was somewhere near me, but I don't remember seeing him. The machine was still in the searchlights, but it was slipping about a good bit and very nearly clear of them. But there was a good moon, and even if he'd got clear we'd still have been able to see him, I think. I switched on the fighting beam at once and pooped off a green Very light at him, as we'd arranged."

Dermott inquired: "Did he take any notice?"

"Not that I saw, sir. He got clear of the searchlights almost directly after that. I could still see him faintly in the moonlight, and brilliantly whenever I got the fighting beam on to him, of course. He slipped right round then, and went away to the west, full out. I went after him."

He paused again. "I didn't gain much on him. I think he must have been very nearly as fast as the Nightjar, sir. I lost all touch with Poddy then. We left the Doves behind. We went away west for minutes on end, and when I'd closed up till he filled the ring of my sight in the fighting light I gave him a burst of tracer bullets, sir. Over his head."

"Did he make any reply to your fire? At any time?"

The boy swallowed violently. "No, sir. I don't think he had a gun."

"Did your fire have any effect at all?"

"No, sir. I thought at first he was giving up after that, because he turned away and I lost sight of him for a moment. I thought perhaps he'd shut off, and was going down to land. And then I picked him up again. He'd turned north, and he was still going full out. We were over the Solent then, and somewhere west of Lee."

Dermott eyed him keenly. "What happened then?"

"I was afraid he would get away, sir. I was running my engine full out with the supercharger. It's not meant to be run like that below fifteen thousand feet, but I was afraid he'd get away from me. I couldn't have kept up with him any other way."

Jackson interrupted. "Mr. Mackenzie means that he could only rely upon his engine to give that excess power for a very short time. He had to act quickly, or not at all. As you know, sir—I had given explicit orders that the machine was to be shot down in those circumstances."

Dermott nodded. "I know," he said. "Mr. Mackenzie did quite right."

He turned to the boy. "So then you shot him down?"

"Yes, sir."

There was a little silence. The pilot was staring uneasily around him, as though he was afraid to meet our eyes. "It was about half-way between Lee and Hamble," he muttered. "I closed right up and gave him three bursts into the fuselage. He pulled her right up as if he was going to loop over me . . . and then he fell out of that into a spin with full engine on, I think, and went down like that. I saw him flicking round. And I saw him hit a tree. . . ."

His voice died away into silence.

"You went back to the aerodrome?"

"No, sir. I flew about low over the fields for a bit, till I found what I thought was a pasture. It looked smooth enough, so I landed in it, with the flares. It turned out to be harrow, but I got her down all right.

"It was two fields from the crash," he said. "I left the Nightjar with the lights on so that anyone flying over would see where I had put down. And I ran across the fields to the crash, sir. And as I went, I heard Poddy Armstrong land behind me."

"You were the first person to reach the crash, then?"

"Yes, sir."

"Was the pilot still alive?"

"Yes, sir." There was a short silence. "The machine was very badly crashed—the fuselage all telescoped on to him. I had to shift the top plane before I could get at the pilot. When I got that out of the way I tried to get him out of his seat, but his legs were caught somehow. And when I tried to move him, he cried out, sir." The boy's face was dead white. "So I had to leave him where he was, and I just did all I could to get him into a comfortable position and find out how he was hurt. You see, sir, it was all dark, and I couldn't see very well what I was doing. I did all I could." He stared round at us, as though he expected us to disbelieve him. "And he kept on trying to tell me something, but I don't speak German, and I didn't understand. And then Captain Armstrong came. And a minute or two after that, he died."

Arner turned away, and sat down quietly before the fire, and began polishing his glasses with a handkerchief.

"Can you remember anything of the sound of the words?" asked Dermott. "Enough to repeat what he was trying to tell you?"

The boy shook his head. "I'm afraid not, sir. I was . . . rather upset."

Dermott bit his lip, and tapped the cloth-covered packet. "You say that these were taken from the breast pocket? In that case they'll be the important ones."

Jackson nodded. "The body was considerably shot about," he said. "Those were the only papers we could find. It's possible that there may be other evidence in the machine. Maps, for example. I have had nothing touched."

There was a pause.

"That's very likely," said Dermott at last. "I'll come back with you to Gosport." He glanced out of the window; it was still quite dark. "It should be getting light soon," he said. "We'll start directly."

He turned to me. "You were quite right this evening, Mr. Moran. Evidently, if the machine landed here on Thursday night, she repaired the trouble and got away again."

Arner raised his head by the fireside. "Why does she keep on coming, night after night? She can learn all she wants to by one visit."

Dermott shook his head. "I don't know. We may find something to explain that in the machine.

"Anyway," he said, "we've got her this time."

He asked if his suitcase could be packed. I went out into the hall and found Sanders drowsing in the gun-room, and sent him off to see about it. When I came back, Dermott was going over the details of the affair again with the other two. Arner was still sitting before the fire, still taking little notice of what was going on behind him, still leaning forward and polishing his glasses. I remember that at the time I was very much impressed with that little action of his. Of all the people in the room that night Arner was most able to appreciate the significance of that affair,, and of all the people in the room he was the least excited, the most detached.

At last Dermott had finished. "Right," he said to Jackson. "We'll start at once. If you wouldn't mind going out to the car. . . ."

And when they were out of the room, he turned to Arner. "We're in for the devil of a row over this night's work, sir, I'm afraid," he said. "We shall have questions in the House."

"Which will certainly not be answered," said Arner quietly. "But in regard to Russia . . . I don't know. It depends on Allen now."

I had a quick impression of the tremendous forces that were massing together for a catastrophe.

Dermott walked nervously down the room, and swung round at the other end. "I don't see what else we could have done."

"Nothing," said Arner. "You could have done nothing more." He rose to his feet before the fire, a short, portentous little figure. "This thing will have to take its course."

And that was all of any importance that was said. In a minute or two Sanders came and told us that the Commander's bag was in the car. Dermott rose to take his leave. Through the open door I saw Jackson and Mackenzie in the hall, buttoning up their coats.

"I am very sorry for that young man," said Arner.

Dermott smiled. "He's young. A good lad, but he's not long out of Cranwell. He'll get over it. Jackson's very good with them. He'll probably send him off on a month's leave, and that'll put him right."

He drew on his coat, and went. I walked with him to the door, and waited outside at the head of the steps till I saw the lights of the car swing round to make a brilliant tunnel of the drive. The night was practically cloudless. The moon was sinking, and the east of the sky was getting a little grey.

I went back into the library. Arner had settled down again before the fire and was slowly turning the pages of the *Studio*, the big volume firmly posed upon his knees. In one hand he held his glasses before his eyes.

I asked if there was anything that I could do. At his instructions I fetched the telephone from the morning-room and plugged it in beside him, and set it on the table by his side.

And then: "You'd better go back to bed, Moran," he said. "There's nothing more."

I hesitated for a moment outside the circle of light from his reading-lamp. "What about you, sir," I inquired. "Won't you go up to bed yourself?"

He shook his head. "I think I shall stay up for a little," he replied, and by his voice I knew that he wanted to be alone.

I went out of the mansion by the garden door, and went round to the stable-yard and to my own house. It was about half-past five, and the sky was getting very grey. I knew that I should sleep no more that night, but I went into my bedroom and threw off my clothes, and got back into bed.

It was full dawn when I gave it up, got up again, and dressed. In the next room to my own I could hear Lenden's steady breathing as he slept, even and regular. I went through into my sitting-room, and the first thing I saw in there was that black box of plates on top of the safe. Looking back upon it all now, I find it very curious to realise how careless of that thing we were. It might just as well have been inside the safe, but we left it lying about on top. As if it was of no consequence.

I moved across the room and took the thing up from the safe, turning it over absently in my hands. I was worried about Arner. I couldn't get any sleep myself, but the thought that the old man might still be sitting over there in the library, still turning over the pages of the *Studio* in the bright morning, worried me more than a little. He was too old for that sort of thing. I decided to go over to the mansion again to see if there was anything that I could do for him; if I could persuade him to go up to bed.

But as I went, I slipped that packet of plates into the pocket to my coat. I suppose I must have known even then what I was going to do.

I crossed the yard and entered the mansion again by the back door. There was a maid in the kitchen, yawning and fiddling with the grate; when she saw me in the corridor her mouth shut with an almost audible click. I passed on into the house.

There was nobody about. The library was empty, and that volume of the *Studio* was replaced in the shelf with the others. Arner had given it up. I went over to the window and drew the curtains; the rings went rattling back along the pole and the sunlight streamed in upon the room. It was exactly as I had always known it. As usual in that room, everything was more or less in its place but not quite; there was no indication of what had happened there during the night. There was nothing to show that I had not dreamed of Dermott and of Jackson, nothing to show that the evidence of that white young man was anything more than a distressing form of nightmare. Till my eye caught the whisky decanter and the scattered glasses, and I knew that it was all quite true.

I don't know how long I stood there like that—I dare say it was only for a minute or two. It was long enough for the sense of a great responsibility to come upon me, and of a great loneliness. I had those plates in my pocket. It was up to me now; I had chosen to conceal the man who took them, and now I had to do something with the ruddy things. I couldn't bring myself to let him get back to Russia with them, unhindered. I discovered, as I stood there in the library that morning, that it is one thing to assist in the escape of a renegade spy from justice, but quite another thing to play the part oneself.

And then I heard steps. They were on the stairs that went up at the far end of the hall in a wide, shallow flight, and then they were on the parquet of the hall itself. I knew that it was Sheila at the first sound. I would have known that two years before. I stood there motionless until she came; I heard her pause first at the door of the drawing-room, and then come on down the hall.

She came and stood in the doorway of the great room, and

looked around. I remember that she was wearing a pale blue jumper and a tweed skirt; she was dressed for the country. There was a patch of morning sunlight that fell across that door, and she stood there with the colours gleaming in her fair hair, staring around the room. For the moment she didn't see me, but stood there, her lips parted a little, taking in the slight disorderliness of the room, and noticing the whisky glasses.

And in the end she saw me. "Mr. Moran!"

I moved across the room towards her. "Morning, Miss Darle," I said. "You're up bright and early."

She glanced up at me, her eyes twinkling. "So are you," she said demurely.

I nodded. "I do this once or twice a month," I replied. "I like to see the men get about their work to the proper time."

For a moment there was silence. "I believe you're the best liar I've ever met," she said at last. I was silent. "Mr. Moran, I want you to tell me, please. What's been happening? Has Commander Dermott gone?"

I nodded.

"When did he go?"

"About an hour and a half ago," I said. "He went away by road."

That seemed to puzzle her. "I heard the car from upstairs. Why did he go away like that?"

I was silent.

She came a little closer to me, and stood there looking up into my face. "There's nothing wrong, is there? Not frightfully wrong?"

I laughed. "It's all about as wrong as it can be, Miss Darle," I said. "But, as you say, I'm the world's champion liar, and I've managed to put Dermott off the track. So I suppose that's something."

She had nothing to say to that.

"I came over to see if Lord Arner was still up," I said inconsequently.

She shook her head. "I came down, and got him to go up to bed about an hour ago. He's frightfully upset over something."

She stared at me. "Something that happened after we went up to bed."

I nodded. She waited for a minute to see if I was going to tell her anything, and then she said:

"I came downstairs soon after the car went away, when I heard you go over to your house. He was still up, and sitting in the chair here, looking at the *Studio*. And I made him shut it up, and go upstairs to bed. . . ."

I was curious. "How did you know that there was anything going on at all?" I asked.

"Because you all made such a row that you woke me up," she replied. "Mostly the telephone. And then I came half-way downstairs in my dressing-gown, and asked Sanders. And then they sent over for you. And after that the car came with the other two."

It was very quiet in the library. In all the house there was nothing stirring then.

"Mr. Moran," she said.

I looked down at her, and looked away again. She was looking very sweet that morning, in the sun.

"Won't you let me know the whole thing? I know most of it. you know. And there's always the chance that I might be able to help, some way or other."

She certainly could. Almost unconsciously, while we had been talking I had made up my mind. I wanted a witness for what I was going to do then. And I knew that whether she thought me right or wrong she'd never let me down.

I glanced out of the window to the Home Farm across the meadow. "Mattock sent over to me to say that his old mare foaled yesterday morning," I remarked. "We might walk over and have a look at that."

She turned with me, and we went through the hall and out of the house into the bright morning.

The farm lies about half a mile from the mansion, and we walked slowly. And as we went, I told her everything that had happened, from the time when I had driven back from Winchester in the dark. I left nothing out. I went straight ahead with the events as they had happened, and I didn't look at her till I had finished. I didn't want to see how she was taking it till she had heard the lot. Not even when I came to tell her about the dirty game that I'd been playing on Arner and on Dermott.

I was hoping that she'd pull me up over that. I was hoping that she'd stop me and turn round in the path, and tell me that I ought to be ashamed of myself. If that had happened, I'd have chucked it up there and then. That was to be the touchstone for my conduct, and I was waiting for it. In her I had an outside view and outside opinion, outside advice that I was ready to take. I'd done my best according to my lights, but I was very uncertain whether I'd done right. And so I say that if she'd told me that morning that I was playing a damn dirty game, I'd have gone back to Arner and told him the whole thing. And given Lenden up.

I wish to God I had. I was hoping that she'd tell me to, I think. But she didn't. She stood there in the path looking up into my face when I had finished, and as I caught her eyes that hope flickered out and died. I knew then that I had to go through with it. I saw that she thought I'd done the right thing. I saw that she was proud of me, and I looked away again very quickly when I saw that. And the next thing was that she was speaking to me.

"What are you going to do?" she asked.

I put my hand to the pocket of my coat and pulled out that packet of plates. "I've got all that matters with me, here," I said.

She glanced at them for a moment, and then back to me. "I don't mean about those," she said. "But about the man."

I stood there, fingering the plates. We were both of us thinking more about Lenden than about the espionage that morning. "He's going back to Russia," I said. "That's quite definite. His mind's made up. The only way of stopping him would be to give him up."

She glanced at me curiously. "He's a great friend of yours? In the war?"

I shook my head. "I hardly knew him. Only just casually in the Mess. But he's a damn good sort, and I don't see that one can give him up. It means imprisonment, and a pretty long spell. Maybe as long as ten years. And frankly, I don't think he's deserved it."

She nodded slowly. "At the same time," she said, "I don't think you ought to let him get away to Russia with the information he's got. That's not playing the game, either."

She glanced up again. "Can't you persuade him to stay here now? We ought to be able to find something he could do."

A little way from the path there was a fallen tree, one of two that had come down a fortnight before and that we were cutting up at our leisure. I moved over to it, and brushed the chips from the trunk, and sat down there in the sunlight. She followed, a little curiously, and stood beside me. "You can't lead a grown man like that," I said. "He's got to take his own course. In that way there's nothing to be done for him. I'm afraid he's made up his mind to go back to Russia, and I don't see that I can stop him."

She nodded gravely. "And then he'll tell them what he's seen."

I looked up at her quickly, and shook my head. "No. He can't do that. He tried to tell me what he saw, and I don't think the Russians will learn very much from that account. He's too vague and confused, and he only got the shortest possible glimpse. But he'll take the photographs back with him, of course."

There was a momentary pause. I lifted the metal box, and turned it over in my hands.

"And by the time we've done with those," I said, "the Russians won't learn much from them."

There wasn't much difficulty about it. A little spring catch at one end of the box loosened the cover plate. Then there was a slide held by a sort of locking-pin, and underneath the slide there was a thin metal plate covered in black velvet. That pulled out in the same way as the slide, and under it I saw the greenish yellow of the first plate.

Sheila stood there beside me, very quiet, and watched me fiddling with the thing.

"Got to be damn careful to remember how this bag of tricks goes together again," I muttered. "Don't want to find any bits left over that I can't put back."

There were twelve plates in the box, each separated from the other by a velvet shield. As each came out I laid it carefully upon the tree trunk in the bright sunlight, until at last I had them all laid out there in a row, and the box was empty.

Sheila stirred beside me. "You're going to give them back to him?" she asked. "To take back to Russia?"

I nodded.

"How long does it take to spoil them?"

"About the hundredth of a second, I suppose," I replied. "We'll give 'em a couple of minutes, for luck."

And when that was over, I put them back again. I laid each plate emulsion-side downwards, each with a velvet plate to separate it from the others, exactly as they had come out. Finally I replaced the slide and secured it with the locking-pin, and when I had snapped the cover plate in place, I turned to her.

"That takes the sting out of it, anyway," I said. "There were only three lots of photographs taken, and they're all accounted for now. There was the lot that he took on the first flight—and they were spoilt. There's this lot that he took on the second flight, and I've done them in. And the third lot were shot down last night. The Air Force will look after those."

She nodded. "Now he can do what he likes."

"That's right," I said. "Now he can do what he likes." And we turned and walked back to the house, forgetting all about the foal that we had come out to see. It wasn't worth seeing, anyway. I told Mattock that that mare wasn't fit to breed from, but he wouldn't have it.

I left Sheila in the rose garden by the pool, and she went back to the mansion. I stood and watched her till she was out of sight, and then went over to my own place. There was nobody in the sitting-room. I took the pack of plates from my pocket and replaced it on top of the safe, exactly as I had found it.

Lenden was up and shaving. He came to the door of his bedroom when he heard me moving about.

"Morning," he said, "I say, did you go out at about four o'clock this morning? I'll swear I heard someone crashing around."

I nodded. "I went over to the house."

He was about to say something, but stopped. He was turning away, when he stopped suddenly and I saw him looking across to the safe. He moved across the room and took up the pack of plates that I had just laid down.

"Oughtn't to leave these lying about," he said.

In the town, a mile or so away, a church bell began to toll. I heard it faintly through the open window.

"This day is Sunday," I remarked. "Are you staying over the week-end?"

He shook his head. "I must get up to Town to-day. I was thinking about it last night in bed. If they don't hear from me soon, they may be sending out the reserve machine to do the job."

I suppose I was tired, and a little sick from the narrative of the night. The cool way in which he referred to his movements stung me up properly.

It seemed to me that it was nothing to him that he was in my house, as my guest, and that he was talking of putting my country in the cart. My country—Sussex—that I'd sweated to make a good show of ever since the war. He was ready to throw all that away.

I leaned against the mantelpiece and grinned.

"The reserve machine," I said cynically. "That's the one that's similar to yours. To be flown by a chap called Keumer. Leutnant Friedrich Keumer. A married man. Lives in Noremburg. Got two children called Elsa and Franz, and his wife writes to him every other day."

He stared at me. "I never told you all that."

I laughed unpleasantly. "No, you didn't. Bit of a pal of

yours, didn't you say? Shares a hut with you, and all that?"

He nodded dumbly.

I jerked myself suddenly erect.

"Well," I said brutally, "he's dead. Got shot down over Portsmouth last night, doing your job. And crashed in a field by Hamble."

CHAPTER FOUR

ALMOST BEFORE I HAD SPOKEN, I was sorry. Lenden stood there staring at me blankly, razor in hand, his mouth drooping a little at the corners. He asked no questions, didn't say anything at all. He just stood there dumbly, till I could stand it no longer, and he went a sort of yellow colour under his tan.

I moved over to the window and stood there with my back to him, looking out upon the garden. "I'm sorry I said that," I said at last. "It's been the hell of a night—and I'm a bit tired."

He cleared his throat. "Tell me what happened."

I turned round and gave him the account in a few short sentences. I put it as gently as I could. It came as a great shock to him, and he showed it. I can remember thinking at the time that this man Keumer had evidently been a closer friend than I had quite realised, and that it was curious that a man of his life and experience should suddenly appear so much alone. That is the only way in which I can describe his reception of my story. He was terribly alone. And when I saw him like that, his wife came into my mind, and it struck me to wonder if she had ever quite realised the injury that she did him when she went. Probably not, I thought.

He made no comment on what I had to say. He listened to the end, and waited for a little, staring irresolutely about the room. And then he moved towards the door.

"One thing," I said, and he stopped.

"What's that?"

"Give it another day. This is Sunday. You'll do better to stay here till to-morrow, and see what's going to happen. This may make a breach with Russia. It's very likely. Arner thinks it will. There might even be war."

I paused. "Give it another day."

He stood there for a minute, irresolute. "Might be best," he muttered. "I don't want to get mixed up out there if there's going to be a war."

He glanced at me. "You don't really think there'll be war?" he inquired.

"I don't see how there could be," I replied. "But . . . I don't know."

He went back into his room, and I went and had a bath, and shaved. A little later we had breakfast together in my room, and during that meal Lenden hardly spoke at all.

And afterwards he began asking me questions about Keumer. He wanted to know how it had happened, but he was satisfied with a very brief account of that. Chiefly he wanted to know whether he had been able to give any messages, and whether he had had any personal papers on him at the time. I told him about the letters, but there was very little solid information that I could give him. For a time I couldn't make out what he was driving at, until at last it became evident to me that Lenden was worrying over the settling-up of his friend's affairs.

He was very muddled and confused about it, and yet in a way he was practical. "He wasn't getting so much as I was," he said, "and I know he hadn't a bean in the world except his pay. If he had, he wouldn't have been at Kieff. None of us would. It ran out to something like five hundred a year, I think. And he used to send over half of it home, so that he was always hard up. He never used to spend anything except on cigarettes. The sort of chap that likes sitting before a fire and smoking, and talking about his home and his kids. And I don't know what's going to happen to them now. . . ."

As we talked it became clear that he was set on doing something for that family in Noremburg, that he felt that it was up to him to do something. He said he knew they hadn't any money, and he didn't think they had any relatives that would be of any value to them. He didn't know if there was any sort of poor relief in Germany; but, anyway, he couldn't let

Keumer's wife go on the dole. He didn't even know their address, except that they lived in Noremburg.

I suggested that Keumer had probably got his fee in advance and sent it home, as Lenden had done himself. Lenden didn't think it likely.

"He was so damn casual," he said. "He wouldn't have bothered about it . . . I don't know what to do."

He said that Keumer used to take snapshots of the aerodrome and of the town and send them home to his wife, with long letters. He said that he had an album full of photographs of his wife and children, and of his house and of his garden, that he used to show round upon the least encouragement.

"You see," said Lenden, "we were more or less the same sort, and keen on the same things. I'd have had a place like that myself . . . one time."

"I don't know what to do," he said.

That part of it, at any rate, was none of my business. I left him, and went over to the house. Lady Arner was at home, so it was no part of my duties to go to church that Sunday morning. She liked some representative of the family to be there; on occasions when the family were away it was my business to attend, presumably to ensure that the Padre read the lessons right. This morning I was free, and I went over to the gun-room to see if I could find the Sunday papers.

There was a copy of the *Scrutator* there, and one of the *World's News*. I opened the *Scrutator* first, and glanced at the political news. There was nothing to add to the situation as I already knew it in regard to Russia. I skimmed through the remainder of the news on the chief page, and idly turned the lesser pages before abandoning it.

And there, in among the motor-car advertisements, I saw an article that brought me up with a jerk. It was headed:

THE ARGENTINE AIR SURVEY

(BY OUR AERONAUTICAL CORRESPONDENT)

At a meeting of the Royal Aeronautical Society held at the Royal Society of Arts on Friday last, at 8.30 p.m., Captain S. T. Robertson, M.C., gave a

detailed account of the conditions governing the
work of the aerial surveyor in semi-civilised
countries. The lecture, which was of a highly technical nature, was entitled "The Survey of Inacces-
sible Areas", and was the occasion of a large attendance.

There was a column and a half about it. It was all about
grids and traverses and rectifying cameras, with a little about
aeroplanes thrown in. I didn't read it all through in detail. It
was clear from the space devoted to the paper in the *Scrutator*
that the lecturer was no slouch at the game, and that on air
survey he must be regarded as a leading authority. That was
certainly interesting; but what concerned me far more than the
technical ability of the lecturer was the fact that Lenden's old
friend and employer of the Honduras affair was in England,
and accessible.

I turned to the *World's News,* and idly glanced through the
scandalous, indifferently printed pages. And there, dovetailed
in between a murder and a rape, I came upon the reverse of the
medal.

AIRMAN IN THE DOCK
CONSTABLE'S GRAVE CHARGE OF ASSAULT

Yesterday morning, at Vine Street, Captain
Samuel Robertson, described as an air surveyor,
and giving as his address the Phalanx Residential
Club, was charged with drunkenness and assault.
P.C. Skinner gave evidence that the offence was
committed near Hyde Park Corner at about 2 a.m.
on Saturday morning. The defendant pleaded not
guilty to both charges.

Captain Robertson stated that on Friday night he
gave a lecture on Air Survey before the Royal Aeronautical Society, and subsequently, in company with
several old friends, he had paid a visit to a club in
Soho known, he believed, as Les Trois Homards.
He stated that it was impossible that he could have
been intoxicated, because he was able to maintain
an erect position without assistance, and, in fact,
was dancing continuously from eleven o'clock till
one in the morning. At the time in question he was
on his way home with two or three companions,
when he was induced to lay a small wager that he
would be capable of hanging by his toes from the

cross-bar of a lamp-post for a period of five minutes, a feat which he had repeatedly performed in England and abroad. A lamp-post situated just inside the park was selected for the purpose of the experiment, which had been in progress for approximately two minutes upon the arrival of the constable, who ordered him to come down. The defendant, in his statement, continued to the effect that his feet then slipped owing to the fact that the toes of his evening shoes were of patent leather, whereas he was accustomed to perform the feat in riding-boots. By good fortune he fell on to the constable, thereby saving himself from a serious injury.

A fine of five pounds, with costs, was imposed.

It didn't strike me as amusing at the time. I sat there for a little in the gun-room, thinking it over, and then I went back again to my house.

Lenden had dragged out an old atlas from the litter on the floor beside the safe, and had opened it on the table at a map of Germany. He turned to me as I came in, and put his finger on the page.

"That's it," he said. "Noremburg. It's right in the middle."

I sat down on the edge of the table by his side. "Are you going out there?" I asked.

He looked up at me in perplexity. "I don't know what to do. I never thought of anything like this."

There was a little pause. "You'll have to let that go," I said gently. "You've got yourself to think about. There's no possible way of finding out about his family short of going out there yourself. And you can't do that if you're going back to Russia."

"I believe I could find the house if I was out there," he said vaguely. "I know the look of it quite well, because he was always showing me the photos he had. It's out in the suburbs, up on a little hill. There's a water-tower near-by. That ought to make it easy to find.

"You see," he said, "somebody's got to go and tell them about it."

I began to see his point. If things were left as they were, that German family would never even know that Keumer was dead. The Russians would never do any notifying of that sort, especially in the circumstances. All that Keumer's wife would ever know would be that the letters would stop coming, and the money. And then things would begin to run short—half-rations, as they used up their little funds and waited for the letters and the remittances that didn't come. And for news.

"They'd think it was the post for a bit," said Lenden. "It's not very regular."

I stirred uneasily on the table. "You'll have to leave it till you get back to Kieff," I said. "You'll be able to get his address from the Russians then. And maybe you'll be able to get the money that he ought to have had for the job, and get it sent off to them."

He shook his head. "They'll freeze on to that."

There was a silence, and then he said: "I don't know what to do. Not much catch going back there, now. It'll be rotten out there without old Keumer. And if there's going to be a war, or anything like that. . . ."

I nodded slowly. I began to see it now. Keumer had been the only real friend he had in Russia, and now Keumer was dead. I hadn't realised before that that might affect Lenden's decision to go back.

I waited for a minute or two, and then said: "Your pal Sam Robertson's in London." And I told him what I had seen in the papers.

He was only mildly interested. "He's doing damn well on that survey," he remarked absently. "They all say so. He asked me to go in on it with him, but I couldn't. I expect he's come home to buy machines."

"Any chance of a job with him?"

He looked up quickly, and stared at me across the table. It was quite a new idea, that. "There might be. Most likely he's all fixed up, though. Still, it'd be damn good fun to get with Sam again."

"It sounds worth trying," I remarked.

He dropped his eyes on the map. "I can't leave this infernal business like this," he said morosely.

I left him to think it over then, and went off to the farm to have a look at that foal I hadn't seen in the morning. There was nothing to be done until he had made up this mind, if that were possible for a man of his temperament. Whatever way he went now, he couldn't do much harm to Sussex, and that was what I was chiefly concerned about. What worried me now was the man himself. I didn't want to see him make a muck of things, and I didn't in the least want to see him cut off back to Russia. I'd got to like him quite a lot. And yet, if he decided to go I didn't see how I was going to stop him.

At lunch-time he asked me a whole lot of questions about the political situation. I told him all I knew, which was precious little. Things were very uncertain, and there was every chance of our turning out the Soviet. What would happen if we did so—I couldn't tell him.

He thought that over for a bit. It was very evident that he was scared of getting caught in Russia if there was going to be a breach with England.

I left him again after lunch, and went down to the office. I was tired and upset, and I had a whole stack of work to get through before the Quarter Day. I thought that if I settled down to clear some of it off it might stop me havering about this other business, and I got out my files and ledgers in the intention of making an afternoon of it.

I never touched a pen. It was quiet in the office. The only sounds were the clicking of the footsteps and the giggling of the couples on the pavement below, and the church clock chiming the quarters. I sat there idle from a quarter-past two till four, leaning forward on the desk, my head in my hands. My work was spoilt, and to the best of my knowledge I was thinking of nothing at all. After all, I'd been up most of the night.

I say that to the best of my knowledge I had been thinking of nothing at all. But at four o'clock I reached out for the telephone and put in a trunk call to the Phalanx Club, in Knightsbridge.

It came in ten minutes or so.

"I want to speak to Captain Robertson—Sam Robertson, of the Argentine Survey. If he's in the club."

"Just one minute, please." There was a pause.

In a little while he came to the instrument. "This is Robertson speaking. Who is that?"

It was an unusual voice, very soft and husky and deep. I put him down at once as a thirteen-stone man, and leaned forward to the instrument, prepared to lie confidently.

"My name is Moran," I said. "Peter Moran. Good afternoon, Captain Robertson."

"Afternoon." There was a hoarse laugh. "I'm real sorry, Mr. Moran, but I'm afraid at the minute I can't place you."

I laughed in return. "Dare say not. But you'll have heard of my brother. Jack Moran, of Stevenson and Moran, in Buenos Ayres. Shippers. Grain trade—you know them? I represent them on the Baltic."

"I know." He was doubtful, but making the best of it. "Never done any business with them myself, but I know of them. Glad to meet you, Mr. Moran."

"Yes. I'm very sorry to disturb you on Sunday afternoon. I've got a long cable here from my brother that I want to come and talk to you about. It means fixing up quick transport between Buenos Ayres and a place up in Santiago, where Stevenson's got an interest."

He grunted. "We run pretty frequently to Rosario. Is it near there?"

"Madreguello," I said, and for the spur of the moment I think that was a pretty good effort. "I'm not sure where it bears from Rosario."

"Is this just occasional trips?"

"That's right. Now look here, when can I come and see you?"

"Sooner the better, when it's business. I'm free all day to-morrow, but for lunch."

"Ten o'clock too early?"

"Not a bit, Mr. Moran. I'll drop round to your office, if you like."

"Don't worry. I'm motoring in, and I'll be passing through Knightsbridge. At the Phalanx, then, at ten o'clock to-morrow morning."

"Right. I'll be pleased to meet you. Good-bye."

I rang off, and sat for a little at my desk, staring out of the window at the timbered house opposite. I've always kept pretty well to myself, and I've never gone about poking my nose into other people's affairs. But when you find a chap down and out and on his beam-ends, it seems to me that the least you can do is to go and tell his friends about it.

For one thing, it rids you of the responsibility for him.

I shut up the office soon after that, and went back to my house for tea. Lenden had disappeared; for the moment I had the wind up that he'd vanished for good, until I saw the pack of plates still lying on top of the safe where he had left it. I knew that he wouldn't have gone away without those, and I didn't think he'd have gone away without telling me.

I spent an hour or two at the piano after tea, running over the passages of my play. I very soon became immersed in it, and I dare say that I may have gone on for an hour or so without noticing very much. And when I looked up in the end and glanced round the room, there was Sheila Darle standing before the fire and laughing at me.

I dropped my hands from the piano and swung round. "I'm most awfully sorry," I said. "I never heard you come in. Have you been here long?"

She stood there on the fender in imitation of my own habit, with the laughter still bright in her eyes as she looked down on me. "About ten minutes or so. What's that you were playing then?"

I looked up and grinned at her. "A fairy tale."

She came a little closer to the piano. "What's it about?"

I turned round again to the keys. "It's a thing I take up now and again when I've nothing better to do. I'll play you a bit of it, if you like."

She came and sat down on a little stool beside the instrument. I played a few bars of the overture, and stopped. "It's about a

Princess who went walking in the forest alone," I said, "and got chased by a bear. And she ran away very fast, which was about the best thing she could do in the circumstances, and the bear ran after her. And they ran faster and faster through the wood—I'll play you that bit—till the Princess really thought she was done for that time. And then a Woodman came along and killed the bear."

"Bit o' luck that," said Sheila phlegmatically.

I nodded. "That sort of thing always happens in that sort of wood. Grimm and Perrault, you know."

"Like a conventional fairy tale, you mean?"

"That's right."

"I see. That might be rather nice. What happened then?"

"The Woodman killed the bear with his knife. And the Princess was so grateful and she thought the Woodman was such a He-Man that she fell in love with him and went away and lived with him in his hut in the woods. Under the trees, in the sunlight. It was always sunny there."

"Was she pretty?"

"Very pretty. As pretty as a picture."

"That was nice for the Woodman, then," said Sheila demurely.

"It was. Frightfully nice. He liked it no end. Never had such a nice thing happen to him in his life before, I should think. I must say, I'd kill a bear with a knife myself—any day —if I thought that'd happen. And all the Court and all the Knights and Squires and Varlets came riding through the woods to look for the Princess, but they didn't find her because she was in the hut with the Woodman. She wasn't going to let herself be caught and taken away."

"How long did she live with him?"

"Weeks and weeks."

"I don't think she'd been very well brought up."

"She hadn't. She wasn't really a very nice girl, but she was pretty and very much in love with the Woodman, so that part of it was all right. But she didn't get on very well with cooking his dinner, and emptying the slops, and washing up, and cleaning his boots. She used to shirk that sort of thing a bit, and then he'd come in tired and all of a muck o' sweat and see it wasn't done, and he'd buckle down and do her job for her. Almost every day."

"He'd have got on a lot better if he'd given her a good spanking."

"I know," I agreed. "But she was a King's daughter, you see, and I expect he didn't like to do that. But the result of it all was that he began to get more and more like a Prince within the hut, and she got more and more like a peasant girl, because she was always shirking her job. He got taller and straighter and handsomer, and she got shabbier and shabbier because she hadn't any new clothes and the old ones weren't standing the strain very well. And at last they were just about as shabby as each other, and it was perfectly obvious then, when you looked at them side by side, that he was a King's son, and she was just an insignificant little person that he'd picked up somewhere or other."

She laughed. "What happened then?"

"Why," I said, "they went back to the castle and got married. And everybody said it was a very suitable match and they were all frightfully pleased about it, and they went about telling each other what a good job it was, because they thought she was never going to get off, and now she'd gone away and found such a nice young man all by herself, and so well connected. And they said he must be the son of the King of Tenebroc, and the Princess whispered to him that that was eighteen months' journey away, and so he said—Well, perhaps he was. And so that was all right, and they lived happily ever after."

"Is that all?"

"That's all. I'll play you some of it now."

She settled herself upon the little stool by the keyboard, and I began upon the overture. That evening stands out very clear and distinct in my memory, even at this distance of time. It came as an oasis, an interlude in that rather trying period. Throughout that evening I was able to forget the whole affair— aeroplanes, espionage, and everything. For that interlude I was grateful at the time, and I have seen more reason to be grateful since.

Some time after that—perhaps as much as an hour later—Lenden came in. I had finished the play by then, and was playing bits of things to her at random—Chopin mostly, I think. And we were talking. Lenden hesitated in the doorway.

I swung round, and introduced him to Sheila. He shook hands vaguely. "I—we've met before. Didn't you come over to look after me the other day?"

She nodded. "Mm. You're much better now, aren't you?"

He hesitated. "Yes," he said quickly. "I'm quite all right again now. It was awfully good of you to come over. Not used to people bothering—like that." He smiled shyly.

"You're quite all right again?"

"Yes. Fine."

"Well enough to come over to the house for supper? With him." She jerked her head at me.

He glanced at me inquiringly. "It sounds awfully nice."

She turned to me. "Did you know that Arner went up to Curzon Street this afternoon?"

I shook my head, surprised. "He didn't say anything about it to me."

She nodded. "I forgot to tell you, with your playing. It was in the afternoon, when you'd gone down to the office. He got a telephone call. It was that I came over to tell you about, really. There's only me and Aunt Maud."

She swung round on Lenden, laughing. "So you needn't be frightened. You'll come, won't you? Both of you?"

I grinned. "We'd like to very much."

"All right," she said. "Half-past seven." And went.

Lenden had been out on the down above Under; he said that he had got fed up with the house and had gone out for a walk. He had taken a dog with him that he had found tied up in the stable-yard; it belonged to Kitter, the chauffeur. Kitter had been only too willing that the beast should get some exercise, and Lenden had gone wandering with his dog over the downs in the direction of Leventer. He told me where he had walked. He had certainly covered a good bit of ground in the time.

"And then," he said, "I came up over a bit of a hill by a beech wood and saw my Breguet, about a mile and a half away. She was covered up and pegged down in the lee of a barn. Did you do that?"

I nodded. "You'd see her from there. It's the only direction from which she's really conspicuous." I thought about it for a minute. "We'll have to do something with her soon."

He agreed that she couldn't stay there indefinitely. He told me that he had walked on over the down to have a look at her. Spadden was evidently sleeping in his house that Sunday afternoon, for Lenden saw nobody.

"She's quite all right," he said. "I slipped off the cover from the oil filter, and it was all bunged up with stuff from the inside of that bit of pipe. It's a rotten bit of stuff, that pipe. Like garden hose. All she wants is a new bit, and the oil tank cleaning out, I suppose. There's eight or nine hours' petrol in the tanks still . . .

"Might want her again yet," he said uneasily. "It'd be the easiest way of getting back to Russia."

His walk had done nothing to resolve his mind. I made no direct answer to that, but presently I said:

"I've got to go to Town to-morrow."

He was silent for a minute. "How long are you going to be away for?"

"It's only a morning appointment. I ought to be back here by tea-time."

"Any news of what's happening about Russia?"

I shook my head. "Nothing at all."

He relapsed into silence again, and presently we went to get ready for dinner. It was clear to me by that time that he was quite incapable of making up his mind. It was becoming more and more evident that he was reluctant to go back to Russia. I began to put considerable faith in the issue of this meeting with Robertson. It seemed to me that Lenden was in such a state of dither that he would go passively in any direction in which he were pushed. I had some hopes that Robertson might provide the push.

We went over to the mansion. That was a quiet evening, one of a type that I had grown familiar with through the years that I had spent at Under. Supper on Sunday evening is always the same in that great candle-lit room; I trust it always will be. There was a cold chicken, a smoked tongue, a potato salad, a caramel pudding, and a Camembert. And rather a good Barsac. Beyond the candles the portrait of Arner's grandfather stared down at me from above the mantelpiece, and I talked to Lady Arner about the garden and the tenants and Mattock's foal—which I didn't think much of. Mattock was a bit disappointed with that foal himself, as a matter of fact, and sold it over at Pit-hurst the other day.

Sheila had taken Lenden in hand, and was being very sweet with him. He was shy and restrained to begin with, I fancy, but by the time we reached the sweet the Barsac was at work, and he was talking to her quite fluently about his joy-riding experiences. I overheard some of it.

"Ten days in one place," he said, "and then move on. Just the two week-ends. However well you're doing, it never pays to stay longer than that. And it's never any good to put on a special show on market day, like you'd think. Never do much business then. Just the Saturday and Sunday—they're the big days. And little bits in the week. . . ."

"I expect you get most people to come up at the big seaside places, don't you?" inquired Sheila. "Places like Bournemouth and Brighton?"

He was entirely at his ease by now, and intent on telling her about the work he loved. "In a way," he said. "You can burn your fingers pretty badly there, though—they're mostly worked out. No, we stick more to the little places now—places about the size of Pithurst and Petersfield. You have to leave them for so long to recover. It's never any good going back for four years. That's the interval that you have to leave before you can do a good week's business again. Four years. . . ."

He mused a little. "Of course, some places you can go back

to year after year, and still take up as many as you can manage. Clapton . . . I've taken money there year after year. And then, some day we'll get Bargate opened up."

Sheila interposed a question. "Does Bargate go on and on?"

He smiled shyly. He had rather an attractive smile, though I hadn't seen much of it since he'd been with me. But when he smiled, I remembered him as he used to be in the Service.

"Can't go to Bargate at all," he replied. "They won't look at an aeroplane now. O'Dare did that in for us."

"Why can't you go there? Won't they have you?"

He shook his head. "Corporation won't hear a word about it —not since 1919. You can't get permission to use a field within five miles of the place—not at any price. They're not going to have the reputation of their town blasted by a lot of flying men. Never no more. I dare say they're right."

He sighed regretfully. "I'd make a fortune in six months if I could get a field at Bargate. I'd be able to retire. . . ."

Sheila was intrigued. "What's the matter with them? What happened?"

Lenden hesitated. "It was a bad show," he said shyly. "It happened just after the war. O'Dare was the first of us to go to Bargate, and it was a little gold mine, I tell you. He got a field there just at the end of the promenade, by a bus stop. He was flying a three-seater Avro—he only had the one machine, and his ground engineer, and a clerk. And there'd never been any joy-riding in Bargate before, and the town was full of visitors. And every day when the boat came in from London they simply made one stream for his field. It was wonderful, I believe. He had a queue half a mile long from eight in the morning till dark, and the sole right for the place for the summer. He was in the air for thirteen hours a day, and in six weeks he'd cleared his expenses and paid for the machine and banked two thousand pounds clear profit."

He was silent for a minute.

"What happened then?" asked the girl.

Lenden smiled. "He took to shooting the bottles off the shelf over the bartender's head with his old service Webley," he explained. "In the Hotel Metropole, where all the Jews go. It was a shame that happened."

"And then?"

"Oh, then it all came to an end, of course. They ran him and his aeroplane out of the town next day, and closed down the field. And now if you so much as fly over Bargate to take a photograph, you hear about it afterwards from the Town Clerk."

He mused a little. "There's a mint of money to be made there," he said regretfully. "It's virgin ground. . . ."

I turned again to Lady Arner. We had bee disease in pretty well every hive that year; they used to come out on to the little ledge outside and die in shoals. I remember that she was very worried that we might not be going to get any honey of our own that year, and we talked bees and bee disease till the end of the meal.

And after supper, in the drawing-room, I played to them. I should probably have been playing that evening in my own house, if I had been there. Lady Arner and Sheila and Lenden pulled up chairs before the fire to study seed catalogues, or talk, or go to sleep, and I went over to the piano and sat for a little polishing the white keys and the rosewood before beginning.

I forget what I played that night—the usual things, I suppose. A little Chopin for myself, a little Schubert for Sheila, a little Verdi for Lady Arner and, incidentally, one or two of the songs from *Butterfly*. Lenden had got hold of one of Bunyard's catalogues and was talking fruit trees with Lady Arner; she told me afterwards that he knew quite a lot about fruit trees, and wanted to know more. She was very much surprised when he told her that he hadn't got a garden of his own. She knew nothing of his circumstances, but she had thought from the way he was talking that he would have been a great gardener.

That was the manner of that evening, and of a hundred similar ones that I have spent at Under. At the end of it we left the house, and strolled back to my place across the stable-yard.

We went into the sitting-room and had a whisky. I yawned.

"Got to get away before eight o'clock to-morrow," I remarked, "if I'm to be in Town by ten. I'm driving up."

I glanced across at him. "Have you made any plans?"

He shook his head. "I'm going to wait till to-morrow night. I expect you'll hear a bit more about Russia up in Town, won't you?"

I nodded. "Should do, if I see Arner."

"In that case, I think I'll wait till you get back."

I set down my glass and got up on my feet. "Better take that dog of Kitter's out again," I said. "He's getting as fat as butter."

And so we turned in.

It saves quite a lot of time to motor up to Town from Under; I had breakfast at half-past seven and got away in the Morris by eight o'clock. It wasn't a bad sort of morning—blue sky and clouds, with a stiffish wind from the north-east. I made pretty good time on the road, and by ten minutes to ten I was rolling into Knightsbridge.

As I had supposed, Robertson was a big man. He must have stood six foot two, and he was broad in proportion. He had a tanned, pleasant face, but he looked as hard as nails, and I judged that he would be a pretty tough chap to tackle if you got up against him. On the whole I liked the look of him as he came across the lounge to meet me, walking with a curious rolling gait. I found out later that that was the legacy of a crash.

He greeted me in his soft, hoarse voice, strongly flavoured with Americanisms.

"G'morning, Mr. Moran. I'm real glad to see you." He moved away across the room. "Come on over here. There's a quiet corner that we can talk business." We settled into a couple of leather chairs. "Now, what'll you drink?"

It was ten o'clock in the morning. I cried off that.

He laughed quietly. "Well then. About this business for your firm—Stevenson and Moran, I think you said?"

For a moment I wondered if I was going to be kicked out of the place. "I must explain that a bit," I said. "The matter that I've come to see you about is pretty confidential—I didn't want to go into it over the phone. There's no such firm as Stevenson and Moran, not that I know of. That was a yarn to get you to give me an appointment."

He turned a very grey eye on me. "See here," he said without heat. "Are you a drummer?"

I grinned, and shook my head. "I'm agent to Lord Arner, down in Sussex."

He looked relieved. "I reckoned that you'd come to sell me something. It didn't take me long to find that there was no such firm as Stevenson and Moran on the Baltic."

"I've not come to sell you anything," I said. "But I've got business to talk, all the same."

He settled down into his chair and offered me a very black and diseased-looking cigar. "Fire away," he said, biting the end off his own.

"It's about a man called Lenden," I said. "Maurice Lenden. I think he was out with you in Honduras."

I had startled him. He paused in the act of taking the bit out of his mouth with finger and thumb, and stared at me.

"What about him?" he asked, depositing the tobacco in an ash-tray.

"What's he like as a pilot?"

There was a long pause at that. "Now see here," he said at last. "If you're thinking of employing Maurice Lenden as a pilot, I'll tell you what I think of him." I wasn't thinking of employing him as a pilot, but I let him run on. "You'll find him a real wizard pilot. He's right out of the top drawer. Barring the float that he ripped up when we were up the Patuca, I've never heard of him doing the slightest damage to a machine. Maybe he's had luck in his forced landings, but if you want a damn fine, safe, careful pilot for any job whatever, then you've got the right man."

He paused. "That's as a pilot. If you try to run him as a manager as well, then your luck'll be out, and I tell you that straight. He's a damn good fellow, and straight as they're made; but he couldn't run a whelk stall to make it pay. He can't manage his own affairs—let alone a business. He's a pilot, and a pilot only, and as a pilot he's right up in the front line. But he's nothing more."

He turned to me curiously. "Do you know where he is now?"

"He's down at my place, in Sussex."

"Is he out of a job?"

"He'd probably take one if he could get it."

"You're not thinking of employing him yourself, then?"

I shook my head. "I came to see if you knew of anything that he could do."

He was puzzled at that. He turned and stared at me curiously. "I don't see that. Why didn't he come up himself? Did he send you to see me?"

I blew a long cloud of smoke from that foul cigar. "No," I said. "As a matter of fact, he didn't. I came up here on my own to see how the land lay." I paused. "As a matter of fact, he's been in a bit of trouble."

Robertson raised his eyebrows.

I eyed him steadily. "In confidence," I said. "You won't go and let him down?"

He shrugged his shoulders. "It's no business of mine what he's been up to. But he's a good pilot and a damn nice chap, and I'm sorry if he's in trouble."

That seemed good enough to me. "He's just back from Russia," I said. "By the back door. He's been flying for the Soviet for some time now. There's nothing really wrong, but the Foreign Office 'd probably like to get him for a quiet talk before sending him to Dartmoor for a bit."

He nodded slowly. "D'you know," he said at last, "we reckoned it was something like that." And was silent again.

After a bit he turned to me curiously. "I don't quite see how you come into it," he said. "Are you one of his wife's people?"

I shook my head. "I came into it by accident. But I've met him before. In Ninety-two Squadron, in 1917."

"Does he know you've come up here?"

"No."

"What's his own idea, then? What's he going to do?"

I shrugged my shoulders. "He talks about going back to Russia."

Robertson blew a long cloud of smoke, and flicked the ash from his cigar on to the carpet. "Doesn't sound as if that'd do him much good. Not the way things are at present."

I shook my head. "There'll be a break with Russia."

He glanced at me quickly. "D'you *know* that?"

"No. It's bound to happen sooner or later, though. And it won't do for him to get caught out there then."

"No," he said slowly. "By God it won't." He turned to me. "Does he understand that?"

"In a way. He's very vague. His trouble is that he doesn't see what else there is for him to do."

I laid the unconsumed portion of that appalling cigar upon the ash-tray. "I understand that a year or two ago you offered to take him into partnership. When you were starting in the Argentine. He told me that."

At that, Robertson leaned forward and began to talk. He said that he wanted me to get this quite clear. He didn't employ pilots as staff—he only had one, or two at the most. He got them in as partners. He wanted capital—he was always wanting capital, and he paid ten per cent for it. His pilots had to operate away from him for months on end, and unless they had an interest in the business he couldn't rely on the show being run properly when he was away. If Lenden could bring capital along with him—say a thousand pounds—he might be able to fix him up with a job, although he would be no party to getting him out of the country. Lenden would have to meet him in the Argentine.

"You see how it is with me," he said. "I'm not a charity show for dud pilots. If Maurice Lenden can come in on those terms I think he'd be a damn good man for me. If not, there's others who can learn the job. That offer that I made him two years ago—you can tell him it's still open."

I nodded. "Right you are," I said. "In the meantime, we'd better fix an appointment when I can have a look at your books."

"Oh." He shot the ash from his cigar on to the carpet. "For a thousand?"

"I could find a thousand."

He glanced at me very curiously. It was quiet in the lounge. "Lenden's got no money of his own at all?"

"Not a bean. He was working in a garage, as a matter of fact, before he got the Russian job."

"Poor devil," said Robertson softly. He glanced at me again, still curious. "I don't quite see what you stand to get out of this."

"Ten per cent," I replied. "Better interest than I'm getting for the money as it is."

There was a long silence then. Robertson relaxed and lay back in his chair, staring at the ceiling. In a far corner of the room a couple of men began talking of the Grand National, and the odds they had been getting.

And at last he said: "You say you've not had anything to do with Lenden since the war?"

I was surprised by that question. I didn't see what he was driving at. "No," I said. "I hadn't met him since 1917, not till a few days ago."

"He'd be better on the survey than Dines," said Robertson softly, half to himself. "And Dines could start in to work up the other side. We want that just as much, way things are opening up. . . ."

He turned to me. "You don't want to go putting money into a show like mine," he said, very frankly. "Nor into any flying business for the next ten years. You'll only go and burn your fingers. But, by Christ, if you're willing to put up a thousand for him, it'd be a queer show if I couldn't do as much, knowing him all these years."

He spat a bit of tobacco out on to his lip, and removed it to the ash-tray. "You can tell Lenden there's a job with me in the Argentine if he wants it," he said. "I was giving him seven hundred when we went up the Patuca together. I can't run to that now. Four-fifty, and a small percentage on profits. I'll have to reckon that out."

I nodded. "I'll tell him. That's very good of you."

Robertson yawned. "Reckon it'll pay me in the long run. He's a wizard pilot. Tell him to come up here and see me— some time in the next week." He ground the stump of that filthy cigar upon an ash-tray. "And now, what about a quick one?"

It was little after half-past ten, but he ordered gin and tonic for us both. And when it came:

"Here's luck," he said, and set down his glass. "Have you met Mrs. Lenden yet?"

I wrinkled my brows. "Mrs. Lenden?"

He nodded. "Mollie Lenden. But perhaps he hadn't told you he was married?"

I shook my head. "He told me that he was divorced," I said.

Robertson went diving into the inner pockets of his coat, and produced a sheaf of at least a dozen dog's-eared letters. He laid this collection out upon his knee and picked out one. It was a letter on thick, pale blue paper, addressed in an upright, feminine hand.

He tossed it across to me. "That's all I know," he said shortly.

I opened that letter, and read it. It was quite a short one.

> *Ye Tea Shoppe,*
> *Winchester.*

Dear Major Robertson,

I expect you've heard from people how things are between Maurice and me. I don't know where he is now, and nobody seems to know at all. The last thing I can find out is when he left the Atalanta when it bust, and after that I can't find out anything about him or what he's doing or anything. And I thought that he's sure to turn up in aviation soon because he loves it so and can't stay away from it, and I thought if I wrote round to you and one or two of his other friends you could let me know as soon as you hear of him. I read the flying papers every week. Please will you try and find out where he's gone to, and let me know as soon as you hear anything at all?

*I wouldn't have written to you like this but you've been so
good to us all through that it seems different.*

> *Yours sincerely,*
> *Mollie Lenden.*

I sat there for a long time staring at this thing. There was no
subtlety in it, no skill. It was the letter, I thought, of a very
ordinary girl who had lost something that she valued, and was
trying to find it again. I remember wondering whether she
was going to pull it off. And then I thought of Lenden, and
realised that whatever might be the outcome of it all, this letter
was going to turn the whole of his affairs upside down again.

I turned to Robertson. "I see she signs herself Mollie Lenden.
D'you know what happened about that divorce?"

He shook his head. "That's all I know. I've been in the
Argentine for the last two years. That reached me about a
week before I started home. Matter of fact, I'd forgotten all
about it till you mentioned him. D'you say she was divorced?"

I wrinkled my brows over it. "Lenden certainly told me
that he fixed it up so that she was able to divorce him. But I
see here that she still uses his name."

Robertson wasn't greatly interested. "I expect they had a
bust-up and he cleared off for a bit," he said phlegmatically.
"Best thing to do, sometimes."

I thought about it for a minute. "What about the Argentine?"
I asked. "Can he take her out there with him if she wants to
go?"

He set down his glass. "My wife's coming out there with me
this time. Fed up with being out there alone. But as for him...."

"I dare say they can do it," he said. "The difficulty is the
screw I'm giving him. Yes, I think they might be able to work
it, the way we live, if they're damn close. Not unless."

He picked up the letter and handed it to me. "Will you take
on this show now?" he asked. "You'd better show him this,
and maybe he'll go along to see her."

"Maybe he will," I said absently. "It's not far from my
place."

Robertson yawned. "Tell him to give me a ring before he comes," he said casually.

There was nothing more to be said or to be done, and so I went away.

*   *   *   *   *

I got to Winchester at about four o'clock, wishing vaguely that I was a clergyman. They seem to have the knack of butting in adroitly. I was very conscious that I hadn't.

It had seemed the only thing to do. I retired to my club after I left Robertson, picked up a novel off the table as I passed into the smoking-room, and sat there for half an hour trying to read it. At the end of that time, I turned back to the beginning and began again. By the time I had got to page forty for the second time, I had come to the conclusion that the only thing to do was to go down to Winchester that afternoon and find out how the land lay. Having once started butting in, I might as well go through with it.

The shop was in between the Close and the main street, in rather a quiet little by-way. At first sight one would not have known it for a shop at all. It was a square, uncompromising Georgian house that stood directly on the pavement; through the open windows of the ground floor one could see that the whole of the front rooms of the house had been knocked into one, and were set with little tables. A small, brightly-coloured sign over the door announced the calling of that house, and a little white notice on the door impressed upon me that it was under the entirely new management of Mrs. Mary Lenden. Home-made cakes, it seemed, were a speciality.

I got out of my car and went up the three steps into the big room among the little oak tables, and stood there for a minute waiting for something to happen. It was evident to me that the tea trade was slack in Winchester on Mondays; it was after four o'clock, but I was the only person in the room. And then there was a rustling in a back region, not unlike somebody laying down the *Daily Mail,* and a girl came out from behind a brightly-coloured curtain that hung across the back of the room.

"Good afternoon," she said quietly. "Can I get you tea?"

I suppose she might have been twenty-six or twenty-seven years old, medium in height, and with brown hair that she wore long and dressed smoothly back over her head, giving her a very quiet air. She was dressed in a long white overall, and I stood there wondering for a minute if she were the girl I'd come to look for.

She looked at me inquiringly. My courage went trickling away through my boots, and I ordered tea.

I sat over that for half an hour. Not many people came into the shop; by half-past four there may have been half a dozen in the room. I was rather surprised at that because the tea was one of the best I've ever had the good fortune to sit down to. Mrs. Lenden knew her job all right, so far as that was concerned.

I very soon came to the conclusion that it was Mrs. Lenden that I had met as I entered. There was another of them there, a red-haired girl of about eighteen who seemed to do most of the running about. It couldn't be her. Unless there were more of them behind the scenes, Mrs. Lenden must be the one that I had spoken to at first. And then, as she came through the curtain with a fresh supply of cakes to set on a little table by the wall, I noticed what I suppose I should have seen before if I'd had any sense. She wore a wedding ring.

That room faced the sun, a wide, airy place, and not too crowded with tables. There was a little jug of snowdrops before my plate, and the sun came in through the window by my side and lit up these flowers, and the light oak of the table, and the bright mats upon it. I nodded to her, and she came over to tell me how much I owed.

She stood beside me, and cast a rapid eye over the table. "Three cakes?" She considered for a minute. "That'll be one and fivepence, then."

I fished it out. "You are Mrs. Lenden, I suppose?"

She nodded. "We haven't been open for very long. I took this shop over from the other people when they went away, about six months ago. Did you know it then?"

She was very grave and courteous and kind, and she stood there eyeing me directly.

I shook my head. "I've never been here before. But Major Robertson sent me down here. He told me that I'd find you here. You know him, don't you? Sam Robertson. He's back from the Argentine."

If I had expected to surprise her, I was mistaken. She showed no change, but she nodded gravely. "Major Robertson is a very old friend of my husband's," she said simply. "We know him quite well."

She wasn't giving anything away, that girl.

"I know," I said. "I saw him this morning. He gave me this, and told me to come and see you." And I pushed her letter across the table towards her.

A donkey cart passed slowly by the window in the street outside, loaded with yellow bananas and red oranges, and all manner of bright things in the sun. She stood there fingering the letter, and she was silent for a minute.

"He gave you this," she said at last. "Then you know something about Maurice?"

"He's staying with me now," I replied.

"He's—he's quite all right?"

I glanced up at her sharply, and looked away again. "He's perfectly fit," I said gently. "Just had a touch of malaria that's kept him in bed for a couple of days, but nothing to worry about. He's quite all right now."

She nodded. "Did he get his mixture made up?" And then, as if she was ashamed to talk to me of trivialities, she said:

"You must come upstairs. Please, if you don't mind. We can't talk here."

She had recovered, and seemed as impassive as she had been when she was giving me my bill. That was a way of hers. She never showed one very much of what she felt, even when things were very difficult for her.

She took me to a room on the floor above, looking out on to an uneven array of roofs and an untidy little yard at the back. It was their sitting-room. There were a couple of basket chairs, and a low smouldering fire in the grate, and a little writing-desk littered with account-books and loose bills. Half sitting-room, half office, this was evidently where they lived.

In the room she turned to face me. "What's your name? I'm sorry. . . ."

"My name's Moran," I said. "I live over in Sussex, about forty miles from here. I was in the same squadron as Lenden in 1917."

She wrinkled her brows.

"I don't suppose you've ever heard of me," I said. "I hadn't seen him since those days—till last week."

"You've come from Major Robertson?" she asked.

I nodded. "He sent me here. Your husband's in a bit of trouble, Mrs. Lenden. I went to Robertson because he seemed to be a pretty old friend, and because he was handy. In Town."

She was quite collected now. "What's the trouble?" she inquired. "Where's he been?"

There was no point in beating about the bush. "He's been in Russia," I said frankly, "and that's the trouble."

And then there was a sudden commotion on the stairs, and there was the red-haired girl, who said there was a party of four asking for poached eggs, and there weren't any eggs, and should she send Lizzie out for eggs or should she tell them that they couldn't have eggs? And when that was settled and the commotion had died away downstairs again, Mrs. Lenden was silent for a little time, and then:

"I knew that was where he'd been," she said at last. "It was the only place." And then she turned to me. "Where is he now? What's he going to do?"

"He's staying in my house for the present. He's going back to Russia to-morrow or the next day."

"Why's he going back there?"

"He's got a job out there." I paused for a moment, and then decided it was best to take that fence at once.

"From his point of view, there's nothing to keep him in England. He hasn't any ties or anything.

"You see," I said gently, "he thinks he's divorced."

She dropped her eyes to the table. "I know," she said quietly. "I know he does."

There was a little silence then. She stood there with her eyes fixed upon the table, and I followed her glance. It was a heavy old refectory table backed up against the wall, and as I stood there waiting for her to say something I took notice of what was on it. Stacked up against the wall there were great heaps of weekly periodicals—I dare say there may have been a couple of hundred there, of all shapes and sizes. A few of them were scattered loose upon the table, and I glanced at the titles.

And then I realised what I was looking at. There was *The Aeroplane,* and *Flight* and *Airways*—all three of the English ones. Then there were the Americans, the *Aerial Age,* and *Aviation,* and *The Flying World.* And there was the *Aero Revue Suisse,* and *L'Air,* and the *Illustrierte Flug-Woche,* and *La Rivista Aeronautica,* and *L'Ala d'Italia,* and a whole heap of others, in all languages. She must have given a wholesale order to some agency and paid a mint of money to have every aeronautical publication in the world sent to her by post. For months.

I could picture her sitting there at that table in the evenings, surrounded by those papers that she couldn't read, very grave and serious.

She saw what I was looking at, and raised her eyes inquiringly.

I indicated them. "These papers," I said. "You've been reading them every week?"

She nodded. With the red-haired girl to help her she had waded through the lot of them, night after night, for over a year. She had let the girl deal with the English ones because they were easier, while she looked for his name in the foreign journals, line by line.

"You see, I knew he'd turn up in aviation some time," she said simply. "He loves it so—it's the only thing he can do really well, and he can't keep away from it. We tried giving it up before, you know, and it didn't work. . . ." She hesitated.

"That's what made me write to Major Robertson and the others. Because I knew that where there was flying, Maurice'd turn up sooner or later."

I could find nothing to say to that.

She turned away, and sat down at the littered desk. She pulled out a sheet of notepaper from a pigeon-hole. "If I write a little note to Maurice," she said gravely, "will you take it to him?"

I nodded. "I'm going straight back home from here," I said. "He'll get it to-night."

She raked about among her papers till she found a little blunt stump of pencil, and bent over the desk. I sat down on the edge of the table and began to turn over a copy of *Aviation*. Before I had looked half-way through that issue she had finished her letter and was sealing it deliberately in an envelope. That must have been a very short note that she wrote to him.

And then she got up and stood there fingering the envelope for a minute. "He thinks we're divorced," she explained. "But we aren't really, and he ought to know, oughtn't he? Because he might be wanting to marry again, and he couldn't, you see. And so I've just told him that, and what I'm doing, and perhaps he'll be able to come over and see me before he goes back. Do you think he will?" She stood there eyeing me gravely, and a little wistfully.

"Why," I said, "I'm sure of it, Mrs. Lenden."

She nodded. "You see, we were going to be divorced," she said. "And it was only when it all began that I saw what a rotten, cheap sort of way out it was, and how it wasn't going to work—not properly. It all depends on how you're made if you can get to be happy that way, and I couldn't. And it might have been different if he'd been well off and had lots of money, but he wasn't; and it was a rotten trick to go leaving him like that, and I've been most frightfully . . . ashamed. And then, when I wanted to find him to tell him about it, he'd gone away."

Her voice died into the silence, but presently she began again.

"A man isn't like a girl," she said quietly. "That's what I didn't know, and it was all my fault, really. A girl gets married, and she wants a home, and children, and a quiet time. And she puts all that first, and she hasn't got much patience with anything else. And I think a man's a bit like that, too, but only a bit. A man gets keen on other things that don't seem to be any good at all, and he goes and spends all his life on them, even if they don't lead to the quiet time that he really wants. Even if he can't make enough money at them to live properly . . . He won't give up."

I could find nothing to say to her.

She went on, speaking half to herself. "It's like a kid with its toys. Music, or the sea, or . . . or flying. A man has to have his toys, and if you try and take them away from him— you just kill him." She stood there gazing at me from her quiet, dark eyes. "I know, because I tried it. Maurice was in the City for two years, you know, and all that time we weren't half so happy as we'd been when he was doing his own job. Even if it did mean that he was out of work half the time. Nothing like."

I nodded, and she stirred a little beside me, as if she had forgotten I was there. "And what I thought we could do," she said practically, "was this. I've got this shop now, and it's doing nicely, and it makes quite enough to keep us both if it had to. And what I thought was that Maurice could go on flying and have this for his home, and then when he was out of a job for a bit he could come back here, and there'd always be the shop to keep us, you see. Before, when he was out of a job, there wasn't any money, and that was so rotten for him. But I thought that this way, it'd be all right."

Her voice died away into a silence. "You'll tell him about this, won't you?" she said. "You're a great friend of his?"

I cleared my throat. "I'll tell him that. I think it's a good idea. It's just what would work with him. You want to leave him pretty free."

She was pursuing her own train of thought. "I don't want you to persuade him, or anything." She gazed at me steadily. "You won't, will you? Because it wouldn't be fair, and it's awfully easy to persuade him into anything. You must just tell

him what you've seen here, and tell him what I've been doing
and why I've done it. And tell him that if he'd like to have a
go at being married to me again, I think it might work this
time."

I nodded. "I'll tell him that."

She dropped her eyes from my face with a little sigh, and
handed me the note. "Then that's all, I think."

She had a great presence with her, that girl. I paused for a
minute before going downstairs.

"You'd better have my address," I said.

She sat down at the little desk and took it down in her neat,
round hand. Then she accompanied me down through the shop,
and came out with me into the street to where my car was
parked. I got in and started up the engine.

"You'll tell him what I said, won't you?" she said wistfully.
"I know he'll be most awfully busy, and I expect he's got to get
back to Russia. But I'd love just to see him before he goes. . ."

"I'll tell him that, Mrs. Lenden," I replied. And then she
stepped back from the car, and I slipped in the gear, and she
was gone.

CHAPTER FIVE

LENDEN DIDN'T RETURN till half an hour after I come in. He had
been out all day with the dog; from what he said I gathered
that he must have been pretty well as far as South Harting
along the down, because he described passing a big white house
in the middle of the hills. I put that down as Beacon House,
where Sir John Worth lives and breeds his bloodhounds. He
must have been twenty miles. Kitter's dog returned in a state
of prostration—and a good job too. It doesn't get enough
exercise, that beast.

I let him have his dinner before I started. There's no sense
in expecting a hungry man to listen to reason, and Lenden
was very healthily weary. He spoke very little during the meal,
but he mentioned Keumer once, and it was clear that he was as
far from a decision on that affair as he had been in the morning.
After dinner he left the table and flung himself down in a
long chair before the fire, and with his first words he gave me
the opportunity that I wanted.

"D'you hear anything more about Russia in Town?" he
inquired.

I shook my head. "Not a word. I left soon after lunch. But
I saw your pal Robertson this morning."

He took the cigarette from his lips and stared at me. "Sam
Robertson? Where did you see him?"

"In Knightsbridge," I replied. "At his club."

"What d'you go there for?"

I crossed the room, switched on the reading-lamp, and sat
down on the music-stool before the piano. "Bit of officiousness,
I suppose," I said quietly. "Can't think of any other reason."

He didn't speak.

"You may as well know what I think about this thing," I
said. "For myself, I don't care a damn what you do. It doesn't

affect me. You can walk out of this place when you like—to-night or next month—and I don't suppose we'll meet again for some time. I'll get rid of that aeroplane for you. But when you do go, I honestly think you'll be a ruddy fool if you go back to Russia. There's going to be bad trouble there, and there'll be hell to pay if you're caught out there then. You can see that for yourself."

He brushed that aside. "I know all that. But what did you want to go and see Robertson for? Was it about me?"

"I went to Robertson because I knew damn well you wouldn't go yourself," I said. "Not my business, I know. But that's what I did."

He thought about it for a minute. "What happened?" he inquired.

I filled a pipe, and lit it before replying. "He ended by offering you a job on his survey," I said at length, and glanced towards him through the smoke. "At four hundred and fifty—to start with. Plus a share of the profits."

He stared at me incredulously. "Did he offer that—on his own?"

"He did."

"Without wanting any capital put into the business?"

"Not a bean."

He laughed. "He must have changed his mind since last I saw him, then."

"You've got to remember that his business has expanded since you saw him last," I said.

It upset the whole apple-cart of his decisions once again. He didn't say very much, but he sat there conning it over for a long time.

"I'd like to go with Sam again," he said at last, a little uncertainly. "It was good of you to go and look him up for me. I wouldn't have thought of it, myself. It's a better show than going back to Russia. But I don't know that I can cut off and leave the job like this. . . ."

I might have told him there and then that his plates were spoilt, I suppose. But I didn't.

"And then there's Keumer and his wife," he said. "I couldn't go shooting off to the Argentine without getting that squared up somehow." He turned to me. "D'you know, I thought of something to-day. Keumer's got an uncle who keeps a retail grocery shop in Mannheim, in a pretty big way of business. I believe we might be able to trace his wife that way." As a matter of fact, it was through that uncle that I found her in the end. But that was much later.

He sat there dithering over his decisions. I saw then very clearly that there was only person in the world who could resolve his mind for him. I suppose I had known it all along, in a way.

"There was one other thing happened up in Town," I said nervously, and went fishing in the breast pocket of my coat.

"What's that?"

I passed his wife's letter to Robertson over to him to read. "Robertson gave me this after we'd done talking business," I remarked. "You've turned up at last, you see."

I didn't watch him while he read that letter, but swung round on the music-stool and began polishing the white keys and the dark rosewood of the piano with my handkerchief. That piano stands beside me as I write, and presently, when I am tired of recalling those bad times, I shall get up and I shall play a little to Sheila before going up to bed. With my three stiff fingers my playing will never be a patch on what it was in the days of which I am writing—and that, I think, is the least price that I have had to pay for interference.

"I've read that letter," I remarked, without looking at Lenden. "Robertson showed it to me."

He didn't make any comment.

"And then," I said, "I went on down there this afternoon, and had tea."

He stared at me darkly. "Oh. You went to Winchester?"

I nodded.

He was about to say something, but stopped. "Did you see Mollie?" he inquired.

"She gave me tea. And then I said I'd seen Robertson, and

she gave me a note for you."

He blinked at me. "She all right?"

I got up from the piano. "She looked pretty fit," I said casually. "She was very anxious to see you before you go back," and I dropped her letter on the table by his side. "I've got to go down to Under this evening for a bit. There's her note."

He took it in his hands and sat there fingering it, and looking up at me. "How long'll you be?" he inquired.

"About an hour or so, I suppose," I said, and left him to it.

I walked down to Under. I had to go down there some time, and this was as good a time as any, because I knew that I should catch the crowd I wanted all together. There was an amateur dramatic show brewing, Gilbert and Sullivan, and because it was for charity they wanted the use of the hall without paying any rent.

I found them hard at it in the hall itself, rehearsing and quarrelling, and having a fine time generally. I might have seen eye to eye with them in the matter of the rent if they'd been red-hot in the cause of charity. But their chief trouble lay in the allocation of their mythical profits between the costumier and the charity; if they were to run to wigs by Parkinson, would there be anything left for Barnardo? I didn't see why Parkinson should pouch the lot, and so I told their secretary that they could hold their show in the street for all I cared, but if they had the hall they'd pay for it.

Having made myself quite clear on that point, I stayed on for a bit and watched the progress of their rehearsal. They were doing *Patience*, and young Saven, whose father kept the Red Bear in the market, was playing some small part in the thing. I liked young Saven. He had recently come out of the Air Force; I think he had been one of the first batch of peace-trained recruits. He had attained the dignity of two stripes before he came out, and now he was opening a little garage at the back of his father's inn.

We sat there smoking and gossiping for a bit. Then Nitter, the hairdresser, joined us, and with him came his brother.

Now, I've mentioned Nitter before—John Nitter, that is, who

keeps the hairdressing establishment in the Leventer Road, and talks Communism in the market on Saturdays. He's a nice little man, and when he isn't talking Communism he's breeding Irish terriers, or children. There's no harm in John Nitter, and for a long time I was puzzled to see where he got his Communist ideas from. And then one day I met his brother, and I knew.

They came from Bradford originally, I think. John was older than Stephen, and left Bradford some years before the war with a lung that required the comparative warmth of the south. In that way the hairdresser's shop came into being. Stephen, on the other hand, was clever, and won scholarships. Eventually he passed on to Oxford and, as befitted the son of a fitter in those less tolerant days, he went to Ruskin.

I don't know what happened to him in the war. He never got into the Army—I know that much. And he never married. He was industrial to the backbone; a little short tubby man in a bowler hat and a shiny black suit. He had very light blue eyes, and he wore his hair rather longer than one would have expected. I saw him on a platform once. It was in Hyde Park and he spoke without a hat, and his hair fell down over his eyes and he kept shaking it back as he put the whole impact of his nature into his tirade. And when I heard him then, I forgot that he was a tubby little man.

There was the inspiration that brought John Nitter to the market every Saturday afternoon. But I can vouch for this, that John wasn't in the same street with Stephen, whatever he might have been ten years before. Living in the south had done it, I suppose. That, and the Lotus.

Stephen used to come down to Under about once in six months to stay with John—partly for a holiday and partly, I think, to ginger up his brother. I expect John needed a bit of gingering up from time to time. The Revolution wasn't getting on very fast in our part of Sussex.

"Evening, Nitter," I said to John. "You acting in this thing?"

He shook his head. "No, sir," he said, and got a scowl from

Stephen for his deference. "Ah could have had a part in t' chorus, if Ah'd a mind. But it's a game for t'youngsters." He sucked his pipe. "D'you know my brother Stephen, Mr. Moran?"

I shook hands. "We've met before," I said. "You down here for a holiday, Mr. Nitter?"

He stared at me uneasily. He was shy and difficult to get on with, was Stephen—all edges and rough corners. "Ay," he said morosely. "For a holiday. Just the three days, and I'm for the north again. I wouldn't stay longer than that."

I took him up. "Why not?"

The south, he said, was a playground. I must condense his ideas into a practicable space, for they dragged out in little short, dark sentences, interminably. The south was where rich men came to live, capitalists who had made their money by the sweat of the workers in the north. A capitalist only needed to work in the north for ten or fifteen years and then, having made a fortune from the labour of the workers, he came down into the south to get away from the reminder of his own misdoings, and to spend his money.

I'm no good at arguing with those chaps. I couldn't refute this slander, because, in cold hard fact, a certain amount of it was true. A lot of industrialists retire to the south when they've finished their life's work in the north, because it's the best part of England to retire to.

"It's like a garden, this place," he said sullenly. "It all runs that smooth and soft and rich. An' up there, where Ah come from, there's the workers sweating in the factories. In the half-dark and the rain, and never to see the sun clear, for the sky's that mucky." He eyed me dourly. "Conditions what you've never dreamed of. You come up north, and Ah'll show you something."

I grinned at him. "You'd better go to Russia if you want to see what sweating is," I said. I suppose he had stung me up a bit, or I wouldn't have said that to provoke him. "You've never seen anything in the north to touch what you get out there. You don't want a revolution to put that right."

I had annoyed him very much. I knew that it was his dearest ambition to visit Russia; to be able to say that he had been there would give him a *cachet* in the counsels of his union, and raise him from the ruck.

"That's not true," he said hotly. "You don't know nothing about it—you, living soft and easy as you do. Ah'm for Russia in two or three days from now, and Ah'll find a better and a more hopeful world for the worker in that country. A better and more hopeful world." He repeated the words as if they were a quotation. "And the time will come—the time will come when we'll see that better time in England. And Ah pray to God that Ah'll be spared to see it."

I eyed him for a minute. "You won't expect me to agree with you about that," I said. "But apart from politics, this is a damn bad time to go to Russia, you know. There may quite well be a break. You want to be careful what you're letting yourself in for." I had a vague recollection of having said that before, quite recently.

"Ye're wrong!" he cried passionately. "Ye're all wrong. This is the time when every thinking man among us ought to go to Russia. Your Capitalist Government—they're slighting and insulting Russia every way they know. And for why? Because Russia sticks up for the worker. That's what it is. Well, the workers must unite. It's us that counts. We've got no quarrel with the Russians; they stuck to us like brothers in the strike. Like brothers. This is the time when every worker in England and in Scotland and in Wales has got to stick to Russia—and Ah'm away to tell them so."

I nodded slowly. I had no arguments to meet this chap's sincerity.

"You want to be careful you don't get caught out there if there *is* a break," was all I said. "Get clear in time."

"Ah," he said rudely, "ye're talking nonsense, and ye know it. But it's always the same with you rich folk." He paused. "Ye won't see what's going on under yer own eyes."

With that he turned on his heel and walked off. John gave me an anxious, uncomfortable look; I grinned back at him, and he hurried off after his brother. I fancy Stephen was a bit of a trial to John at times. Especially in the Red Bear.

I left soon after that, and walked back to my house. Lenden was still sitting there in that chair before the fire, but the fire was practically out and the room was filled with the smoke from his cigarettes. I stirred him up about the fire with a few winged words, and he got down on his knees to make it up, a little apologetically. He said that he had forgotten all about it.

I threw off my overcoat and went and sat down at the piano. "What'll we have?" I inquired. "Spot o' sugar?" He stared at me uncomprehendingly. "No," I said absently. "All right. Spot o' Chopin, then."

And I played him a couple of mazurkas. And when I had come to an end of that I glanced at him, and he was sitting there exactly as he had been when I first came in, and I thought he was asleep. And I swung round on the stool, and I said:

"You can have the Morris if you want her to-morrow. I shan't be using her myself."

He stirred in his chair. "Thanks," he said quietly. "I was going by train. I've been looking up the trains in your time-table, but it means going by Portsmouth and Southampton to get there. You're quite sure you won't be using the car?"

I shook my head. "I'm going to London again. I've got some insurance business to get through up there, but I got side-tracked on to this thing of yours this afternoon."

"Sorry."

He hesitated. "I was going to pinch the car as a matter of fact, and run over there this evening," he said. "And then—I thought it'd be better not to go over there so late . . . and it'd be nicer if I went over there after breakfast."

He paused, and then he said: "What's the shop like? She was always wanting to have a shop like that."

"It's not a bad place," I said. "There's two of them there, that I saw. She's got a red-haired young woman in to help her run it." And then I started in and told him everything that I had done or said, so far as I could recall. He heard me to the end in silence and then, with only the briefest excuse, he got up to go to bed. He made some remark to the effect that he was tired, I remember, and I remember that he paused in the doorway for a moment.

"This puts all the Russian business in the cart again," he muttered. "I don't know what the hell's going to happen about that."

Then he was gone. I played a bit of my own stuff, sat there idly for a quarter of an hour, kicked the fire to the back of the grate, and followed him to bed.

An early breakfast suited us both next morning; I was aiming to catch the 8.32 myself. Before I left I went out with Lenden to the stable to make sure he'd got the hang of the Morris; he started her up and got in.

He was wearing my ulster and my driving gloves. He nodded to me from the car. "See you this evening, then," he said, and with that he swung her round and out of the yard gate on to the western road to Petersfield, and he put his gloved hand up in salutation as the car shot up the road. And so he drove away out of my life and on to meet his wife and all the promise that she held for him. I only saw him once after that.

I had meant to go to Town. But as I turned back from the stable to my house, they came to fetch me to the telephone in the mansion. A cowhouse in one of our farms out by Leventer was blazing merrily, and it was up to me to go and see that they did something about it.

It was the usual sort of thing. A chimney in the farmhouse first; they hadn't worried about it—in fact, they were rather pleased than otherwise when it happened. It saves sweeping the chimney if you have a little fire in it to burn away the soot. That went on while they were having breakfast and thinking no evil, till a lump of red-hot soot fell on a little stack of straw, and then half the outbuildings went up. We got it in hand by eleven o'clock, and then I went on with the farmer into Pithurst to see the insurance agent about the claim. By the time I got back to Under it was three o'clock.

I might very well have given up the idea of going to Town

that day. But when I got back to the office my clerk showed me a telephone message from Lenden that had arrived about an hour before. He wasn't coming back that night unless I wanted the car, in which case I was to ring up a number in Winchester. Otherwise he'd be over first thing in the morning.

I told the clerk to ring up and tell him he could have the car for as long as he wanted it. He could have had a second honeymoon in it for all I cared. There was the little Talbot belonging to the mansion which nobody ever used except myself when the Morris was in dock. And, apart from that, there was the Siddeley.

There didn't seem to be much point in stopping in Under, and so I went up to London that afternoon, and put up at my club. That gave me the whole of the next morning clear for my business, and I reckoned to catch an afternnon train down again. If I didn't get away from Under while I had a chance, I thought, there'd be another fire, or a cat 'd kitten, or something, and I'd have to stop and see to that.

I had a certain amount of luck next morning, and went on to Curzon Street for lunch to report progress to Arner. He told me that things in connection with Russia were still very bad. He didn't think that the evidence in the machine that had been shot down had been worth very much. There was little direct evidence to connect it with the Soviet. He was of the opinion that the break would not come at once, but on the next opportunity. Things were getting very difficult, especially in regard to Arcos, where all sorts of fishy work was going on. He thought that Arcos would be able to provide all the material that was necessary to make a breach with Russia, if that were considered necessary.

I gathered from the way in which he spoke that the espionage had sunk rather into the background. I wasn't sorry about that. It gave far more chance for Lenden.

I left Curzon Street at about half-past two, and took a taxi for Waterloo. There was a train down at three-fifteen; I went to the time-tables on the platform to verify that it stopped at Petersfield. There's always a bit of a crowd about that board, and while I was looking at the list I felt somebody press in beside me. And somebody said:

"There's a luncheon-car as far as Exeter. And after that it seems to stop everywhere between Exeter and Instow."

And a girl's voice said: "Oh Lor. Can't you find one that doesn't?"

I wasn't paying much attention, because one never does in a crowd like that. But as I stood there following the figures in the list it seemed to me that I had heard the first voice before, quite recently, and I glanced back over my shoulder.

It was Mackenzie, the young pilot with the fair, sandy hair, who had flown the Nightjar from Gosport. He was dressed in mufti and he had a girl with him even younger than he was himself. He was pressed close up against me, and without reflecting I nudged him with my elbow.

He turned to me, and I was pleased to see him. "Afternoon, Mr. Mackenzie," I said amicably. "I think we've met before." I paused. "My name is Moran."

The crowd came surging round us, jamming us more closely together. His face was chalk-white, but whether it had been as white as that before I can't say. He forced his way backwards out of the press, and I followed him.

"Are you from Under Hall?" he asked, and there was something in his tone that shook me rather.

"I'm the agent there," I said quietly.

He seemed about to say something impetuous, but stopped. I became aware of the girl, who had pressed close up against his side and was holding his hand, regarding me anxiously. "Look here," he said, with evident restraint. "What's the matter? What the hell do you want with me?"

I eyed him steadily for a moment. I think he must have been on the very edge of a breakdown that day. Dead-white face, blue eyes, and sandy hair. That sort takes things very hard.

"Nothing at all," I said. "It's pure chance that you got shoved against me there."

"Pure chance . . ." he repeated scornfully. He dropped his eyes to the girl, and smiled at her. "I told you it was no damn good going away. There's no place where one can get shut of it."

The girl looked up into his face, and I saw her squeeze his hand. "It's quite all right," she breathed. "This is just an accident." They stood there for an instant very close together, in common defiance of the enemy—myself.

"God damn you!" he burst out suddenly, and shook her off. "Get along back to Under, where you belong!" And then to the girl: "Come on," he said. "Let's get along out of this."

He swung round, and went off up the platform. The girl cried—"Alan!"—after him, but he never turned. She hesitated for a moment, and decided she must say something to me.

"I'm so frightfully sorry," she said. "He—he's not quite himself."

I nodded. "I know. That's perfectly all right."

She was going off after him, but she stopped dead at that and came back to me. "What do you mean by that? How much do you know about it?"

I hesitated in my turn, and then: "I know he shot down a machine the other night, under orders," I replied.

He was fifty yards away by that time, walking with his head down among the crowd. He stopped for a moment, and looked back. The girl stared at me most urgently. "Tell me, was it fair?" I didn't understand what she meant. "Oh, was it a fair fight? He's so frightfully upset because he says it—it wasn't. He says all the time that it was . . . just murder."

In the bustle of the crowd it seemed to me that there came a little pause at that, as though all the world were waiting for my answer. She had courage, that girl. "I'm afraid the other fellow wasn't armed," I said. "He hadn't got a gun. In that way it was—very easy for him."

She stared at me wide-eyed for a minute. "I see," she said. "Thanks for telling me." And then she turned and ran off up the platform after him, and I stood there watching till I saw her take his arm, and they went away together.

I turned away depressed, and went and found a corner seat

in the train. And then, as I opened my evening paper at the middle page, I got a shock. There was half a column of it, and it began:

BUTLER SHOT

OUTRAGE IN A SUSSEX MANSION

Under Hall, the residence of Lord Arner, a historic mansion prettily situated near the old-world village of Under in West Sussex, was the scene of a violent affray early this morning, when Mr. Albert Sanders, butler in the mansion, was shot in the shoulder in an endeavour to detain a burglar. Mr. Sanders is understood to be in a serious condition.

It is understood that the outrage occurred in the Steward's House, a building situated at a short distance from the mansion and normally occupied by Mr. Peter Moran, agent to the estate. In the absence of Mr. Moran it is presumed that Mr. Sanders entered the house and surprised a burglar, who shot him and escaped by the open window. The shot was heard by several of the employees of the house, who rushed in and found Mr. Sanders lying on the floor of the sitting-room. The assailant made good his escape.

There were several paragraphs more of it, but no more news. They gave a little bit about Sanders, another little bit about myself, and a condensed biography of Lord Arner. I had plenty of time to think about it while the train meandered down to Petersfield, and I cannot say that I found my reflections very pleasant.

There was only one possible explanation of it, that I could see. There was only one possible thing in my rooms worth burgling the house for—only one thing that could possibly involve the use of firearms. It was only then that it came home to me what a ruddy fool I'd been about those plates. I'd left them sculling about where anyone could see them, thinking that they were harmless now that I'd exposed them. The up-shot of it was that some Russian organisation had got wind of the situation, and paid me a visit to collect their property. I was dead certain that that was what had happened. Sanders had blundered in upon them by chance, attempted to defend my property . . . and they'd let fly at him.

I cursed myself most bitterly for all sorts of a ruddy fool not to have foreseen something of this sort. I might have known that to hang on to that box of plates was simply asking for it.

I got down to Petersfield at about five o'clock, and Kitter was on the platform there to meet me. I swung out of the carriage and gave him my case. "How's Sanders?" I asked.

"Doin' fine, sir. You've heard about it then?"

I nodded. "Is he much hurt?"

"They shot him through the shoulder, sir." He touched his shoulder to show me exactly where the bullet had gone in. "It went in here and came out at the back, sir. Doctor Armitage said it was providential it wasn't higher up, sir, or it'd have bust his shoulder-blade. It do seem a terrible thing to happen, and nine o'clock o' the morning, in England."

"Do you know how it happened?"

He shook his head. "Not rightly. The safe was all shut up when we went in. I don't know as they had time to pinch anything. I think Mr. Sanders surprised them in your room, like. And then they shot at him, and Mrs. Oliver was out in the yard near the door and she heard the shot, and she heard Mr. Sanders cry out. And she called to me and I got Watson because he was just in the garden there, and he brought a fork with him, and we went into your house and the window was open and Mr. Sanders on the floor, sir. And then we telephoned for the doctor, but I don't know what we'd have done but for the lady. She put him to rights before the doctor came, an' got him up to bed, an' that. And he's going on quite all right, sir."

I wrinkled my brows. "What lady is that?"

"I forgot to tell you, sir. She's waiting to see you when you get back. That gentleman what's been staying with you—his wife."

"Mrs. Lenden?"

"That's right, sir. They arrived together in your car not a minute or two after we found Mr. Sanders, and long before the doctor came. And the lady knew just what to do, and she and Mrs. Richards bound him up a treat with bandages and all. And then the doctor came, and the police, and Sanders told them what had happened, but I wasn't there then, only Mrs. Richards and the gentleman and his wife. And then we got Sanders up to bed, and a little while after that the gentleman went away in your Morris, sir."

"D'you know where he went to?"

"Yes, sir. He was going to Dover, and he was in a great hurry. I filled up the Morris with four gallons, sir, and lent him a couple o' maps." He paused, and then he said: "The lady's at your house now, sir. Waiting to see you."

I stood for a moment on the platform. The train had steamed away down the hill to Portsmouth, and I was the last passenger to leave. Over the downs the sun was going down; from where I stood I could trace the hogged line of the hills from Butser to South Harting. Beyond that lay my own country and . . . I didn't know what.

I turned to the Siddeley. "We'd better get along back there then," I said. "And pretty quick."

He made that car move faster than she'd ever gone before along the road to Under, and he got there long before I had time to make my plans. The car swung round the gate-post on two wheels and came to rest in the yard. "I'll see Sanders first," I said to Kitter. "If he's awake."

I went into the house by the back. A maid that I met in the passage told me that Mrs. Richards, the housekeeper, was sitting with Mr. Sanders in his room. She had heard that Mr. Sanders was getting on nicely, and had had a little sleep during the afternoon. It was a terrible thing, she said, and she hoped I wouldn't find anything taken, papers or that, and not as if he was a young man, neither.

I went on upstairs. He had a little sitting-room of his own in the servants' wing, with a bedroom opening out of it. Both were furnished very profusely in the Victorian manner, with furniture that I think had once graced the house and had been turned out to make room for older stuff, or newer. An ornately framed photograph of a forbidding old woman who had been his mother hung above his bed; in the sitting-room there was a brightly-coloured oleograph of King Edward and Queen Alexandra at their coronation.

Mrs. Richards was sitting by his bed, and reading the leading article in the *Morning Post* to him aloud, with long pauses of non-comprehension between the sentences. I heard them at it as I came upstairs. He had his own copy of the *Morning Post* every day—a perquisite that I had not dared to curtail when I took over the reins after the war. I don't think he has ever read anything else, except possibly the Bible. Country-bred—gardener's boy, footman, valet, and finally to butler. It makes a difference.

Mrs. Richards got up as I entered, and began to talk. I let her run on for a little, and then moved up to his bedside. I don't know how old he was, but old enough to be very badly shaken by a thing like that. His flannel nightgown had had one sleeve cut off, and the arm was bandaged closely to his body.

I said the usual things that one does say at a time like that. He was as comfortable as they could make him in the circumstances, but he was in for a bad night of it. They had sent for a nurse from Portsmouth, and were expecting her very soon, they said. Sanders himself was pretty cheerful; I was relieved by the way he greeted me. He wasn't very badly hurt. And then I asked him how it happened, and he looked about him for a little without speaking, and finally he said something inconsequent. I divined what he wanted, and sent Mrs. Richards on a vain errand.

He said that he had gone over to my rooms with a bottle of whisky in his hand to fill up my decanter.

"The window was open wide, sir. And there was two men there, one of them just outside the window and one right inside the room. Right inside. They must have come in through the kitchen garden from the lane, and then through the little green gate. The only way they could have come, sir."

I nodded. "Did you recognise either of them?"

145

"That brother of Nitter's was one, sir—the one outside. Not the one that had the pistol, but the other one. I didn't tell that to the police, sir, seeing that it touches the town and thinking that I should rightly tell you before saying anything. But that's one of them."

He had barely given a glance to him. The other man, he said, had rather a fat, white face, and was taller and broader than Nitter. He had a brown soft hat on. He was standing by the safe, and as he entered Sanders saw him pick up something black.

"One of your books from the safe, or something of that, sir," he said. "A black one, and rather fat. Would that be anything important?"

I shook my head slowly. "It sounds like the cash-book. I don't think that'd do them much good."

Sanders had made some exclamation as he entered. The man who was inside the room whipped round at that and made for the window, taking the black packet with him. Nitter was already outside. And then old Sanders, who had lived all his life in Under and found London a confusing place and terribly expensive, acted promptly and with decision. The man with the fat, white face was at the window when Sanders lifted the whisky bottle that he was carrying and flung it straight across the room with all the force of his old arm. It hit the chap on the shoulder, cannoned heavily off his head, and burst against the wall. Sanders ran forward to grapple.

He never saw the man draw his gun. He only knew that two shots were fired, and he was sure it wasn't Nitter. Something went singing past his ear in an explosion, and another crashed through the soft part of his shoulder. "And then," he said naïvely, "I seemed to get one foot in front of the other, sir, and I fell down." He stayed down till Kitter and Watson came bursting in, a minute or two later, and found him on the floor.

"I gave Mrs. Richards the key to the silver cupboard, sir," he continued. "And there's eight dessert-spoons and four table-spoons in the left-hand drawer in the pantry, and a tea-spoon in Miss Sheila's room what she has for her medicine. And I told Arthur that when he lays the table this evening he's to go to Mrs. Richards and she'll give him the silver out of the cupboard, and he's to take it straight back to her when it's washed, and no nonsense. And then there's the tea-pot what was used for breakfast. That will be in the pantry on the shelf, unless Mrs. Richards thought to lock it up with the rest."

"I'll see her about that when I go down," I promised him.

I stayed up there with him for a quarter of an hour longer, listening to his instructions about the silver and the wine. He insisted on giving me the key of the cellars. I could have left him much earlier but—well, I suppose it comes to this, that I was shirking. Waiting in my house was the girl that I had met in Winchester, and I was afraid to go and meet her.

I realised that at last, and went downstairs.

There was nobody about in the mansion. I don't know what happened to Lady Arner that day; I suppose she was keeping to her room. Arner himself was up in Town, and Sheila had gone off early in the morning to visit friends in Hornsea, and was still away. I went out of the mansion into the yard, and crossed over to my own house.

And there was Mrs. Lenden in the sitting-room by the window. She had turned on the reading-lamp by the piano and she was sitting on the window-seat, in the gloom outside the circle of light. I do not think that she can have been doing anything at all, but wait for me.

I crossed the room to her. "Good evening," I said. "I'd have come over before, but I went up to see Sanders. They told me that you were here."

She inclined her head gravely. "They've told you all about it?"

"I think I've probably heard most of it," I replied. "All but one thing, that I don't quite follow. Where's Lenden gone off to?"

She didn't answer at once. "He left a letter for you," she said. "He wanted to do that, because he was a bit worried about taking your car away again without asking. There it is, on the table."

I took it up. It came in an envelope, and gummed down. I stood there fingering it for a minute, but I didn't open it at once. And while I was hesitating there, the girl got up from the window-seat and came over to me by the table.

"Do you know what it was that they stole?" she asked.

I moistened my lips. "The plates, I suppose."

She nodded. "That was it. Maurice told me about it last night. The whole thing—everything that he told you. And he told me all about what's happened since he's been here. You've been most frightfully good to us, Mr. Moran. To us both."

I cleared my throat. "That doesn't matter," I said at last, and I was startled for the moment by the strangeness of my own voice.

She shook her head. "But it does matter. You don't see it, but it matters—frightfully. It was because you were so decent to him that Maurice stayed here after the first day when he was ill. If it hadn't been for that, he'd have gone straight back to Russia directly he was well enough to travel. And the plates would have been there by now. And developed and everything. . . ."

I couldn't have found anything to say to her then in any case. But I didn't want to say anything. The less I said the better, until I had heard the whole of what she had to tell me. And so I stood there looking at her dumbly, and she thought that I was embarrassed at her praise, and she smiled a little to make me feel less awkward. Even at such a time she could do that.

"It's because you were so frightfully decent to him about it all that we've got just the one chance to put it right," she said.

I nodded slowly. "I see," I muttered, and stood there fingering the letter.

She went wandering in her narrative, and I didn't dare to recall her to the point. "One reads about spies in books and things," she said absently, "and it all seems—unreal. Not the sort of thing that could possibly happen in one's life. And then—well, it does."

She raised her eyes to mine. "Maurice didn't think about being a spy," she said. "Honestly—I know he didn't. All he

148

ever thought about was the job—the flying, and whether he'd be able to keep his course all right, and how he'd be able to find out what the wind was doing, and what height he'd have to be when he let off the firework. And whether a thousand pounds was the right fee for all that night flying, and what he'd have got for a series of long night flights like that if it had been in England. You see, it's his profession, and it's all he thinks about. It's—it's the only thing he lives for, really."

She paused for a minute, and then she began again: "I know him so well. I've helped him so often with his plans for long flights like that. I used to sit and write down things for him in the evenings when he was plotting his route on maps and things, and I used to make little lists of things that he mustn't forget to tell the mechanics in the morning. We used to do everything like that together. And so you see, I do know. Honestly. He gets so keen upon a job, and he does his job so well for its own sake, that he forgets about the rest of it."

I said something then. I don't know what. At all events, she didn't heed it.

"Do you know what we came over here for this morning?" she inquired. "To get those plates back again. And then he was going to expose them." I think she may have thought from the expression on my face that I didn't understand her. "You know, it's an awfully quick plate, because it was for using at night. It's quite easy to spoil a plate like that, and ruin the picture on it. You've only got to take it out of the case and expose it to the light for ever so short a time, and it's done for. I know, because I used to have a Kodak once, and I spoilt some. And Maurice says it's just the same with plates as it is with films."

I crossed over and kicked the fire up into a blaze. "You were going to do that this morning?" I inquired. It was the shortest, the most non-committal thing that I could find to say.

She nodded. "We talked it all over last night, at Winchester. You see"—she glanced up at me wistfully—"we couldn't possibly let those plates go back to Russia. It's not the thing to do.

Maurice saw that for himself, just as much as I did. It only wanted someone to put it to him."

There was a little pause at that. "It wanted you to put it to him," I said. "I can't say that I had much success."

I really think that was a new idea to her. "I suppose that's true," she said. And then she went on to tell me how they had driven over from Winchester after an early breakfast, and had arrived not five minutes after the burglary had taken place.

"It was rotten luck, that," she said quietly. "If we'd only been just a minute or two earlier—this wouldn't have happened. You see, we were going to expose the plates at once—directly we got here. Maurice thought it'd be a good place if we were to lay them out on the window-sill for a minute or two." She turned vaguely towards the curtained alcove. "This window-sill."

"Bad luck," I said.

There was a long silence after that. I broke it at last with the inquiry that I knew the answer to.

"Where's Lenden, then? Did he go off after them?"

She nodded dumbly. "He wanted to," she said, a little pitifully. "He said he couldn't possibly let it go like that, and he said he knew which way they'd be going." She pulled herself up, and stared at me gravely. "I think it was the right thing to do," she said.

"It's a damn risky thing to do," I said practically. "Where's he gone to?"

She had quite recovered her control. "He's told you in his letter, I think. It's somewhere between France and Italy. It's the same way as he went to Russia, when he went out there first of all."

I glanced furtively at my wrist-watch. There was still lashings of time to catch the Havre boat, but by this time he would be in Paris. He had an eight hours' start.

I ripped open the letter. It was written in pencil on some sheets torn out of one of my ledgers with the cash lines running down the edge; I suppose that was the only paper he could find, being in a hurry. I have that letter beside me now.

Dear Moran,

Mollie will be able to tell you all about what's happened here. It's those plates I took of Portsmouth. Somebody's pinched them. I expect they're in with the communists here, or something. And they've shot up your butler, and I'm terribly sorry that's happened, old boy.

I'm pushing off now to Dover to get the boat there. I think those plates are on their way to Russia, and there's only one way that they can go. The way I went. You go first to the Casa Alba by Lanaldo; that's a bit off the track, but it's the clearing house and they tell you which way to go from there, and they fix you up with a new passport. The villagers reckon it's smuggling across the French border and they do a bit of smuggling to keep up the blind, but it's the clearing house really. All the funny business goes that way since the Kleunen show.

I want to get to the Casa first and spill a line of innocence before the plates arrive. Then when they come I'll be quids in, anyway enough to get my fingers on the plates with any luck. After that I don't mind if they do blot my copybook for me, because it'll be worth it.

Now, I'm taking your car to Dover. I'll leave it in your name at the nearest garage I can find to the boat, and say you'll call for it in a day or two. You'd better bring the registration book with you to claim it.

And now, there's just one other thing. I've fixed things up with Mollie all right, and I want to say thank you for your share in that. If this show goes all right we'll probably have a go at being married again, which'll be just what the doctor ordered. And if it doesn't, Mollie's got enough money to get on with now, and then there's the shop. But what we fixed up last night was that we'd do in these bloody plates and let the Soviet whistle for me. And we thought we'd go out to Germany pretty soon together, and we'd run it as a second honeymoon, and we'd hunt up old Keumer's wife and make her a present of the thousand because I know she'll be on the beach and I'd

*like to do that for the old lad. Mollie knows all I do about where
to find her.*

*If anything goes wrong in this show I'd be most awfully glad
if you'd try and do something about that for me, because it's
the only thing outstanding really, except for a fiver that I owe
Morris of the Rawdon Aircraft Company, and you might see
that he gets it. And I think that's all.*

*Thanks a lot for putting me up like you've done and all the
rest. I wish to hell I was well out of this; but you see Mollie's
point of view, and it'd be pretty rotten for her having me
about the place without this thing being squared up O.K.*

Yours truly,

M. T. Lenden.

I stood there staring at the last page of this letter long after
I had read it through. I was afraid to look up, I suppose. By
this time he would be in Paris. The Havre boat was the next;
so far as I remembered, it left Southampton at about eleven
o'clock. That would mean reaching Paris about ten o'clock in
the morning. But by that time he would be in Marseilles, or
Modane, or however it was he went. He was going out hell
for leather, in order to "spill a line of innocence before the
plates arrive". There was no possible chance of catching him
up that way.

And then I knew that Mollie Lenden had seen that I had
finished the letter, and I must say something to her.

"He'll be in Paris now," I remarked. It was the only thing
that I could think of to say. "I expect he'll be catching a night
train on from there."

She nodded. "I expect so," she said absently. "He'll get out
there to-morrow afternoon—to this place in Italy. That's what
he said." And then she turned to me. "What was it that he
took photographs of?" she asked. "Do you know?"

In the grate the fire was dying very red. "It was of Portsmouth," I said. "It was something at the entrance to the
harbour, but I don't know what it was."

152

She eyed me wistfully for a moment, till I knew what she was going to say. "It's most frightfully important, isn't it?"

There was only one way in which I could have answered that. "I don't know what it is," I said again. "But it was important enough for them to shoot down the next machine that came over to repeat the job."

In the red glow from the dying fire she inclined her head, her lips quivering. I would have left her to herself then, but it semed that the least that I could do now was to assure her of the urgency. "I know," she said at last. "That was Mr. Keumer's machine."

"They went so far as that," I said. "Just murder, because he hadn't got a gun to answer with. That wasn't done for fun, you know."

She had her eyes fixed on my face. "I know," she said quickly. "I know it wasn't."

I had only half my mind on what I was saying to her. I hadn't got a passport. I hadn't been abroad since just after the war, and it had lapsed years ago. I knew that one could get into France without a passport by taking a cheap day-return ticket. But not Italy. To get a passport meant at least a morning's delay in London. It meant that I couldn't start after him till midday to-morrow. I should be twenty-four hours late. At least.

And suddenly she startled me with a question.

"You're agent here, aren't you?" Her voice was clear and strong again.

I nodded.

"Does that mean that you look after the land and the people?"

"In a way," I replied. "The farms, and the rents, and things like that. Repairs, and a bit of stock-breeding, and any building that's going on. I've got a finger in most pies in this part of the country."

"Do you know the country very well?"

I couldn't imagine what she was driving at. "Pretty well," I said. "This part of Sussex. I was bred here—out past Leventer. My father was a doctor there."

She eyed me for a minute, and then she said: "Well, you're country-bred. What did you think of Maurice when he told you what he'd been doing?"

That came as a complete surprise. I was still thinking about that passport, as a matter of fact. "Why—nothing very bad," I replied. "I don't know that I thought about it much. Not till he told me himself what was the matter with him, and then I thought——"

She stared at me. "What was it that he told you?"

I had let myself into that blindly, thinking of other things. I could see no way out of it now but to tell her the truth.

"It wasn't much," I said gently. "It was just that he hadn't got a stake in the country. He hadn't got a home to go to, or a wife and kids, or anything like that. That was when he thought he was divorced, you see. And so he thought it didn't matter a damn what he did."

She had gone very white.

"One has to put oneself in his shoes," I said slowly. "It's different for me, and I think it's different for you. I've got this place, and my job in this part of the world, and my friends. And you've got your shop, and your home, and Winchester. Little things—but what else would you call patriotism? Just being fond of the little things you've got at home, and that you don't want to see changed. A house with a bit of garden that you can grow things in, and a dog or two, and all the little inconveniences and annoyances that you couldn't really get along without. That's your patriotism, and that's all there's in it. And that's what Lenden hadn't got."

She didn't speak.

I glanced down at the letter. I was still holding it in my hand, those blue red-lined leaves from the ledger. "And now," I said, "you've gone and given him back his patriotism." I bit my lip, and turned away towards the window.

I knew then what I'd got to do—the only thing that I could possibly do to put this thing right. It was only a fifty per cent chance at the best, but it was one that I had to take. I stood there for a minute staring out into the darkness beyond the window and trying to master my cold feet, and for that reason I kept my back turned to her.

And then I heard a little noise behind me, and I swung round. She was crying. It was time that came, I thought. She had buried her face in her arms against the mantelpiece and she was crying there, quite quietly. I can remember that I wished to God that Sheila was at home.

I let her carry on for a bit, hesitating irresolute by the window. At last I crossed the room, and presently I touched her on the shoulder. "I wouldn't cry like that, if I were you," I said, as gently as I could. "There's nothing to cry like that for, you know. It's only that he'll be away for a few days longer, till this thing's cleared up."

I suppose it was a silly thing to say. But she raised her head and began dabbing at her eyes with a handkerchief. And then:

"You don't understand," she muttered wearily. "It's me . . . that's been such a beast. He'd never have gone out there at all if it hadn't been for me, and none of this would ever have happened. And now there's this. It's so frightfully dangerous, and I let him go—just as he'd come back home. He wouldn't have gone if he'd thought I didn't want it. . . ."

She dropped her head down to the mantelpiece again.

"If those plates get back to Russia there'll be hell to pay," I said.

I had caught her attention. "I know," she muttered.

I laid my hand upon her shoulder, and she stood up. "There's nobody else in the whole world that stands a better chance of putting this thing right," I said. "It's up to him. He's the only Englishman that has the entrée, that can get access to expose those plates now. You see that, don't you?"

She had her eyes fixed on mine. "Yes," she said quietly. "I see that."

I dropped my hand from her shoulder. "Well," I said, "there you are. It's a damn fine thing that he's up to, and a thing that you can be proud of. He's the only man who has the power to put this thing right now, and he's gone out to do it. I don't reckon that's a thing to cry about."

And then I heard a car in the yard outside, and from the beat of the engine I knew it was Sheila in the little Talbot. And I can remember that I was very thankful.

I smiled down at Mrs. Lenden. "There's a friend of mine outside," I said. "A girl. I'm going to send her in to you, and she'll take you somewhere where you can wash your face and blow your nose. And I wouldn't cry any more. Not if I were you."

I left the house and went out into the yard. Sheila's car was there, standing beneath the stable lantern on the wall; the headlights made two narrow pencils of light out into the darkness of the garden. I crossed the yard to her.

"Evening, Miss Darle," I said. "I'm afraid we've had some trouble here."

I told her briefly what had happened, in the dim light from the lantern on the wall. She listened to me in silence till I came to the part about Lenden going off to Italy. Then she broke in.

"Do you mean to say that he's gone off to Italy to get those plates back?" she inquired, and in the half-light I saw her brows wrinkled in perplexity.

I nodded. "He's going to expose them."

"But, Peter," she said, "they're exposed! We did it that morning over by the farm."

There was a moment's silence, and then I laughed. "I know they are," I said.

She stared at me wide-eyed. "Is it dangerous?"

I was sick of evasions, and there was no need for them with Sheila. "I think it's about as dangerous as it can be," I said. "If he gets into that house among the Russians and makes any effort to destroy those plates, I wouldn't give twopence for his chance of coming out of it alive."

She had nothing to say to that.

I dropped my foot from the running-board of her car, and stood up. "It's up to us now," I said heavily. "I'm going after him. There's just one sporting chance of catching him up before he gets there, if I get away at dawn. I'm reckoning to catch him just the other side of the Italian frontier."

She nodded. For the moment she was satisfied with that, and I went on to tell her about Mollie Lenden.

"All right," she said at last. "I'll go in and see her, and look after her. I'll take her up to my room, and she can lie down for a bit. She'll be sleeping here to-night, won't she? I can lend her things."

"I expect so." And then I hesitated a little. "You'll be careful what you say, though?"

"What about?"

I eyed her steadily. "I haven't told her that we exposed the plates ourselves. It didn't seem much good telling her that. And I funked it."

She stood there for a minute, chewing the corner of her glove. "I don't think it's any good telling her that just yet," she said. "It won't help her much, will it?" She glanced up at me in the dim light. "It was very sweet of you to think of that, Peter," she said softly. "Very kind, and very considerate. You know, you're rather a dear."

And then she turned, and went away across the yard towards my house. I stood there watching her until she disappeared.

CHAPTER SIX

PRESENTLY I WENT INTO THE HOUSE, and up into the library. There was a copy of the *Encyclopædia Britannica* there; I opened it at a map of Italy and stood staring vacantly at the Ligurian Riviera. I had been along that coast as far as Monte Carlo from Nice; farther than that it was quite unknown to me. In the end I had to turn to the Index for information about Lanaldo. I found it on the map then. It was one of a dozen very small towns up in the hills, rather more behind Ventimiglia than Mentone.

That map was on too small a scale. I had taken on the job of re-arranging the library one winter, so that I knew my way about. There was a series of atlases there called "Maps of Europe". I dragged out one of the volumes and found quite a good map of the country behind San Remo, to a scale of about two miles to the inch.

My heart sank as I studied it. Lanaldo lay about six miles inland from the sea, and about three from the French frontier. It stood on the side of the Roja valley, about three hundred feet above the main road that runs up the valley from Ventimiglia to the north. No road was shown leading to the town itself. I knew what that meant. It would be one of the walled, cavernous little mountain towns of that neighbourhood, where every street serves as a sewer and every cellar as a stable. That would not have worried me, but that I knew the sort of country that those towns stood in.

As I stood there studying the map upon the table before me I was appalled at the mountainous nature of the country. Literally, it was all up on end. Beyond the bed of the river, I could see nothing to indicate flat country of any description there. Behind the town the hills rose up into a peak about three thousand feet high, called Monte Verde; the country was simply studded with things like that. There was no possible place where one could put down an aeroplane, unless it were in the bed of the river. And I knew what sort of landing that would be.

I lingered for a little while longer over the map. The scale was too small to show houses, but I was able to make a pretty good guess at the probable position of the Casa Alba. I decided that if it were a centre for Soviet activities it must be near the road; if then its address was Lanaldo, it must be on the road immediately below the town. I didn't think that there'd be much difficulty about finding the house if once I got out here.

I left the maps lying open on the table, meaning to come back and consult them again later in the night. In the stable-yard I found Kitter putting away Sheila's car. We should want that car before the night was out, I thought.

"Kitter," I said, and he turned and came towards me. He was a young chap, and very smart on his job; I don't suppose he was thirty. "Ever had anything to do with aeroplanes?"

He shook his head. "No, sir. I was with the Tanks in the war."

I nodded. "I've got a machine out on the down, this side of Leventer. She wants a new bit of oil pipe—about a foot of seven-eighth stuff, or it may be inch. Rubber pipe. Can you find that for me—to-night?"

"For an aeroplane, sir?"

I nodded.

He shook his head. If he was at all startled, he didn't show it. "Young Saven might have a bit at his place, sir. I've got nothing like that."

He was a sound man, and I knew that he'd be for me in this thing. I rested one foot upon the running-board of the Talbot and stared at him reflectively. "This has been a damn bad day's work, Kitter," I said quietly.

"Yes, sir," he said.

I put it to him frankly then. I forget exactly what I said, but told him straight out that there was fishy business on hand,

and that it hadn't been quite an ordinary burglary.

And then I told him something about the Breguet, and I told him that I was going to fly it out to Italy at dawn.

And I told him a little more than that—that if he was to help me he'd be putting himself well within the reach of the law, and it might be that I shouldn't be able to get him out of the mess. I told him all that, and that it was up to him to make his own decision as to whether he gave me a hand with that machine or not. And at the end of that he scratched his head and said:

"I don't know where you'd go to get a bit of pipe like that," he said. "There's just a chance that we can get a bit off young Saven." And then he said: "Will we be working all night, sir?"

I nodded. "Most of it, if I'm to get away at dawn."

He considered for a minute. "I think we ought to get young Saven in on this, sir," he said. "I do, straight. He's only just come out of the Air Force."

"Can he keep his mouth shut?"

Kitter laughed. "He'd kill his grandmother for the chance to handle an aeroplane again, sir. Tell him this is on, and he'll never rest till he sees you in the air. If he gets to know that the police'll stop you flying if they get on to it . . . I do think we ought to have Saven, sir."

And so we had Saven, and we got out Sheila's car and ran down to Under in it, and ran Saven to earth in his father's pub. Kitter went in to broach the matter with him while I went on to the police station. They kept me there discussing the burglary for over half an hour; in the end we came to the conclusion that Sanders must have disturbed the burglars before they had had time to get to work on my safe. I signed a deposition that they had stolen my cash-book, since Sanders had admitted to seeing them with something black. The Inspector congratulated me that nothing more important was missing.

I got away from there at last, and went back to the pub. Kitter and Saven were in the little garage in the yard, turning over a heap of scrap and junk in the light of a candle stuck in a bottle.

Saven turned to me as I came in. The flickering candle flung great shadows around the little place as I stood in the doorway, peering around among the wrecked and derelict ten-pound cars that Saven deals in.

"Evening, Saven," I said. "Kitter told you about this machine?"

He came forward, and nodded. He was a little short man, quite young, and with a shy, bird-like manner. "He told me as you wanted a bit of oil union for it, sir. This stuff the right size, do you think?"

I took the pipe he handed me. "I couldn't say till we try it on the job."

"What's the machine, sir? That's what they use on Avros, and the like o' that."

I shook my head slowly. "She's a Breguet Nineteen."

In the flickering darkness he stared at me in amazement. "The French Breguet—what they done the long-distance flights on?"

I nodded. "That's the machine."

"Lord, sir," he said. "She's as big as a Fawn."

I nodded. "I've never seen a Fawn," I said. "But this one's pretty big."

I had aroused his interest thoroughly. "How would it be if I was to come along with you and fit this bit o' pipe, sir?" he inquired. "I've never worked on one o' them, but I've got a ticket for most of our Service types, and I expect it's about the same."

In the darkness I was suddenly aware that I was very tired. "I came to ask if you could give a hand," I said.

We went out of that place and got into the car. Saven was talking to Kitter in low tones. From what I heard, Kitter was telling him he'd got to keep his mouth shut. I thought, as I drove, that the gods had been very good in sending me a couple of first-rate mechanics at this time. With their help I had just a sporting chance of getting this machine into the air; without them the odds would have been so heavily against me that I do not think I should have had the courage to go through with it. They were local men, both of them, born and bred within ten miles of the place where I was born and bred myself. West Sussex, all of us. I had known of them, and they of me, since we were ten years old. I knew they wouldn't let me down in this affair, however fishy it might seem to them, and that knowledge heartened me.

It was very dark, but a fine, overcast night. I remember that I turned to Kitter once during the drive. "We'll take this car right up to the barn," I said. "We shall need the lights."

And so we left the road not very far from the spot where I had picked up Lenden on that first night of all, and we went wandering over the grass upon an ancient track, barely distinguishable in the darkness, down the incline of the slopes. It was rough going but we went slowly, and so we arrived at the barn at about eight o'clock in the evening of that night. Behind the barn the broad overhanging wings of the Breguet loomed deserted in the headlights, exactly as she had been when I saw her last.

"Lumme!" said Saven. "She isn't half a size!" He turned to me as I got out of the car. "Did you say you're going to take her up yourself, sir?"

I nodded at him in the dim, white light. "That's the big idea."

He seemed about to say something, but didn't say it. We swung the car round behind the barn until the lights bore on the engine cowling of the Breguet, and then we got to work. It was a pleasure to watch Saven on the job. In five minutes he had stripped the cowling with our help and had got a clear idea of the run of the petrol and oil systems. He had brought with him in the car a great assortment of stuff, with many tools.

By nine o'clock the job was done. He had examined every oil and petrol pipe, and had remade the majority of the flexible unions. He had examined the water system, and had run over every other component of the engine very systematically. And then, at the last, he dropped down from the nose of the machine and stood wiping his hands upon a bit of rag.

"Well," he said quietly. "She should run now."

It took us about twenty minutes to get her started. She went off with a rush then and surged forward against the pig-trough that we had fitted for chocks, till Saven caught her on the throttle. We let her run warm for a bit, and then we ran her up to full power. She ran up sweet and true, for all her week out in the open. In the end Saven throttled her down, and we saw him begin to clamber from the cockpit. He hesitated up there for a minute, and then climbed slowly to the ground.

"She's running very sweet," he said. He turned to me. "About the petrol, sir. Will she have enough for what you want?"

I had been thinking about that. "Lenden said she had fuel left for seven hours," I muttered. "We'd better make it up to ten. What'll she use an hour?"

He eyed her thoughtfully. "I couldn't rightly say. Twenty-five gallons an hour, cruising, perhaps—maybe thirty. Say we'll want another forty to forty-five tins of Shell. That'll mix up with the stuff what's in the tank, if it's Aviation, and she won't notice the difference, I don't think."

I nodded. "Can you get that quantity to-night?"

He said he thought he had that much in store.

I clambered up into the cockpit, and Saven came up and sat on the cowling beside me, and for a quarter of an hour he coached me in the massed controls till I knew every tap in the petrol system and every gadget on the dash by heart, with its appointed function in the scheme of things. Essentially the flying controls were the same as when I used to fly. Those were straightforward, and my skill was the only criterion for their proper use. The engine and fuel controls had to be learned by heart, and he coached me till I was word-perfect. It worried me that all the labels were in French.

Finally Saven and Kitter got out on to the wing-tips, and we set to work to taxi her up the hill.

There was a south-westerly wind that night. I had decided

with Saven that we would take her up to the top of the down, and then along as far as we could get her to the east. That would give me about half a mile in a south-easterly direction for my take-off before I came to the telegraph wires bordering the road. I'd got to get her over those.

Those wires were a worry to me. The first three or four hundred yards of that run was flat; from there the ground sloped gently down to the road. I didn't know how much run a machine like this would want; I only knew that that old B.E. that I used to fly in the war would have got off in about half that distance if she was ever going to get off at all. Things might have changed a bit, however, since last I flew. It scared me to think how long ago that was.

I knew what would happen if she didn't clear the wires, of course. She would trip up on them and go crashing down nose first into the field beyond, and with all that petrol in the fuselage she was pretty certain to take fire.

It's sometimes an encumbrance to know too much. The thought of that fire didn't help me a bit.

We got her up on the top of the down all right, and then we began to manœuvre her into the correct position. Finally we settled her quite comfortably at the extreme end of the run, with her tail in among the gorse bushes that formed the limit of the good ground. That was the last that we could do with her for the present. I stopped the engine, took a last look round the cockpit, and clambered down to the ground.

Kitter and Saven were talking together by the wing-tip. They broke off as I approached, and Kitter came towards me.

"I've been talking to Saven, sir," he said. "You don't want to start away before it's light, do you?"

I shook my head. "I'll get away directly we can see the road from here."

"You'll go back to the Hall, an' get a bit of sleep now, sir?" He eyed me anxiously. "Reckon you'll want a bit of sleep before starting, sir. Flying all that way. I'd come and call you when you want. There's nothing more to do here, bar filling her up, and Saven and I can do that."

I hesitated. "Somebody's got to stand by the machine all the time she's out here," I said. "It won't do for her to blow away now."

"That's so," said Saven. "I tell you what. I'll run you back to Under while Mr. Kitter stays out here, sir. Then I can get the petrol from my place, and come back. And then Mr. Kitter can come and call you when you want. . . ."

I considered for a moment. "It will be light enough by half-past five," I said. "I should have to be called soon after four."

"That's right, sir," said Kitter.

And we arranged it so. I knew that a little sleep might make all the difference to the upshot of this flight; I was tired and, sleepy as it was, and I was most terribly worried about those telegraph wires. I should want to be absolutely on the spot when it came to getting over those, I thought. Curiously enough, I cannot remember that I worried very much about the other end of the flight. That was hopeless, I suppose.

We left Kitter with the pickets and the mallet in case the wind got up, and I went back to the Hall with Saven in the Talbot. He dropped me at the entrance to the yard, swung her round, and went back, by the way that he had come, to load the little car with petrol cans.

I went into my house. There was nobody there and the fire was nearly out; on the mantelpiece the clock showed five minutes to eleven. I kicked the fire together and threw on a little more coal, poured myself out a whisky and soda, and then I went over to the mansion.

Everyone had gone up to bed, for I had to let myself into the mansion with my key. The lights were all out, and in the darkness the great house was very still. I went up into the library and settled down there for half an hour; in the stillness of the house the small rustling of my movements startled me with their immensity. I was very tired.

I had only indifferent material for my study. There was a good map of France in the *Encyclopædia Britannica,* but to a lamentably small scale. I settled down to plot my course with that and with the "Maps of Europe", which were on much too large a scale to give me much assistance. I had no protractor, and only a slip of paper for a scale. But as I bent over the maps the old practice began to come back to me in flashes; there was the Mediterranean—a big mark to hit—and there was the straight course to it. I noted the compass bearing. For windage, I must try to correct my course by landmarks as I went along.

I stayed up there for half an hour, but there was very little that I could do. I tore the map out of the *Encyclopædia* and folded it carefully, and I tore out three pages from the "Maps of Europe". Those three are still missing, and one can see the pruned edges in the volumes; I replaced that volume of the *Encyclopædia,* but the others were irreplaceable. And then, having done what I could to lay my amateurish course, I went back to my house.

In the sitting-room the fire had burnt up well, and was throwing great flickering shadows upon the walls and ceiling. I lit the reading-lamp by the piano and busied myself for a time in minor preparations for the flight. I had an old automatic pistol with a few clips of cartridges that I used to carry in the war in case of fire. I got out this thing, saw that the mechanism still worked freely, and slipped it into my pocket. Then I set to looking out warm clothing.

By a quarter to twelve all that was done. There was nothing for it now but to go to bed till Kitter came to call me.

I stood in the middle of the room, and stared around. Lenden would be in the train on his way south from Paris by now, getting on towards Dijon. I could picture him huddled in the corner of a French second-class carriage, nursing his new-found patriotism and the image of his wife, awake and dark-eyed in the night. I could see him in the long pauses of the train in the stations, his long hair ruffled and falling down upon his forehead, rubbing the dew from the window to try and find out how far he had gone upon his way, while the train went "Whew . . ." and a little horn sounded from the rear. I wondered if he was armed. I wondered what story he was going to tell at the Casa Alba.

I moved over to the piano and sat down, wondering impersonally whether I should live to see him again.

I sat there for a little time before the piano, thinking about the work I'd done in Sussex since the war, and the small noises from the fire made me company, so that I was not quite alone. And then, after a time, I stirred a little on the stool and began to play.

I cannot rememher what I played that night. There was almost certainly a strong vein of Chopin, and I dare say I played a little Grieg, because I was in that mood. I may have gone on playing for twenty minutes or so. And then, in a pause, I dropped my hands sharply from the keys and swung round on my seat. There was somebody coming in by my front door.

Long before she came in sight I knew that it was Sheila. She came and stood in the open doorway of my room, and I smiled at her from the music-stool.

"Good evening," I said. "I hope I didn't wake you up by my playing?"

She shook her head. "I wasn't asleep," she said. "I heard you playing, and so I came over."

She moved closer to the fire, and crouched down before it. She had only a coat on over her pyjamas, and bedroom slippers on her bare feet; she had, in some queer way that I am not competent to describe, the appearance of having slept in her hair, and being only recently awake. And because she hadn't got the proper quantity of clothes on, I didn't go over to her, because I was afraid of making her feel awkward, and so we sat at opposite ends of the room, she crouched down before the fire and I on my music-stool. And for a little while we sat like that in silence.

And then she said—"Peter!"—and I went over to her by the fire, and drew up a chair near her.

"Where have you been?" she asked. "I've been trying to find you all evening, but nobody knew where you were."

She paused for a minute, and then she said: "We've made a frightful bloomer over this thing, Peter."

I nodded. "It was a mistake not to tell him that I'd exposed those plates. But it didn't seem like that at the time, did it?"

She shook her head. "I thought it was the best way then, doing it like you did."

"What's happened to his wife?"

"She's asleep—I think. I put her to bed quite early—about half-past nine. She's quite happy about it now. She thinks he's doing a perfectly splendid thing. Heroic. She's most awfully proud about it all."

I grinned, but there was very little laughter in me at that time. "That's what it is," I said mechanically. "Heroic."

She twisted round and looked up at me puzzled. "It seems so funny," she said. "I didn't know that heroes were like that."

"Nobody ever does," I said.

There was a little silence then, and we sat together there before the fire in the dim light of my room. I had a vague feeling that she oughtn't to be there at all at that time of night, especially in her pyjamas, and that instead of sitting there with my hand upon her shoulder I ought to be packing her off back to the mansion and to bed with a few delicate, well-chosen words. Instead, I did nothing about it, and we sat there till she turned to me again.

"Where do you suppose he is now?"

"In the train," I replied. "Round about Dijon or Macon, or somewhere down that line. So far as I can see, he must be going out by Ventimiglia. That means going through Marseilles; he gets there about nine o'clock to-morrow morning, as I reckon it."

She stared up at me pleadingly. "Isn't there any possible way of getting at him to tell him? What was that you said about going after him to catch him up? Wasn't it any good?"

I didn't want much to tell her about that. I had meant to slip off in the early dawn before she was about and so prevent an explanation, but there was nothing for it now. "I think it may work all right," I said, and smiled down upon her. "Anyway, it's worth trying."

She twisted round upon the floor and stared up into my face. "What is it? You can't catch him now?"

I hesitated for a moment, and leaned forward and chucked a bit more coal on the fire. "There's only one way of doing it, so far as I can see," I said. "That's by air. His aeroplane's still out there on the down."

"Oh . . ." she said softly. "Do you mean you're going to fly it out there after him?"

Beneath my hand her hair was very soft. Like spun silk. "Why yes," I said simply. "That's the big idea. I've been out there all evening with Kitter, and with Saven from the Red Bear, getting the machine ready. I'm pushing off in her at dawn."

I paused. "According to my reckoning, that'll get me out there just before noon, or about noon. She'll go all the way without a stop, that machine. The real trouble will be at the other end, I'm afraid—after I've landed. I haven't got any papers for myself or for the machine. The machine hasn't got any registration letters. I haven't even got a passport. That means they'll jug me for a cert in Italy, if they can get hold of me. After I've landed I've got to keep out of the way of everybody, and yet get into touch with Lenden before he reaches this house—the Casa Alba. That's the real difficulty."

She eyed me seriously. "It's a ripping scheme, Peter," she said. "If there's anyone can make it work, it's you."

"It's a fifty per cent chance," I replied. "I don't put it higher than that."

"What are you going to do when you've landed?" she inquired.

I left her for the moment, got up and fetched my maps from the table, and came back and sat down as I had been before. She knelt up before the fire and leaned against my knee to see the maps. I spread out the large-scale one of that district and showed her the main features of the land.

"You see his hill behind Lanaldo," I said. "Monte Verde, it's called here. It looks to be all woody, and I think these little squiggles mean it's pine trees. I'm going to put the machine down up there—it's about three miles from Lanaldo and looks to be pretty desolate. Then I'm going to work down through the woods—down here—across that little col and down that sort of ravine till I get out on to the main road—there. It looks as if there might be pretty good cover all the way. When I get to the road, I shall have to wait there in a sort of ambush. If he comes by Ventimiglia he's got to get to the house by that road, and I suppose he'll be in a car. I should be able to stop him there."

I didn't tell her the rest of the plan—which was simply that I was going to wait there upon the road till five o'clock. If by that time I had not succeeded in intercepting him, then I should have to assume that he had passed, and the only thing to do would be to go up quietly through the woods and see what was going on at the White House. I didn't know what that might lead to, but it was with that in mind that I had resurrected my old automatic. I hoped to God that the cartridges were still all right.

She leaned across my knee, pulling the map towards her and studying it with brows wrinkled in a frown. "Peter, I don't see where you're going to land on Monte Verde from this map," she said slowly. "I thought aeroplanes needed a great big open space for landing. It doesn't look as if you'd find anything like that there."

Girls in these days know too much. I didn't quite know what to say to that.

"They don't need so much room as all that," I said uncomfortably. "Not the way I'm going to land this one."

She looked up very quickly at that. "Do you mean you can't land it properly out there?" she asked. "I don't understand."

I smiled at her in what I hoped was a reassuring way, though if anyone needed reassuring it was me. "There's two ways of landing an aeroplane," I explained. "One so that you can use it again afterwards, and one so that you can't. The second one is quite a good way, if you don't happen to want the aeroplane particularly."

She was about to say something, but I stopped her. "In a

place like that," I said, "it's pretty certain that there'll be clear-ings. If there's a really flat, eligible bit of greensward, I shall put her down the first way, because I don't like waste. But if there isn't anything like that, then I shall put her down on the tree-tops. In the war, I always used to look for two things when I had the wind up or engine failure. A good big field, or, failing that, a wood. Trees are soft, you know."

She was staring up at me intently; beneath my hand her shoulder was very still. "You mean you're going to crash?"

I laughed at her. "That's a hard word to use," I replied. "I'm going to put her down on the tree-tops. Nobody ever got hurt doing that."

She was still staring up into my face. "Peter," she said. "Don't go and get hurt."

I shook my head. "All right," I said, and smiled a little. "I'll be careful about that."

She wasn't satisfied at all, but she looked down and began playing with the poker in the ashes of the hearth. "Must it be done like that?" she asked. "Isn't there any place where you could land ordinarily?"

I shook my head. "You see, it means being arrested if I put down on an aerodrome with that machine. At one time I did think of going to London and chartering a machine from Imperial Airways. But I haven't got a passport, and it'd mean spending all the morning getting one. No, this way'll be all right."

A new idea struck her. "Is this a very big machine? Very powerful?"

"Bit of a lump," I said.

She twisted round again to look at me. "Peter, when did you fly last? Are you in practice?"

I shifted a little uneasily in my chair, and because she was leaning up against my knee she noticed it. "One doesn't lose practice in a thing like that," I lied. "That'll be all right."

"D'you mean you haven't flown at all since the war?"

"Not very much," I said.

I had done it by saying that. She slipped round and stood

erect, pulling her clothes a little more closely about her. I got up too, and we stood looking at each other before the fire. "You can't do this, Peter," she said. "It's a most frightful risk you're taking. I won't have it."

I smiled at her. "I'm afraid you don't come into it," I said.

"Peter. You simply mustn't. Please . . . Peter." She stood there before me, flushed and dishevelled, and very sweet. If there had been less at stake between us at that moment, I would have been no gentleman and kissed her. But I didn't do that, and so I only stood there grinning at her. And when she saw me grinning at her like that she gave up, and there were tears in her eyes when she spoke again.

"Peter dear," she said unsteadily. "You mustn't do it. Really. It's frightfully dangerous."

I took one of her hands in mine. She has very small hands, not half the size of my own. I had never had the chance to examine one of them before. "But I must," I said.

She looked at me dumbly for a moment. "I don't see why."

I stood there with her in the glow of the fire, playing with her hand and wondering at the littleness of it. "Because I've got to live with myself," I said. "You can't shirk that. And because I'd like to see Lenden have another cut at living with his wife again. That's all."

And we stood there silent like that for a long time. In the end she looked up at me. "You really mean it, Peter?"

"I'm afraid so," I replied. "I don't see that there's any other way of getting in touch with him in time. If there was any other way, I'd take it. God knows I don't want to fly the ruddy thing."

I was still examining her fingers; she had made no movement to regain her hand. "When must you start?" she asked.

"At dawn," I said. "Kitter will be coming to call me soon after four. He's getting the machine filled up with petrol now —with Saven."

She looked up at me anxiously, and tried to withdraw her hand. But I didn't allow that. "You must get to bed," she said softly. "At once."

I nodded slowly. "I know I must," I said. "And so must you. You oughtn't to have come over, really."

In all the years that I have known Sheila she has never been quite repressible. There was a glint of humour in her eyes when she looked up, like a spot of sunlight in a puddle of rain. "I suppose not," she said. "But then you oughtn't to be holding my hand like this, in the middle of the night."

I slipped my arm round her and drew her a little closer to me. "In regard to that," I said, "I suppose no gentleman would take advantage of you so far as to tell you that he loved you, in the middle of the night and when you've only got about half the proper complement of clothes on."

She stood there very quietly in my arms. "Peter," she said softly, "are you asking me to marry you?"

I grinned down at her. "Lord, no," I said. "Not at this time of night. It wouldn't be proper. I'll do that one morning before breakfast in the cold light of day, when I can see your freckles and you can see the cigarette stains on my fingers. But for to-night, I just wanted you to know that I love you. Before I pack you off to bed."

She drew a little closer to me. "Peter dear," she said, "I've known that for the last two years."

There was hiatus then—an interlude which must have lasted for ten minutes or so. I sometimes think that no gentleman— and certainly no lady—would have enjoyed that interlude so much as we did, or indeed would have permitted it to happen at all. But at last:

"It's time you went to bed," I said, and I wrapped her cloak more closely round her, and we went out of my house and across the stable-yard in a still, moonlit night. In the hall, at the foot of the great staircase, she left me, and I stood and watched her mounting in the dim light till she was lost in the shadows of the passage at the head. I let myself out of the mansion and went back to my house across the yard, and then, since it was one o'clock, I threw off my clothes, and took a couple of aspirins, and went to bed. And I slept at once.

I was roused almost immediately, before I had had time to

realise that I was asleep. The reading-lamp by my bed was switched on, and I became drowsily aware that somebody was shaking me by the shoulder. I rolled over and opened one eye, and it was Sheila.

"It's time to get up, Peter," she said softly. "Kitter's just come with the car. It's four o'clock."

It was still quite dark. I stirred, sat up in bed, and looked at her sleepily. "All right," I muttered, and I sat there looking at her sleepily for a minute while she smiled at me. "I say . . . was I dreaming, or did I tell you that I loved you last night? Because if by any chance I didn't, I'd like to tell you now."

She laughed softly. "You did tell me something about it, Peter," she said. "But it's sweet of you to say your piece all over again." And she then leaned over the bed and kissed me, and I put an arm round her and returned it sleepily, as I have done a hundred times since then. And when that was over:

"Now you shoot off," I said, "while I get up." And as she moved away I noticed for the first time that she was fully dressed in a light-blue jumper and a tweed skirt. She paused in the door.

"What d'you want for breakfast, Peter?" she inquired. "I've got some coffee here, and toast and marmalade, and there's some eggs. Would you like one poached?"

I passed my hand over my forehead. "I don't know that I can eat anything at this time of the morning."

She nodded slowly. "I'll poach a couple, anyway. If you can't eat them you can mess 'em abaht a bit. But I expect you can."

And then she was gone, and I got up.

I dressed as if I was a starter for a Polar expedition, and when I was ready I went sleepily through into the sitting-room. Sheila had turned my fireplace into a sort of camp kitchen, and breakfast was in train. Kitter was crouching over the fire and helping her; I crossed the room to them. "Have you been to bed at all?" I asked.

She nodded. "Mm. I've only been up half an hour. Now sit down and have something to eat."

"Morning, Kitter," I said. "How's the machine?"

"Saven's been having another go at her, sir," he said. "We got the juice into her all right, and we've been running the engine again, so's she'd be warm to start when you want her. She's running a treat."

"Glad to hear it," I remarked, and sat down to breakfast. "It should be light enough by half-past five."

I didn't eat very much. Sheila ate one of my eggs, and she cut a couple of packs of sandwiches for me. I took these in the pocket of my ulster, together with a fair-sized flask of brandy. And then, having swallowed a couple of cups of coffee, I was ready.

We left the house at about five o'clock, and set off for the down. That was a silent drive. Sheila was beside me, and Kitter in the dickey-seat behind. I was preoccupied with the details of my course. I remember that I was very much concerned whether I should be able to fix my position when I came to France on the other side of the Channel. The wind was from the south-west, and light. That would help, I thought.

We came to the down at about a quarter-past five, and left the car by the roadside. It was light enough to see fifty yards or so by then; as soon as I stopped the engine of the car I heard a low rumble in the distance, away to the east. Saven was running the engine of the Breguet. That walk over the short grass to the machine seemed to take an infinite time. It was trying, that. I remember that Sheila and I were speaking inconsequently of little trivial things, in short, disjointed sentences. I promised to send her a cable as soon as I got an opportunity, telling her what had happened. It was in both our minds that she would know what had happened if she didn't get the cable, but we didn't talk about that. I hurried on to other subjects hoping that she hadn't noticed the break; long afterwards she told me that she had hoped the same of me. Funny, in a way, but I didn't see it then.

At last we got to the machine. It was very nearly light enough for the take-off by then; already I could see the line of the road half a mile away. Saven was up in the cockpit of the machine, and the pig trough was securely wedged beneath the wheels as chocks. I clambered up to the cockpit beside him, out of earshot of the others on the ground.

He throttled the engine till she was just ticking over. "She's running fine, sir." He put his hand on the lever controlling the adjustable propeller. "You want to leave this just like it is. I wouldn't touch it at all, not if I was you. I've set it right for you from the static revs."

I nodded, and asked him one or two questions about the machine. I went over the fuel system with him again to ensure that I had forgotten nothing. And then:

"You'd better get along down to the road for the take-off," I said. "Behind those telegraph wires. I want somebody down there."

He stared at me blankly for a moment, and then: "Lord, sir," he said, "she should go up over those all right. It's only half a load, or something o' that. You want to hold her down on the ground, you know, with the tail well up, till she flies off of herself. And then if you feel she's a bit close, just give her a yank up and she'll be all right."

I nodded. "I know. That's how I used to take off my B.E. with a full load of bombs. But get along down there, all the same." I paused, and then I said: "I'd hate to get singed."

He grinned. "Reckon you won't be able to keep her on the ground. But I'll get along down there, sir, just in case. She's all ready for you to take off. You've got the chocks under now, but Kitter can take them out when you've run up."

I climbed down to the ground again and began putting on my helmet. Saven followed me to the ground, spoke for a moment to Kitter, and set off for the road.

Sheila turned to me. "Where's Saven going to?"

"Down to the road," I said. "He's going to give me a signal as I go over if the engine's running all right."

She nodded, satisfied with that explanation. I finished settling the goggles securely on my forehead—I have never worn them either taking-off or landing—and made sure that I had everything that I wanted in my pockets. And then I turned to her.

"Good-bye, Sheila," I said, and stooped to kiss her.

She could only reach half-way round my shoulders with her arm. "Good-bye, Peter," she said, and kissed me in return. That was all we had to say that morning.

I straightened up and spoke to Kitter. "I'll run her up a bit," I said. "And then, when you see me wave my hand, get that pig trough out of the way and stand clear. Look out you don't run into the prop while you're doing it."

He hesitated for a moment, and then: "Good luck, sir," he said shyly.

I climbed up into the cockpit again and stowed away my maps; in the machine the controls fell naturally to my hand. I settled myself comfortably into the seat, strapped myself in, and saw that everything in my pockets was accessible.

Then I waved Kitter to the tail; he took Sheila with him and together they lay over the tail plane in the blast from the propeller while I ran the engine up. She ran up very smoothly; the revs and the oil pressure were steady as a rock, and the beat was true. I can remember that in all sincerity I thanked God for having sent me Saven at that time.

I throttled the engine down again, and waved to Kitter. He crept under to remove the pig trough; I saw him come out with it and stand clear. Straight ahead of me, on the far side of the road half a mile away, I could see Saven waiting in the field.

I became very cold, quite suddenly.

I smiled down at Sheila.

And then I settled myself again into my seat for the take-off. It was nine years and seven months since I had last flown an aeroplane.

CHAPTER SEVEN

BEFORE I BEGIN upon the account of that flight of mine, I would like to digress a little in order to explain a little more fully to what order of pilots I belong.

I learnt to fly in England, early in 1916. If this account should be read by anyone who shared that experience with me he may skip the next few paragraphs, because he will know all that I have to say upon that subject. But for those who have learnt to fly since the war in the quiet schools and flying clubs, and for those who have never piloted a machine themselves, I would like to try and point out something of the peculiar terrors, legacies of my early training, which infested all the flying I have ever done.

I was trained in the days of ignorance. That ignorance has been written about in other places, and the only aspect of it which I propose to touch on here is the great ignorance that existed in those days on the subject of spinning. We knew that a clumsily executed turn might have the effect of putting an aeroplane into a spinning nose-dive—a Parke's Dive, some of us called it, because Lieutenant Parke was one of the very few people who had come out of it alive. In general, a spin once started continued to the ground, the machine hitting very violently. And that, literally, was all we knew about it.

When I was taught to fly there was a rumour in the camp that it was possible to put an aeroplane voluntarily into a spin and get it out again. Somebody said that somebody had told him that he had seen somebody do it at Farnborough. Closer to hand, one of our own instructors, a Bachelor of Science and a schoolmaster in civil life, claimed that he had done it. So far as I remember, he had the peculiar idea that the way to get out of a spin was to force the machine into a steeper dive still; as nobody had seen him do it the first time, he was disbelieved.

Whereupon he set out to show us how to do it, and it is a fact that the rotation of the machine had practically stopped before he hit the ground. I forget his name now. That made us think that there might be something in it after all; that given sufficient height it might some day be possible to recover a machine from a clumsily executed turn before it spun into the deck.

I would like to try and impress upon the reader the intense moral effect that this spin had upon us. It was a ghoulish thing, waiting to spring out upon you in an unguarded moment. All kinds of legends and exaggerations cloaked its path. My own instructor told me that if one got into a spin on an Avro the wings fell off; he, of course, had never dreamed of trying it. Another legend was that the machine frequently turned upside down in its rotation to the ground, throwing the pilot out. Most terrifying of all was the uncertainty of the commencement of this thing. We knew that it began from an imperfectly executed slow turn, but just how bad the turn had to be to loose this frightful thing upon us was what none of us quite knew. For most of us, that made our turns a nightmare, and increased our consumption of alcohol to an extraordinary extent.

I crashed five times during the war, not counting the occasion on which I was shot down. Three of those were ordinary landings upon an aerodrome, and came from shutting off the engine at the wrong moment, I think. The other two were forced landings away from the aerodrome due to engine failure; those at the time I regarded as an Act of God, and a certain crash for any pilot, good or bad. I am told that things are not quite like that now. They tell me that no pupil is allowed to fly solo in these days till he can loop, spin, and pull off a forced landing in considerably better style than the crack pilots of my day. Well, things change.

But what I would wish to point out in connection with this flight that I made upon the Breguet is—simply—that I am a 1916 pilot who stopped flying in 1917. A relic of the past.

The take-off went better than I had hoped. I settled into my seat, pulled the stick back central, and opened up the throttle gradually. Straight before me, half a mile away, I could see the white line of the road against the greyness of the down, and the line of the telegraph wires. The Breguet stirred, and moved forward. I thrust the throttle forward to the limit of its travel, and sat tight.

We began rolling over the short turf towards the road. I held the stick a little bit forward, till presently the tail rose from the ground, and the fuselage came level. Then I just sat very still, not daring to try and pull her off the ground, while the telegraph wires loomed closer and the wind came whistling over the windscreen and around my head. She reached the end of the level ground and began to run down the incline to the road, but by that time she was travelling at great speed and I could feel that she was getting light. And then, perhaps three hundred yards from the road, she came off the ground. I made no movement of the stick, but shot a glance at the air-speed indicator. It read a hundred and thirty kilos. She touched ground once more, very lightly, and then without any conscious movement on my part, she was ten feet up. Mindful of my precautions I tried to hold her down a little. The tiny move-ments that I dared to make were ineffectual; I had her trimmed to climb, and climb she would, so that we were fifty feet up when we passed over the telegraph wires.

She went up very quickly. It cannot have been more than three or four minutes before the altimeter showed a thousand metres. I was well past Leventer by that time, and the earth was getting very faint. It was still half-dark, and there was a sort of haze over everything; but I could see a glint of open water on my left which I thought was Portsmouth harbour.

I made up my mind to turn then and fly back over the down, in order that they might see that I was all right and that Sheila might be comforted about this business. I had the wind up of that turn from the first, but it had to be done some time and I began to make my preparations for it. I was then at about four thousand feet.

As a preliminary, I levelled the machine out and throttled the engine a little. The speed increased tremendously; every wire seemed to scream at me. The indicator rose to about two hundred kilos. A rapid mental calculation showed me that that was nothing like her top speed; I hardened my heart and thrust the nose down till she was doing about two hundred and forty, which I interpreted as a hundred and fifty miles an hour. I set the tail trim for that speed, and then I began my turn by pressing lightly on the rudder.

The machine swung slowly to the left on an even keel, and the cold air came in over the side of the cockpit like a blast from a hose, drenching and stifling me. I shifted the stick over to give her a little bank, and trod more heavily upon the rudder. The nose of the machine dropped suddenly below the horizon, and continued to drop. I didn't know what to do then, and took off all rudder in a panic. The turning stopped and the air came in over the other side of the cockpit; I was sideslipping violently with the nose of the machine down and the engine on. I pulled her up a little and tried a bit of rudder again, completing the turn in a heavy sideslip upwards and outwards.

I was too high up in that dim light to be able to see them on the ground, but by the landmarks I passed more or less over the spot that I had taken off from. And then I set off on my course.

I was at about twelve hundred metres at that time, and the clouds were close above me. I had had enough of properly banked turns, and got the machine on to her course by skidding round with a very gentle application of the rudder alone. That turn must have taken me five miles to do ninety degrees, but I got her round without incident and settled on to my compass bearing. I set to work then to adjust my controls till I was flying at two hundred kilos without either losing or gaining height; by the time I had done that I was over the coast by Chichester. Before me the sea stretched away dimly into the distance as far as I could see, grey and corrugated in the morning light.

That crossing took an hour, and for the majority of that time I was out of sight of land. The clouds got lower as I approached the French coast, and I had to drop off height till I was down to about two thousand feet. I came in sight of land at about twenty minutes past six, and crossed it five minutes later.

Visibility was getting quite good by then. I missed Havre by seven or eight miles, passing to the east of the town and crossing the Seine estuary at the point where it became evidently a river. That gave me the information that I wanted to correct my course for wind; I headed a bit more to the west and went trundling out over France at about two thousand five hundred feet.

Everything seemed to be going very well. For the first time I began to feel real confidence that this venture of mine would prove successful. If all went on going so well, I was confident that I could get to Lanaldo before Lenden, and I was pretty sure that I should find somewhere to put the machine down gently. If the landing went off all right, it seemed to me that I stood a really good chance of intercepting him before he reached the house. That heartened me for the flight.

I passed over Evreux and Chartres, and so to Orleans, which I reached at twenty minutes to eight. The clouds had gone higher by this time, and I was back at about four thousand. I was getting very cold and stiff. After Orleans I managed to get down to my flask and had a drink of brandy and water, and I nibbled a sandwich in little handfuls from my pocket. It may have been the distraction of eating that made me lose touch with my surroundings, because after Orleans I saw nothing that I recognised.

That didn't worry me much. I had checked my course by each of those towns, and I was confident by then that I was on the right road. The clouds got higher and higher as I traversed France; I followed them up until I was flying at about six thousand feet. At about half-past eight I came to the end of the clouds; they thinned out and vanished altogether and from there onwards I was flying in bright sunshine. I went up to about seven thousand feet at that, and stayed there. I didn't want the French to notice the machine more than was necessary.

I came to some hills at about a quarter-past nine, and guessed rightly that I was somewhere round about the Puy de Dôme. I carried on rather to the east of them and presently I saw a great river winding parallel with my course, far away to the east. I searched my map, and had very little difficulty in identifying it as the Rhône.

I had no trouble after that. At about ten o'clock I ran through a great flock of small birds at about seven thousand feet; I saw none of them clearly owing to our relative speed, but I think they may have been swallows. None of them hit the machine. At a quarter to eleven I came in sight of a great sheet of inland water that stretched far away to the west, and a minute or two afterwards I saw the sea beyond.

I went close enough to pick out Marseilles in the distance, and then did another of those long gentle turns with a scrap of rudder and no bank at all, till I was heading about south-east. I carried on like that until I came to the coast, and set to flying down the French Riviera. I once spent a fortnight in Nice, and I knew the look of the great bluff that stands up above Monte Carlo. I flew on down the coast keeping a sharp eye open for that thing, and at about ten minutes past twelve I saw it.

That brought me to my journey's end. I was very tired by then, very thick in the head with the noise of the engine, and painfully cramped. I had a final drink from my flask and got out the large-scale map of the Lanaldo district in readiness to fix my position.

I passed Mentone, flying at about five thousand feet a couple of miles out to sea. The hills here ran down into the sea, with very little foreshore. It struck me as I looked about and saw the smoke of a train that I must have passed Lenden by this time. In the strain of flying I had forgotten all about him, but the sight of that train recalled me to the object of my journey.

Ventimiglia was marked on my large-scale map, and from there I turned inland up the Roja valley to Lanaldo. The air here was very bumpy due to the proximity of the hills, and once or twice I hit a rough patch that put the fear of God into me. I carried on, dropping off a little height as I went, and so I came to the little grey town on the hill-side above the road that could only be Lanaldo. Beside me, to the east and scarcely lower than the machine, was a thickly wooded hill that seemed to be the commencement of a range running away inland. That could only be Monte Verde.

The air grew frightfully rough. I flew straight on up the valley, peering over the side of the cockpit and trying to spot a likely landing-ground. Now that I saw the wooded slopes, I was not so sanguine about putting down upon the trees unhurt. These pine-woods weren't quite like our English trees. There the woods, seen from the air, appear soft and downy; these looked thin and spiky. In many places I could see the ground between the individual trees.

Then I saw that there was a clearing, right on the top of Monte Verde. The pine trees seemed to come to an end about five hundred feet below the summit, and then there was a belt of some scrubby foliage of a different colour, that I found afterwards to be stunted oaks. The very summit of the hill was bare, and seemed to be covered with grass. The space available for landing would have been about three hundred yards square, I suppose.

I determined to try it.

I was well past the hill then, and a long way past Lanaldo. I gained a little height before attempting the turn, then slewed the machine round clumsily in a wide sweep till I was facing back on my tracks. The bare top of that hill was straight before me then; I throttled back the engine and put the machine on a straight glide down to go and have a look at it.

I passed over the grass at about four hundred feet, I suppose. It looked pretty smooth for landing. The wind was more or less from the south, and the southern side of the grassy patch was bounded by a sort of scree from which the ground sloped away steeply in the direction of Lanaldo. I made up my mind that I should have to bring the machine in slowly over the oak trees on the northern side and try to stop her before she ran forwards over the edge.

That survey rather reassured me; it didn't look too bad at all. I put the engine on again and eased the machine round in a very long, gentle turn to the north. I flew some way to the north before I came round again in another of those long, easy skid turns. Then I throttled the engine and put her on the glide down to land.

I raised my goggles on to my forehead, and rubbed my eyes. I can remember that the air felt very fresh and sweet.

I was gliding short. I came to the oak trees perhaps half a mile short of the grass, and put on a little engine at about fifty feet above the tree tops. I had one eye on the air-speed indicator all the time, and eased her down slowly towards the final fringe of trees.

Then I was there. I shut off all power and passed over the edge of the grass at a height of about thirty feet, thrusting her down to land. She gained a little speed as I did that, and I knew that the screw was getting very near. I flattened her out a little near the ground, irresolute. Then I thrust her down again, and the wheels crunched heavily upon the grass; the Breguet quivered and bounced high into the air again. Slowly she sank until the wheels bounced on the grass again—and we were barely thirty yards from the edge, travelling at about seventy miles an hour.

With a sudden decision I did what I should have done twenty seconds before—thrust forwards the throttle. The engine came to my rescue with a roar, and we surged forwards over the edge of the scree and up into the air again.

The first shot had failed, but I was convinced it could be done. I had not flown slowly enough in the approach, and I had come in too high over the oak trees. As a preliminary to the next attempt I throttled the engine as I was flying north, till we were crawling along in a manner which felt curiously slack on the controls, with the indicator showing about a hundred and fifteen kilos.

I was about three hundred feet above the trees when I began my next turn, a turn to port which was to bring me southwards again for my second shot at landing. I went into it at that slow flying speed, and, to begin with, it was a slow, gentle turn such as I had been doing up till then. When I was half-way round I realised that unless I turned quicker than that I should miss Monte Verde altogether.

I banked a little more, and trod hard upon the rudder.

The nose of the machine dropped suddenly. Very quickly I pulled the stick back to level her. I do not think I touched the throttle or the rudder.

And then that ghoulish thing leapt out at me, bred of my own ignorance, that had been lurking for me ever since I learnt to fly in those old days when we knew so very little about flying. The air under my port wings seemed to give way, so that the machine lurched down in a heavy sideslip; at the same time the nose dropped and she swung round in a fantastic turn. I wrenched the stick hard back, but the spin tightened. She had the bit between her teeth by then. We flicked round one or two turns at a wild, incredible speed, and I became aware that the trees were very near.

I thrust the stick away from me, and threw up my elbow to protect my face.

We hit nose downwards in a little glade between the trees. I can remember that I saw the port wing crumple up, for I was thrown that way.

That was my seventh crash.

*　　*　　*　　*　　*

By all the rules of the game I ought to have been killed. I have seen so many people killed that way that it seems all wrong that I should have got out of it alive. But there is a special Providence that guides the steps of fools and drunken men, and I think it must have been under those auspices that I came out without a great amount of danger from that crash.

I don't know how long I was unconscious, but I do not think it can have been longer than a few minutes. I woke sharply in the end to the intolerable pain of my three broken fingers, and the dull agony of a dislocated shoulder and a twisted elbow. My left arm had caught it badly—the one that I had flung up to protect my head. Apart from that, there wasn't much the matter with me when I came to my senses.

The machine was standing on the crushed forepart of the fuselage and the remains of the port wings, with the tail and my seat high in the air. I was lying forward with my head upon my left arm against the windscreen, and held from sliding forward by the broad safety belt around my body. My nose was bleeding freely—it may have been that that brought me round—and the blood streamed all over my mangled arm as I lay forward in the seat, so that at first I thought that I was more hurt than I really was.

I raised my head, and the slight movement made the crashed fuselage of the machine totter and sway perilously. I was about fifteen feet from the ground. I began to move my strained body to draw my left arm nearer to me. The pain in my broken fingers made me stop that for a minute; I lay there sweating a little with the pain and considering the position.

A goldfinch came out from somewhere beyond my range of vision, hopped on to the trailing edge of the wrecked top starboard plane, cocked his head at me, chirruped, and flew away.

I began again then. I don't know how long it took me to get out of that seat and down on to the ground—it may have been as much as half an hour. I took it very slowly, nursing my left side with my uninjured right hand, and resting after every movement. I slipped once when I was half out of my seat on to the cowling, and that gave me a great jerk so that everything went black for a few minutes and I had to hang on tight. But after that I got going again, and in the end I found myself on the dry mast that was the ground of that wood beneath the trees.

I found that I had to stoop when I wanted to draw a breath then; it was impossible to stand erect and breathe at the same time, owing to the pain of my bruised ribs where the belt had caught me and held me in the seat at the moment of impact. But that soon passed out of my mind when I sat down upon a stump and set to work to put my fingers into splints.

The middle one had the best part of an inch of bone sticking out through the skin. I didn't quite know what to do with that, but decided that it had better go back inside again if I could persuade it to do so. I got up and moved round the crash, stooping painfully to pick up any little splinters of wood or twigs that I thought might do for splints, and then I went back to my stump and set to work to pull my two handkerchiefs into strips by treading on them with my foot and pulling with my right hand.

By the mercy of God that flask of brandy was unbroken, and was still half full. It was empty by the time I'd done that bandaging.

I made a pretty good job of the fingers, but I could do nothing at all with the shoulder. It stuck out backwards into my coat in such a manner that the arm couldn't lie along my side, and it hurt too vilely for me to try and shift it. My scarf was a very long one and I made a sort of sling of that, and had enough of it left to take a turn of it round my body to lash the whole arm securely to me, with my helmet and goggles beneath the shoulder as a pad. I don't know how long it took me to do all that, but I can see now that it must have been a long time.

At last I finished, and rose unsteadily to my feet. The empty flask was lying by the stump on which I had been sitting, but I hadn't the courage to stoop down to pick it up, and so I left it there on the ground. Then I fell to searching in my pockets for the large-scale map of the Lanaldo district. It was time I got about my business; I had wasted time enough in sitting still and licking my wounds.

The map showed me that I was about four miles from Lanaldo, and five as the crow flies from the point on the road that I should have to reach if I wanted to intercept Lenden on his way to the town. I looked at my watch, and then back to the map. It was a quarter-past one; I had none too much time if I was to get down to the road in time.

On the map the way looked pretty straightforward. I had to find my way down the ridge on which I was then standing into the valley below—a distance of perhaps three miles. There was another ridge to be crossed, and then I should be on the hill-side above the road. It should be simple then. The woods ran straight down the hill-side into the valley and the road; from the look of the signs upon the map it seemed that they might be olives. I put the map back into my pocket, and started.

It was easy going. The trees in that oak grove were thin and sparse, and there was smooth walking between them. I left the Breguet and began to make my way along the ridge towards the open patch of grass where I had tried to land. That walk was then, and will remain to me, a dream. My bruised ribs made every motion a sharp, slight twinge of pain—not great in itself, but very wearing. In the shoulder there was a dull, throbbing ache. I'd made the fingers pretty comfortable, and I didn't get much trouble with them until I fell down.

I stopped near the edge of that grassy space, and was very sick. I felt better when that was over, and went on.

From the edge of the scree I could see my way clearly. The hill sloped sharply down from there, and a little way below the pines began. I paused there for a minute or two with the map, and conned my path. It was pretty clear which way I had to go; I put the map away again and began the descent. About seven miles away, over the foothills, I could see a wide expanse of sea gleaming very silvery and blue in the sunshine of that afternoon.

It was rough going down the ridge. Once or twice I found a goat track leading in the direction in which I wanted to go, but for the most part it was a cross-country walk. The side of the hill among the pines was littered with great boulders, and under foot there was a carpet of pine needles and rosemary. It was intensely hot. I was thickly muffled in the flying clothes that I had put on for leaving England in that March dawn, and I could do little to open or remove them without unsettling my shoulder. And so I went plodding on down the hill till I had gone perhaps a couple of miles and was getting down towards the bottom of the valley. It was there that I put my foot upon a loose stone, staggered desperately for a moment, and fell down.

I was able to twist a little as I went down, to avoid falling on the shoulder, and I fell with my bandaged forearm and broken fingers beneath me. That shook me properly; I can remember that I began to weep with the shock of it, and with the pain. I lay as I had fallen for a minute shedding buckets of tears, and when I managed to sit up again I found that the bandages had come off my fingers and the splints were loose and broken.

It took me a very long time to do them up again—I don't know how long. I was very tired and in a lot of pain, and I had no brandy to help me through it this time. I dare say it was twenty minutes before I was on my feet again and plodding on more carefully down into the valley.

In the bottom of the valley I came to a spring, that welled out of the hill-side and ran away in a little trickle down the path. Someone had dammed it up to make a little pool. I was getting frightened at the passing of the afternoon by that time, but I stopped there for a minute and sluiced my head, washing away the dried blood from my mouth and nose with my un-injured hand. It was a sound thing to do, in spite of the loss of time, I think; I went faster afterwards. I put my lips down to the water and took a long, satisfying drink. Then I left the well and crossed the valley towards the opposite ridge.

I went faster, although it was uphill. By the map I had covered three miles out of the five, and it was a quarter to three. I pressed on up the hill, and came presently to the top in a drip of sweat and a dull throb of pain. Before me lay the valley of the Roja. I could see the little grey town of Lanaldo almost immediately below me, and away at the end of the valley there was the blue gleam of the sea.

The pines came to an end here, and were succeeded by olive trees arranged on terraces. I found paths winding down here, and before I had gone far I passed a sort of châlet, with a litter of ragged children round the outbuildings who looked at me curiously as I passed. I pressed on down the hill through the groves, and presently I came to the end of the olives. The terraces continued, and were filled with rose bushes and carnations in neat rows, all very well tended and watered from great circular cement tanks stuck about all over the slopes. I had noticed these things from the air, and wondered what they were.

I struck a paved mule-path then that led straight down the hill to the road, and pressed on down it. Now and again I passed a peasant trudging up; occasionally they spoke to me but mostly they let me by without a word and stood in the path when I had gone, staring after me. And so, at about half-past three, I came down on to the road.

That road ran in thick, white dust along the very bottom of the valley, winding along beside the dry bed of the river. Only a trickle of water ran over the round white stones that made the watercourse; it was a river that only ran full once a year. I was terribly thirsty. About a quarter of a mile down the valley a bend of the stream approached the edge of the road; I went on till I reached that place, stepped aside from the road, and lay down and lapped the water like a dog.

I was fresher after that. The place that I had reached was quite a good one for my purpose; I could see the road for the best part of a mile down the valley. Olives lined the hill that ran down to the roadside; I crossed into the shade of these and sat down near a great bush of mimosa in flower. To wait.

There wasn't much traffic on that road. The first thing to come was a one-horse diligence from Ventimiglia, a little covered thing like a pill-box on wheels and full of women. A farm-cart, drawn by a dejected-looking horse yoked with a donkey, followed that, and flowed on slowly past me. Several peasants came by on foot, and a couple of priests in their black, flowing soutanes. And once there was a cart full of barrels, driven by a very bleary, merry gentleman who spoke to me, and, I think, offered me a lift.

These, and a few more, all passed at long intervals throughout that afternoon. I sat there straining my eyes down the road, that white dusty road that ran down the flat valley with the white-stoned river beside it till a spur of the hill hid both from my sight. I sat there from half-past three till half-past five, shifting uneasily from time to time to find a less uncomfortable position for my arm and shoulder, and shuffling the white dust up into little heaps between my shoes. I sat there till the sun began to throw long shadows of the hills across the white stones of the river, till the bright sunlight turned to the softest gold and the little white clouds above the hills to crimson. I sat there, dumbly straining my eyes down the road, while the light lasted. I sat there till I knew that I had failed.

It was about six o'clock when I gave up. I knew by then that Lenden must have passed before I reached the road; that I had missed him. I discovered afterwards that I must have missed him by about half an hour. He reached Ventimiglia at half-past two, and drove straight out to Lanaldo. If I had managed to land that Breguet properly, I should have had ample time to get down to the road in time to intercept his car. There's no good crying over that. I did the best I could, and that must suffice.

It was nearly dark in the valley. I got up from my seat, stiff and cold. I was in a strange country, without a passport and rather hurt; I didn't know two words of the language and my French is that of the schoolroom variety. I had been in no great pain during the long rest, but when I got to my feet in the twilight and moved forward in the thick dust by the roadside, a wave of pain and sickness came over me quite suddenly, and I sat down again in a hurry.

I had to make a plan of what I was going to do next, and from my experience of the moment before it seemed to me that I could do that more easily sitting down than standing up. I knew that by that time Lenden must be in the Casa Alba, and the Casa Alba must be close at hand—say within two miles. My original plan, if I missed him on the road, had been to find the house and trust to luck and my own strength and resource to get me into touch with Lenden among the Communists. I had only to get two words with him, and I should have done my bit.

Luck I might still have—and I should need it—but I had neither strength left, nor resource. I was getting very tired by that time; the throbbing in my shoulder and the aching pain of my clothes pressing upon it were drowning all my power of action. I could carry on no longer by myself. I sat there by the roadside for a long time as the darkness fell, and in the end I got the rudiments of a plan thought out.

I must have help in this affair. That was the first conclusion that I came to—that I must get allies. I was up against a Bolshevist organisation; the most obvious people in Italy to set against the Bolsheviks were the Fascisti. If I could get the local Fascisti to believe my story, if I could convince them that they had the chief agitators of their country right under their noses, then it might be possible to get them to raid the house. Such a raid would give Lenden a good sporting chance; in the confusion he might be able to escape, or get himself arrested with the plates. It would create a disturbance, perhaps a panic. In a panic a resolute man with his wits about him can do pretty well what he likes. Was Lenden a resolute man? In any case, it seemed to me that to try and create such a diversion was the best thing I could do.

Lanaldo must be the starting point. It was the nearest town, and from what I had seen of it it was a fair-sized place. There was a road leading up to it, not shown on the map, that branched from the main road in the valley and wound in hair-pin bends up the hill-side among the olives till it came to an end on an open terrace before the walls of the town. Inside the walls the streets were not more than six feet wide, mere passages for men and donkeys, and cavernously spanned with earth-quake arches between the house fronts.

That was Lanaldo as I saw it later; a rabbit warren of a place where every house was more or less in communication with its neighbour, with the stables on the ground floor, the high, vaulted living-rooms above, and the kitchens in little attics opening on to the flat roofs. At that time I knew nothing of it but that it looked to be a moderate-sized town with the build-ings crushed together within walls; a solid block of masonry rising above the grey shimmer of the olives. There were other towns dotted about the hill-sides that I had seen in my descent from Monte Verde, but none so large as Lanaldo and none that was approached by a bona-fide road. That seemed to mark it out from the rest as an important place. I came to the con-clusion that I should find all the material there for the diversion that I wanted to create, if I could find a means to set things moving.

I sat there for a minute or two longer, piecing together phrases in my schoolboy French that I hoped would serve me in the town. In the end I got slowly to my feet again and stood there for a minute, trying my balance after the long rest, and shifting the sling and the pad under my shoulder. Then, when the first nausea was over and the world had stopped revolving round me, I moved off up the road towards Lanaldo.

I had to go about three miles, I suppose, for the road that led away up the hill wound interminably in its rise of a few hundred feet. I didn't have much in the way of sharp pain on that journey, but I was growing infinitely tired. I went plodding up that hill mechanically; I didn't count the hairpin bends on the road, but from my impression of that night I should say that there were about forty-seven of them between the main road and Lanaldo. It was half-past seven when I arrived on the terrace before the town.

There were people moving about there, strolling up and down and taking the air, for it was a wonderful moonlit night. They stared at me curiously, but I went straight on and up into the town through an old masonry gateway approached by a sort of cobbled ramp. Inside the walls the place was cavernous and badly lit; I went on towards the heart of the town through an acrid, vegetable smell. That street was about six feet wide. I had to stop once and shrink into a doorway while a string of donkeys felt their way carefully past me over the slippery cobbles, their backs piled high with bundles of wood fuel. And once a peal of music from some mechanical instrument streamed out from a brilliantly lit room above my head, and I heard a burst of laughter and paused for a minute wondering.

That alley led me straight into the central square of the town, an irregular open space between the tall flat-fronted houses, and paved with stone blocks. One side of this square was occupied by a great church, painted pink and yellow, very bright. Another side gave on to a sort of bowling alley; there were many people there, and a clear view of the hills in the moonlight above the roofs of the houses. The third side had little shops all along it, and one large one with the branch of a tree hanging over the door and the legend "Ristorante delle Monte" painted with many flourishes across the front.

The fourth side of the square was occupied by a great barrack of a house in a severe style, the ground-floor windows heavily barred. In one of these windows there was a light. In the light of the solitary street-lamp that stood in the middle of the square I saw a great shield above the door of that house, with the Royal Arms of Italy emblazoned on it.

I crossed the square, and went into that house beneath the shield. On my left was the room that had the light in it. I felt for the handle of the door, opened it, and went in.

There was a man in there, a seedy-looking sort of clerk, sitting at a very dirty table and working among a litter of buff forms. The room was thick with the smoke of his cigarettes. He looked up as I went in, and said something sharply that I didn't understand.

There was a second chair by the wall. I crossed the room to it, moving a little heavily, dragged it forward to the table opposite him, and sat down with a sigh. That annoyed him very much. He got up, leaned across the table, and began shooting off Italian at me nineteen to the dozen.

I raised my head and smiled at him. "D'you speak English?" I inquired.

Evidently he didn't.

"Parlez français?"

He checked his flow of oratory at that, and took thought. And then he began to speak in a language that I recognised as French, though not the sort of French I was taught at school. I had reckoned that it was pretty safe to assume that all these people could speak French. The border must be within a couple of miles of that town.

I shook my head. "Pas comprends," I said. "Attendez un moment." He stopped talking, and stood there watching me curiously as I searched laboriously for my notecase with my one sound hand. I had had the forethought to bring plenty of money.

I extracted a pound note and tossed it across the table to him. "Ça vaut cent francs, français," I said. "C'est pour vous." His eyes became as round as pennies; I had at last succeeded in establishing a means of communication with the people of the country. He began to speak again, but I stopped him.

"Maintenant," I said, "attention." He sank down into his chair again and sat there fingering the note, his eyes fixed on me.

Very carefully I laid my left arm on the table in front of me and took the sling off it, shifting my body to get it into a comfortable position. As I did that I took the helmet and goggles from under my arm and tossed them across the table to him. They would help my explanation.

"Suis aviateur anglais," I said heavily. "Tombé sur la montagne, et un peu blessé. Comprenez?"

He did, and rose quickly to his feet making a little clucking noise of sympathy. I scowled across the table at him. "Assyez-vous, monsieur, un moment," I said, and he sat down again.

I raised my heavy head and stared at him, leaning forward so far as the strained position of my body would allow. "Je désire reconter—désire voir, ici—le capitaine des Fascisti de Lanaldo. Comprenez?" I couldn't make out if he did or not. "Vous m'apportez le capitaine des Fascisti. J'ai des nouvelles les plus importanes des communistes dans ce pays-ce Comprenez communistes?"

He began to talk again, and to my intense relief I heard among his blather of words the essential features of the information that I was trying to get through.

"C'est bien," I said wearily. "Moi, je reste ici pendant que vous m'apportez le capitaine des Fascisti—et quelqu'un qui parle anglais. Toute suite, monsieur, si'il vous plaît. Cet argent-là—c'est pour vous."

He got up from his seat, went and opened the window, and called to a small boy outside in the square. I stopped him for a moment.

"Et un peu de cognac, monsieur," I said.

CHAPTER EIGHT

THERE WAS A HIATUS THEN. I sat at the table drowsily examining my injuries. The clerk, having seen the boy away on his errand, came back and began rolling cigarettes. He offered me one, but I didn't like the look of them and refused. I spoke to him again about the cognac, and he said something that sounded like "subito", and did nothing about it.

In about ten minutes' time we began to have visitors. One or two men came into the room together, and amongst them a short, fat little man with curly black hair. I liked the look of that one from the first. He was a man of about fifty, and I discovered later that he answered to the name of Luigi Ribotto.

He spoke for a little to the clerk, and then they turned to me. He addressed me a little hesitantly, but in quite good English. "Good evening, saire," he said. "I am ver' sorry to see—that you have hurt yourself."

He told me that he had had a little place of his own at one time in Greek Street, Soho, where he had served a one-and-sixpenny dinner of four courses in the happy days before the war. I told him that I remembered the place and had often dined there—and that might possibly have been true, because I often used to dine in Soho before the war. He nearly fell on my neck when he heard that—I quite thought that he was going to kiss me, but it didn't come to that, thank God—and I spoke about the cognac, and he sent the small boy flying to his Ristorante delle Monte across the square.

His big idea then was to send for a doctor at once, but I managed to put him off that. With the shoulder in the state it was I was afraid of what a doctor might do to me; I had work to do, and so long as I remained sitting in the position at that table I was pretty comfortable. Plenty of time for the doctor later, and I began to talk to Ribotto about the Fascisti. He said that the man I wanted to see was Il Capitano Fazzini, and he packed off another boy to look for him.

The brandy came then, and with it a plate of biscuits. I had eaten practically nothing since the early morning, and ate a couple of biscuits from a sense of duty. I did better by the brandy, though.

There was a stir by the door at last, and a man came in. Ribotto beamed at me. "This will be—the Captain Fazzini," he said, and shot off a string of Italian at the newcomer.

I sat and studied the chap in the yellow lamplight while Ribotto was speaking, and liked the look of him. He was a man of about my own age, very tall and straight, and with a tanned, unshaven face. He had a very high forehead, and in some peculiar way he had the look of a leader about him in spite of his three-days' beard. He was wearing rather a dirty civilian coat over a black shirt; his breeches and gaiters were covered with white stains and dust, and his hands were rough and tanned. I discovered later that his father was mayor of the place, and that he himself was manager of a vermouth distillery somewhere down the river.

The clerk broke in upon their conversation, and I thought I heard the word communist. Then the three of them turned and stared at me.

"You have—ah, something that you want tell him?" asked Ribotto. He thought for a minute, and corrected himself. "That you want telling him?"

I raised my head. "This is a confidential matter," I said. Ribotto translated, and Fazzini said something to me in Italian.

"All of us," said Ribotto, "in this room, we are Fascist. All the town is Fascist. That is, in your country . . . Volunteers." He considered for a minute. "The party, not Socialist. You can understand me, what I say?"

I nodded slowly. "I understand," I replied. "You'd better sit down. My story will take a little time to tell."

I told them a much shortened version of what had happened. I made Lenden out to be a flying officer who was responsible for certain confidential photographs which had been stolen from his office. It sounded a thin tale to me as I was telling it, but it went down all right. I told them how he had come out after them. I dwelt for some time on the danger that he must be in, and urged the necessity of an immediate raid upon the Casa Alba. I pressed these points for all I was worth.

The impression that I made was very puzzling to me. They were quite prepared to believe all I said; for one ¿hing they had seen the Breguet flying over and had marked it as it disappeared behind Monte Verde. They were genuinely shocked and horrified at the presence of Communists in their district, being all good Fascists. They were willing to believe that the Casa Alba was full of Russians, and they seemed to think that it might not be a bad thing to have an unofficial pogrom there. Yet they were very difficult to move.

I could make nothing of their attitude. They drew a little way apart when they had heard all I had to say, and began talking in low tones among themselves. I remained sitting at the table with my arm stretched painfully upon it, puzzled and anxious.

Once I got impatient. "There's no time to be lost," I said. "It's urgent. For all you know, they may be getting across the border while you're talking. What's the trouble?"

Ribotto raised his hand. "Presently," he said. "We believe what you have said to us. Yes. But this is a difficult decision that you do not know about. Presently." And they went on talking in the corner.

They talked interminably. It was clear that they were un-easy about something, but I couldn't make out what it was that was worrying them. There was some factor in the situation that I didn't appreciate; something that made them most unwilling to take any action. It was maddening.

Nine o'clock struck on the bells of the campanile, and then the quarter. Now and again they turned to me, and asked me something that I couldn't answer. Did I know the name of the chief Russian in the Casa Alba? How long had this been going on for? What was their object in coming to Lanaldo? I could give no satisfactory answer to any of these questions, and at last their low whispering began to peter out. I don't think they had come to any decision.

I think if that had been the whole story of that night, I should have failed to stir them. I had no strength left with which to combat what I took to be their indifference, what I now know to have been their business interests. But at that point a man came to the barred, open window that faced into the square, and peered into the room, and said something in Italian. I caught the word "Inglesi".

All three of them crossed to the window, with a glance at me. They interrogated the fellow for a minute, and then Ribotto turned to me.

"Your friends, they have come to find you," he said. "You have expected them—yes?"

I raised my head heavily, and stared at him. "I've got no friends here," I said. "There's nobody in this part of the world that knows me. Who's asking for me?"

He smiled broadly, and shrugged his shoulders. "I do not know. They have said they are friends to you," he remarked. "It is by your name they have asked where you are. They have arrive on the terrace. A man and a young lady, both the two of them English people. With a motor-car."

The man at the window said something.

"Yes," said Ribotto again to me. "From Nice they are come."

Fazzini said something to the man, who moved away across the square into the darkness.

"In a few minutes they will be come here," said Ribotto. "He has sent to bring them. We will then see them, whether they are truly friends to you."

But I had little doubt about it from the first. I couldn't place the man at all, unless it were some Englishman that she had picked up on the way. I tried to reckon up how Sheila could have got out in the time. Short of flying out as I had done, I didn't see that it was possible.

I first saw them through the window, when they were half-way across the square. I knew nothing of the man who walked beside her. He was obviously English; a broad-shouldered, stocky sort of chap with a very hard, tanned face. He was dressed in a golf jacket with light fawn breeches and gaiters. At home, if I had met him in the village, I would have set him down as a horse dealer or a vet. from Leventer, but I couldn't place what he was doing here.

I heard them at the door, and turned painfully to face their entrance. "Evening, Sheila," I said. "You've been pretty quick." It was about sixteen hours since I had kissed her on the down.

She came quickly to my table. She was wearing her leather motor coat, a blue one with a furry collar that brushed my face as she stooped to kiss me on the forehead. I could not move to meet her.

"Peter, dear," she said, "you're hurt. They told us outside."

The man that she had brought with her was already talking rapidly to Fazzini in Italian that had a very English ring to it, helped out with frequent gesture and a word or two of French. He was speaking to them most energetically and with more confidence than accuracy, but it did the trick. They understood what he was saying all right.

"Who's that?" I asked.

She bent towards me, and spoke quietly in order that we shouldn't interrupt their business. "His name's Captain Stenning," she said. "Directly you left this morning, Kitter and I drove up to London. I've got a passport, you see, so I didn't have to wait for that. I simply couldn't just sit there in Under and wait till I heard from you, Peter."

I smiled at her. "You mean you flew out?"

"Mm. I went to Imperial Airways, and they got me a special machine from the Rawdon Company, and we left Croydon at about ten o'clock. Captain Stenning was the pilot they sent with it. We had to stop at Paris for petrol, and directly that was done we went on again, but we could only fly as far as Nice. I had a little talk with him at Le Bourget when he wasn't cursing the French mechanics. And I asked him if he knew Lenden, and he knows him quite well. And then at Nice I told him all about it, and he offered to come on with me and see it through, if I'd let him. I was all alone, and I thought it'd be a good thing, and so we left the aeroplane with the people there, and came on by car."

She glanced across at him. He was still talking nineteen to the dozen to Fazzini, but there was a humorous set to his hard face, and Ribotto was laughing quietly. "He's frightfully rough," she said, and smiled. "He was swearing most dreadfully all the time we were at Le Bourget, but we got through the Customs and the machine filled up and all in twenty minutes from the time we landed till we were in the air again. And in all that hurry, he got me a cup of tea and a lunch basket. It was just the same at Nice. He's a lovely man when you're in a hurry."

She bent over me. "What's the damage, Peter?" she inquired. "This arm looks all funny."

I pressed her gently back. "You're requested not to handle this exhibit," I replied. "That shoulder's where it hadn't ought to be, and I've bust some fingers. Bad for the piano, I'm afraid."

She slipped off the table. "Peter," she said, "I'm going to get you a doctor."

I stopped her. "No you're not," I said. "We've got to get this thing straightened out before anyone starts mucking me about."

I raised my head. "Captain Stenning."

He broke off his conversation, and swung round on me.

"Glad to see you," I said. "Can you make out what's the matter with these blokes? I've been trying all I'm fit to get them to go and have a look at the Casa Alba. They agree it ought to be done, but I can't shift them."

He laughed sharply. "That's just what I'm coming to. It's the smuggling, I think," he said curtly. "All the frontier towns live on it, these days." He turned again to Fazzini and began rallying him in Italian with a torrent of words and gestures. The Italian replied with a shy smile. Already these two were good friends.

And presently they came to some agreement. Fazzini and one of the others left the room together, and the man called

Stenning came lounging over to my table and sat down on it casually, swinging one leg. "Well, Fats is all right now," he said casually. "He's going to raid the house for us."

He stared down at me, and at my arm extended on the table. "You look as if you're suffering from impact. Miss Darle here tells me that you came out on one of the Breguet Nineteens. You want to be careful with that chassis. D'you tip her up on the ground?"

I laughed ruefully. "No," I said. "I spun into the deck."

He stared at me. "From what height?"

"About three hundred feet."

"Christ," he said succinctly. "Might have bust your ruddy neck, cart-assing about like that." He was staring at the hump of my coat. "D'you mean to tell me that's your shoulder sticking up like that?"

"I expect so," I replied.

He swung his leg off the table. "We'd better put that back, for a start," he said. "Can't leave the ruddy thing like that all night."

I didn't move. "We'll get along a doctor in a minute or two," I said. "What's happening about this raid?"

He shrugged his shoulders, and got back on to the table. "As you like. None of the Dago doctors I've had anything to do with could bring a kitten into the world without an accident. But have it your own way."

I hadn't thought of that. First-class medical attention in Lanaldo was a good bit to hope for.

Sheila moved forward. I think—and hope—that Stenning had forgotten that she was there while he was talking to me. "Can you put it back?" she asked.

He shrugged his shoulders again. "I can't say till I've had a look. It may be too much swelled up. Probably is, after this time. I'll soon tell you whether I can or not—and if I can't, I'm damned if I'd let any doctor here muck about with it. Better leave it like it is till you can get it seen to properly."

There was a pause. He had said all that he was going to upon that subject, and it sounded good sense to me.

"Ever done it before?" I asked.

He blew a long cloud of smoke. "Lord, yes. Shoulder—twice, no, three times. I play rugger for the 'Quins. But lacrosse is the game for that."

I glanced at Sheila and saw her nod to me, ever so slightly. "You'd better have a cut at it," I said. "But let's get this other thing squared up first. What's happening? Where's Fazzini gone off to?"

Stenning lit a fresh cigarette from the butt of the old one, and offered the case to me. I refused. "Fats is all right," he said. "He's a two-fisted he-man."

"I know," said Sheila dryly. "I heard you tell him so, in Italian. He's gone to telephone, hasn't he?"

Stenning spat a shred of tobacco from his lip. "He's not allowed to go messing about like that on his own," he said. "He's gone to telephone to his boss in San Remo. This is an international affair. But you'll find he's a stout lad, that. He's all for it now."

"What was the trouble before you came?" I asked. "You said something about smuggling."

Stenning laughed shortly. "This town lives on running things across the border," he said. "It's the local industry. Take that away from them, and you put the whole ruddy place on the dole. Well, this Casa Alba of yours is a sort of agency for them, from what I could make out. Fixes the freights and all that. They've got everyone in the district squared to shut their mouths, and paying damn good money. I tell you, these lads don't like the idea of raiding that house one little bit."

I could see it clearly now. "Lenden told me that they ran the smuggling as a blind," I muttered. "Of course."

"That's right," said Stenning. "And a damn good blind too. It's kept everyone here as quiet as a mouse about what goes on in that house, for God knows how many years. Not that they didn't smell a rat now and again. Old Fats there, it wasn't any news to him that they were Russians. But they could shut their eyes to it. And now you've come along and put them in the cart properly over it."

I thought about it for a minute. "What's made them change their minds? Why don't they just shove us all down the sink and forget about us?"

He flicked the ash from his cigarette. "Because they're Dagoes," he said sharply. "North Italians, and a ruddy good crowd with a sense of responsibility and a sense of humour. I tell you—if we'd been five miles the other side of the border in a French village and told them to go and raid a place like that, we would have been down the sink and no mistake. But this lot, you can jolly them along and make them see the joke of it."

He eyed me seriously for a minute. "You'd better get up on your hind legs and say the kind word to Fats when he comes back," he said. "I've said it already, but it'd look well coming from you. They're going to halve the income of the town by this raid—pretty well. And all old Fats said about it was——" he shot off a phrase of Italian, thought for a minute, and translated—"That it's a bloody shame, but it can't be helped."

He thought for a minute. "Give me the Dagoes," he said quietly. "These North Italians, anyway." He chucked the stump of his cigarette out of the window and turned to me. "Let's have a look at that shoulder of yours while we're waiting," he said. "Fats may be some time."

I don't know where that man picked up his medical skill. He was the son of a most tragic marriage between a Naval officer and a chorus girl, I believe. Later in the evening he told me something of his life; he had been a chauffeur before the war. The beginning of the war found him building cycle-cars— the Stenning-Reilly car—in a lean-to shed at Islington. He enlisted, and in 1916 he was commissioned into the R.F.C. I might have met him, because when we came to compare notes I found that his squadron was only twenty miles down the line from my own, but I can't say that I remember him. There were so many of that type. He had been a civil pilot since the war, and knew Lenden well.

He took off his coat before starting on me: I remember

noticing the Froth-blower cuff-links that he was wearing. And then he set my shoulder like a professional. The worst part of it was getting the clothes off, because we didn't want to cut them more than necessary. He had a very sure and gentle touch, that chap. I think that may have been the effect of his manual profession; I only know that the worst of my twinges came from Sheila when she was assisting him. I know that's a rotten thing to say, but it is true. He had the surest hands of anyone I've ever met.

We got the shoulder opened up at last, and he made a very careful examination, prodding the swellings with those sure fingers. In the end he stood up. "Ruddy good job you've kept it still," he muttered. "That'll go back all right."

He spoke for several minutes to the clerk and to Ribotto in mixed Italian and English. He wanted the chemist and not the doctor, but he'd forgotten the word for chemist and Ribotto had forgotten what chemist meant. That got cleared up at last, and the clerk was despatched across the square with a message.

Then he set to work to put my shoulder back. The first shot failed, and I was very nearly sick on the table. The second time it went all right. By the time I had stopped seeing whorls and spots the shoulder was back in place all right, and I could move it a very little.

After that we started on the fingers. Stenning wasn't satisfied with the splints that the chemist brought with his bandages. By a torrent of Italian and pantomime he got what he wanted in an incredibly short time—a pair of tinsmith's shears and a biscuit tin. Out of that he set to work to fashion three little troughs of tin for each finger to lie in on a bed of cotton-wool. After that exhibition I was content to let him set them for me, and they stayed like that until I reached London.

Fazzini came back as we were finishing those, and began talking to Stenning in Italian. They spoke together for a few minutes, and then Stenning turned to me.

"He says his boss is coming over from San Remo for this show," he said. "They reckon to start at about five o'clock in the morning and get to the place at dawn."

I moved uneasily at the table. "I don't see that. Why can't they start before?"

Stenning turned to Fazzini with the question. The Italian hesitated, lowered his voice, and the talk became confidential. Finally Stenning burst out laughing and clapped the Italian on the shoulder; the other smiled his slow, shy smile. Stenning turned to me.

"This is what it is," he said. "The fellow who's coming from San Remo—Fazzini's boss—he isn't in on this smuggling. I reckon he's outside the radius of the people they bribe. He never touches a bean of what these lads get, and he doesn't know about it. Old Fats here has a party out on the border to-night, and they'll be making for the Casa with their stuff. He wants to give them time to get clear away before the Field-Marshal arrives from San Remo. That's why he's fixed his raid for five o'clock."

It was then about eleven. "I suppose it's all right," I said. "What if they start skipping in the meantime?"

Stenning nodded. "I thought of that—and so did Fats. He's put a guard on the road to Ventimiglia, and he'll hold up any car from the Casa. I don't see how Lenden can get away from there except by road, and that's the only road."

He paused. "I think it's all right," he said, and I agreed.

We got most of my clothes on to me again, and lashed the arm up stiffly with a sling. Then we all went across the square in the bright moonlight to the Ristorante delle Monte and had a meal with Ribotto. I managed to eat a little and to drink quite a lot; so that by the time that meal was over it was midnight and I was more or less myself again. That was the brandy, of course. I had a bad time of it when that wore off, but for the next twelve hours I was very little troubled by my injuries.

There was no talk of going to bed. We made Sheila comfortable before the stove in an English wicker chair, and covered her over with a rug. I think she slept a good deal. Stenning and I sat upon rather a hard sofa before the stove, smoking and drinking, and talking together drowsily. It was then that he told me something of the experiences of his varied life. Nothing that he told me lessened the respect that I had formed for him, from the account of his month's imprisonment for being "drunk in charge" to the almost incredible story which culminated in his marriage.

Ribotto was up and about at three in the morning, and we had a sort of breakfast. He went out into the back premises and fried up a dish of veal and sausages, helping it out with spaghetti. I roused Sheila, and when we had had a little walk around the square to get an appetite we settled down to it.

That meal was never finished. There was a commotion in the square, and Fazzini appeared in the doorway. He spoke rapidly to Stenning for a minute or two, and disappeared. Stenning turned to me.

"The road patrol have stopped a car," he said. "From the Casa Alba. There was an Englishman in it, with the chauffeur. They've got him in the Town Hall over there."

I had no doubt who it must be. It seemed that a great weight had been lifted from my mind, that our anxiety was over. Whether Lenden had the plates with him or not was a matter of no consequence to us now. The important thing was that he was safe.

I wondered how he would take the news that I had already exposed the plates. I was a bit nervous about telling him that, I remember.

"What's the matter?" asked Sheila. "Who is it?"

I got up from the table, nursing my arm. "Maurice Lenden," I said. "They've got him in the Town Hall over there."

"Oh . . ." she said.

Stenning grinned slowly. "Seems to me we'd better see if we can't call off that raid," he remarked. "It seems a pity to spoil their business, doesn't it?"

"Well," said I, "let's get across the way and have a look at the Duke," and we tumbled out of that Ristorante and crossed the square to the Town Hall again. There was a light in the same little room and we went crowding in at the doorway, Stenning first. There were many people in the room now, mostly in black shirts. And the prisoner.

There was a little pause in the talk as we entered and stood motionless in the doorway. It was as if all movements were suspended by our disappointment.

"Damned if I know what we've got here," said Stenning, a little heavily. "I thought it might be Maurice, myself."

He moved forward, and we followed him into the room. "I know who this is," I said. "He's got relations in my part of the world. He's a Trades Union official."

From the middle of the crowd of black-shirted Italians the little man peered forward at the sound of my voice. "It's not Mr. Moran, from the Hall?"

I sat down on the edge of the table, and they cleared away so that I was facing him. "That's right," I said. "How's the Russian trip going, Nitter?"

He glowered at me, and was silent. In the background Stenning was translating to Fazzini in a low tone.

"Well," I said evenly. "Let's try again. Where have you come from now?"

"Ye know the answer to that," he said sullenly. "From the big house up the valley."

"And may I ask what you were doing there?"

Silence.

"Is that on the way to Russia?"

Silence again.

"Well," I said quietly, "suppose we have another shot. Was it you that murdered Sanders, my butler at the Hall?"

That shook him. I saw his lip quiver and he went very white, but he pulled himself together. "I know," he muttered, half to himself, I think. "It had to come. Ye don't say he died, Mr. Moran?"

"Was it you?"

He faced me steadfastly. "Ah'll come back with you to England and stand trial for that, Mr. Moran. I was there. But it wasn't me that fired, and if Ah'd known that Manek had a pistol, Ah'd not have gone with him."

I made a mental note of the name. "You'll certainly stand

trial for that," I said grimly. "Now, tell me about this house up the valley. Why did you go there, and where are you going to now?"

The tubby little man stared me down.

"What's that to you?"

"Quite a lot," I said. "And you're going to tell us about that house pretty damn quick."

I must say, I had something of a respect for the little man. "Find out for yourself," he said coolly. "I don't see why I should tell you anything."

Stenning shoved his way forward. He had picked up a drover's whip that was lying on a dusty shelf in the corner. "By Christ, I'll tell you why!" he cried. "Because, unless you tell us everything you know about that place, I'm going to run you out into the square and whip you till your guts fall out."

I am half inclined to think that he would have done it. The little man looked up into his face and laughed. "Is that the best reason ye've got?"

"No," said Sheila unexpectedly. The Italians made way for her, and she came forward to the little man. "We want to find out where Maurice Lenden is, Mr. Nitter. That's all we want—really. Is he in the house?"

He stared at her. "He'll be the other Englishman, the one what they don't trust? Tall chap, with dark hair?"

Sheila nodded.

The little man considered for a minute. "Ah'll tell ye about him," he said at last. "Ye'll do well to get him out of that, if he's a friend of yours." He turned to Sheila with a smile. "If ye'd be so good as to call off your friend with the dog whip?"

He told us that he had travelled out via Paris with Manek, reaching Ventimiglia at about seven o'clock. Manek, he said, had the plates with him. They had taken a car at the station and driven straight out to the Casa Alba; they cannot have missed me on the road by longer than half an hour.

They reached the Casa in time for dinner. He refused to tell us any names or to give any descriptions, but he said that there were seven people there besides himself and Manek, and amongst them he saw Lenden. He didn't have a chance to speak to him. He said that he had a feeling that Lenden was on trial in some way, or under suspicion. They never left him alone for a moment; there was always someone at his elbow. So far as he knew, at this time Manek was still in possession of the plates. After the meal Lenden was taken away by two of the others. Jews, they looked. He was sorry not to have had a chance to speak to him, because he knew that Lenden was a countryman and he had heard that he had done good work for the Soviet in England. He thought that they would have had a lot in common, and might have had a pleasant chat.

After dinner, he was taken into another room and given a passport and one or two other identity papers for his journey into Russia. At about half-past nine they ushered him politely to his bedroom.

He said he wasn't very sleepy. And so he sat in his bedroom and tried to read some seditious literature, printed in French, that he found there, but he wasn't much good at French and didn't get very far with it. At last, for very boredom, he fell asleep.

He was roused by Manek at about two in the morning, who told him to get his things on and come downstairs. They were abandoning ship in the rooms below. News had reached them —Lord knows how—that the house was to be raided at dawn, and they were packing up. There were more people about than he had seen before—country people, he said they looked like, and that was very puzzling to him. He knew nothing of the smuggling side of it, I think. Manek told him the position, gave him his final instructions for the next stage of his journey into Russia, and told him that a car was ready to take him to San Remo, where he would be met.

He spoke to Lenden before he went. Lenden was standing in the hall, unmoved among the flurry, watching the work of departure. Nitter had gone up to him to greet him and to say good-bye. He was sorry that they hadn't had the chance of a talk.

"You going into Russia?" Lenden had inquired.

Nitter had replied that it would be a great experience, and one which he had looked forward to for many years. Lenden had smiled at him queerly.

"You want to live there some time, like I did," he said. "Jolly country, when you get to know it really well. You may like it."

That was all, but something in the way he spoke upset Nitter rather, and made him a little uneasy. He wasn't quite sure that Lenden meant what he said. Then the car was ready for him, and he had driven off straight into the arms of Fazzini's patrol three miles down the road, who had turned the car round and brought him back up the hill to Lanaldo.

That was all he had to tell us, and I think it was true.

"Gosh," said Stenning. "The sooner we get after them the better."

He swung round upon Fazzini, but the Italian needed no gingering. Already he was barking out little short sentences that were orders, and men were slipping out of the room to his obedience. His Field-Marshal might follow in our tracks when he arrived; so far as Fazzini was concerned that house was going to be raided within the hour.

His force of Fascisti paraded in the square. It took some time to get them out to parade, in spite of all his efforts—they must all have been in bed—but I liked the look of them when they came. They were a fine, straight body of young men, dressed in field-green breeches and black shirts and each armed with a sort of truncheon. There were about thirty of them with three officers; the officers seemed to be distinguished mainly by the addition of an automatic pistol in a holster at the belt.

The place was about three kilometres distant from the town. Fazzini gave us the first couple of men to turn up on parade as guides, explaining that he intended to double the main body most of the way to the house as soon as he got them out on to parade. Stenning, Sheila, and I set off with our guides at a walking pace; we had arranged with Fazzini that we would halt and wait for the main body a few hundred yards short of the house. I wasn't up to doubling that night.

It was a warm, starry night, and getting on towards dawn.

Our way led out through the cavernous passages of that town and down the hill-side by a paved mule track through the olives. We went almost entirely in silence—God only knows what each of us was thinking. Stenning had no particular object except a vague friendship for Lenden, and a great feeling that he must see the end of this show. Sheila, I think, had very little concern but for me; I only knew that she kept very close to me all the way, and whenever there was a bit of scrambling to be done she was there to help me. I had been a bachelor for so many years that I didn't quite know what to do about that, and for the most part I did my scrambling unaided.

And for myself—if I was thinking of anything at all I was thinking of Mollie Lenden in that shop at Winchester, and how I should face her if this thing went wrong.

Half-way to the Casa there was a clatter of feet on the mule track behind us. We drew in to the side, and Fazzini's platoon came swinging down the path past us at the double, Fazzini at the head. He dropped out as he passed and had a word or two with us. Some of the smugglers, for whose return he had put off the time of the raid, had come into the town before he left. They had told him that everybody was leaving the Casa Alba. One party of Russians had already started across the frontier by the hill paths, guided by a couple of men from the town.

He swung off down the road after his vanishing platoon, and we followed at the best speed we could.

We came out at last on the main road running up the valley, and followed it in the thick dust for half a mile or so to the north. Then, as we came round the spur of a little hill, one of the guides said something to us, and pointed.

The house was a few hundred yards away, standing a little above the road on the slope of a hill. In that dim light it seemed to be a long, low, white plastered place, with a long piazza before the doors and windows of the front. The rooms were uncurtained and brilliantly lit up, great shafts of light running out into the gardens between the stone pillars of the piazza.

We pressed on. Already there must have been a little light

in the sky, I think, for I can remember that that house was standing in a most beautiful garden. A garden full of yellow mimosa and paved walks, and a little stream that ran through it in cascades down the hill. I wondered who the woman was who had cared for it.

We passed a couple of Fascist sentries at the gate, and pressed on to the floor. It stood open for our approach, showing a very wide, empty hall paved with great square slabs of red and white marble like a chessboard, roughly smoothed and unpolished. There was nobody to be seen.

One or two papers rustled across the marble floor as we went in.

CHAPTER NINE

ON THE RIGHT of the hall as we went in there was a door, leading into a dining-room. I paused on the threshold and looked in. The lights were all on, flooding the room with light, but the room was deserted. There was an unfinished meal on the table and places for about ten people, in great disorder.

We went on down the hall. From a side passage we heard the sound of voices, and we pressed on till we came to a room that was full of a light blue smoke and an acrid smell. Fazzini was there with a couple of his officers and a few men; they seemed to be holding a court over a white-faced, contemptuous stranger, held in the grasp of a couple of Fascists. One of them was going through his pockets.

Stenning barked a question or two at Fazzini, got a few short replies, and turned to me.

"This is the last of them," he said. "The only one they found in the house. Burning things." And I saw that the ornate, square stove that stood out in the middle of the room was full of charred paper. There was a great safe by the door, open and empty but for one or two ledgers and a little stack of printed matter.

I moistened my lips. "Ask him what's happened to Lenden."

Stenning spoke rapidly to Fazzini. The Italian answered him at some length. Then Stenning spoke to the prisoner.

The man smiled, and said nothing.

For a minute Stenning and the Italian stood there motionless, staring threateningly at the prisoner. The deadlock was evident. Then Fazzini said something, apparently in explanation.

"By God," said Stenning harshly, "then we'll ruddy well *make* him talk." He spoke rapidly with Fazzini for a minute. The Italian smiled, and shrugged his shoulders. I don't think physical violence to a prisoner was much in his line, though he was willing to give us all the assistance that he could.

Stenning stepped forward threateningly, and spoke to the prisoner again. I heard the words "Il Capitano Lenden, l'Inglese", followed by a few more words. He paused for a moment, and repeated the question very slowly and distinctly.

The man gave a little contemptuous laugh—and Stenning's fist crashed straight into his face with the whole weight of his body behind it. The prisoner was thrown backwards with his guards against the wall, coughing and streaming blood. I have never seen a more brutal blow struck.

Fazzini stirred uneasily, and said something in Italian. Stenning turned to reply, and if ever I saw the devil in a man's eyes it was then. He said something harshly to Fazzini, who seemed to acquiesce, and then he swung round on Sheila and myself.

"You'd better get out of the room if you don't like it," he snarled. "We can't stay here all the bloody night. I want to know what's become of Maurice, and this fancy man's going to tell me in a minute." He turned to me, and jerked his head to the door. "Get the girl out of the room."

He swung back to where the prisoner was still spitting by the wall. I turned to Sheila. "Come on, dear," I said. But she stood rigid in the doorway, her face very white and set.

"That beast!" she said. "Peter, you can't let this go on."

I met her eyes. "Yes, I can," I replied. "If he won't tell us what's happened, it's probably something pretty sticky. Stenning's quite right. We can't wait all the ruddy night."

She wavered, and I took her by the arm and led her away down the passage to that empty dining-room. There was a bottle of some red wine there, half-emptied; I poured out a glass for her and made her drink it. We said nothing to each other, but after a little she began to busy herself with re-arranging the coat about my bandaged arm.

In an incredibly short space of time Stenning was with us again, followed by Fazzini and one or two of his men. "That fancy man wants a new arm," he said harshly. "I've gone and broken that one for him."

I felt Sheila stir beside me, but I touched her on the shoulder. "What about Lenden?"

He wiped his bleeding knuckles absently upon his trousers. "Lenden got away about an hour ago," he said. "An hour to an hour and a half. He took the plates with him—managed to get hold of them in the confusion, when they had the safe open. And shot off for the hills."

"D'you know which way he went?"

Stenning jerked his thumb eastwards. "That way. Fazzini says there's a hill path over to Rocchetta that way—in the next valley to this. That's the way he's gone."

"D'you *know* that?"

"Yes. Half an hour after he'd got away they got news here that someone had seen him on that path. A couple of these Russians went after him then—maybe three-quarters of an hour ago. They're not back yet." He paused. "Manek—a chap called Manek was one of them. That's the name that Trades Union bloke was talking about, isn't it?"

I nodded. "A big chap with a fat white face, I think. He's a gunman."

"Probably," said Stenning. "Anyone here got a gun?"

I tugged my old automatic clumsily out of my pocket. "You'd better take this thing," I said. "It'll be more good with you than with me."

He took it, and stood for a moment in thought. "We'll get Fazzini to wake up the Rocchetta crowd on the telephone," he said. "Then we'd best push on up the hill after Mr. Ruddy Manek, and have a look what he's up to."

He swung round to Fazzini, and they talked rapidly together for a minute. One of the officers joined them, and then we were all back in that room with the safe, where a weeping man with a hideously battered face and helpless arms was being roughly tended by his Fascist guards. One of the officers stood to the telephone on the wall. In a minute or two he said something.

"Still working," said Stenning. "That's all right. Now we'd better get away up that hill, and pretty damn quick." He swung round on me. "What about you and Miss Darle? D'you think you can keep up?"

Sheila broke in. "We'll try. Give us a man as a guide to stay with us in case we drop behind."

"Right," said Stenning, and swung round into a brisk conversation with Fazzini.

With Sheila's help I slipped off my overcoat and jacket, and started on that walk in my cardigan. Sheila left her overcoat. Already the light was growing in a cloudless sky; in another hour the sun would be up. It was going to be a hot day on the hills.

We started from the house immediately—six Fascists and ourselves. Stenning and Fazzini marched at the head, Sheila and I brought up the rear. They set the devil of a pace up that hill. All the Italians were as hard as nails; Stenning was in fine training, and Sheila can outwalk most men that I know. I was the one who felt it most. I dare say I was as fit as any of them normally, but I was very tired and the exertion played hell with my arm and fingers. Still, I managed to keep up.

The track led straight up the hill-side from the Casa, winding up among the olives and the carnations. We went straight up at a five-mile-an-hour walk, and as we went the dawn lightened upon us so that in half an hour it was light. By the time we had left the terraces and were pressing on up one of the spurs of Monte Verde the path had shrunk to a foot-track that made us walk in single file.

That country was all pine trees and rosemary. It was cool walking in the early morning, and we made fine speed over the ground. Presently we topped one of the spurs and got a view of the mountainous country to the north and east; it was at this point that the sun rose upon us. Over the foot-hills to the right there was a wide expanse of steely, misty sea, just beginning to show up.

I had thought that we should dip down into the opposite valley for Rocchetta there, but the path went winding on up the side of Monte Verde in a more gentle incline. Soon we came to a place of grassy slopes, and the path began to wind along the hill on the edge of a set of miniature precipices, thirty or forty feet deep. It was sinuous here, so that one would round a spur with no knowledge of the path ten yards ahead.

I was getting very tired by then, and the arm was hurting me more than a little. I was plodding along in the rear, intent only on keeping up, when there was a sort of scuffle from the front of the line, a burst of Italian and a good round oath from Stenning. Pressing forward in the clamour, I saw what had happened.

Standing against the rock wall of the path, their hands crooked above their heads, there were two men. A Fascist was standing by them and going through the contents of their pockets, while Fazzini and Stenning held them covered by their automatics and interrogated them in Italian.

They had been coming down the path towards us, and we had run straight into them.

One of the men was very broad in build, but I should not have called him fat. He had a broad, white Mongolian face; a powerful man of his type and something of an athlete. The other one was plainly Italian; I found later that he was a local man.

The Fascist who was searching Manek took from him an automatic pistol; the Russian eyed it phlegmatically as it passed from hand to hand. Stenning slipped out the magazine and glanced into the breech.

"About four shots fired," he said quietly. He smelt the barrel. "And not so long ago." He turned to Fazzini. "You must make the little one talk, Captain," he said in Italian. "This one is no talker."

Fazzini stood closer to the little Italian and began speaking to him, automatic in hand, the barrel pressed close to the prisoner's stomach and waggling a little. I do not know what he was saying, but they were townsmen and one can see the trend. I was watching Manek as he stood there covered by Stenning and I saw his head turn anxiously, perhaps threateningly, to the man beside him. Stenning said something harshly, and the man looked stolidly to his front again.

But by now the little man was talking and gesticulating volubly.

I saw Stenning's face harden to a mask as he jerked his head for me. "They've shot up Maurice," he said curtly. "Shot him up, and left him on the hill. We've got to get on. This chap says he's alive, all right."

There was a sudden cry from one of the Italians who had gone ahead a little way up the path. He was coming back with a black case in his hand, a rectangular black box made of some oxidised metal. I reached out my sound hand and took it from him as he approached. It was closed and intact.

The Russian's eyes were fixed on it intently. "What's that?" asked Stenning.

"The plates," I said. "They must have dropped them back there when they heard us coming." He glanced at me inquiringly, and I shook my head. "They've not been touched, so far as I can see."

"We'd better get along," said Stenning. He jerked his pistol at the Russian. "Get on up that path. And, by God, you give me half a chance and I'll put a bullet in your guts. Get on."

We pressed on up the path, Manek leading with Stenning's pistol hard against the base of his spine. Behind them came Fazzini with the Italian prisoner, walking free and talking all the time. The rest of us followed in a tail. By that time the sun was getting up above the hills and clearing away the mists. In another hour it would be hot.

We carried on like that for half an hour or so longer. Then we came out upon the true shoulder of the hill; before us lay the valley of the Nervia with Rocchetta below. The path went level here and crossed a couple of little grassy swards among the pines. And in this place we came to a little ten-foot cliff below the path that dropped down to a glade of rosemary and brush, a little sort of cup with a grass floor that trended away down the hill below. The guide stopped, and said something.

"This is the place," said Stenning quietly.

And there, at last, we found him.

He had been shot upon the path, because we found blood

there. And then he had rolled, or they had tipped him over the edge of this little cliff into the bushes below. He had crawled forward a little way from the rock face and he was lying face downwards on a patch of grass. I saw him raise his head and stir a little at the sound of our voices, and the clatter of the two Italians who were scrambling down to him.

Stenning swung round to the remaining Fascists and pointed to Manek with his gun. "Guard him well," he said harshly in Italian, "for, by the Mother of God, if that man dies he hangs for it."

Then we went scrambling down into the little glade.

He had been shot from behind at very close range; each of the three bullets had passed through the upper part of his body. He was fully conscious, and knew us all. Very gently we turned him over and began cutting his clothes away to get to his wounds, and while we were doing that he spoke to me.

"Manek's been to the pictures," he said thickly. "He did it with his little gun."

Sheila sat down beside him, lifting his head and making a pillow for him with a coat that one of the Italians offered her. And then she began wiping the blood and dirt from his face with her handkerchief, brushing the long black hair back from his forehead.

"Manek won't use his little gun again in a hurry, old boy," I said. "We've got him safe up top there."

And as I spoke there was an uproar from the cliff above our heads, and Stenning and I started from the glade. Manek had kicked his guard in the stomach and made a dash for it. He came leaping down the hill towards the valley, some twenty yards from where we stood.

There was a sharp report beside me, and I swung round.

Stenning was leaning against a tree, his face hard set. I saw the smoke curling from the barrel of my automatic, as he steadied his hand against the trunk, and I saw him fire again. That shot flicked the ground by the feet of the running man, but he never stayed.

Stenning fired three shots more, three shots in very quick

succession. I saw the fugitive check for an instant. He seemed to stumble; it was as if he had put his foot on a loose stone. Then he pitched forward on to his face and went slithering face downwards down the steep slope of the hill, till the curve of the ground hid him from our sight.

There was a long sigh beside me. Stenning stood up from the tree and glanced at me.

"That's the end of Mr. Ruddy Manek," he said brutally. And with that, he handed me my gun. He had done with it, and he went back to Lenden in the glade and knelt down beside him.

"Cheer-oh, Maurice," he said quietly. "How's ye're wattle?"

He made a quick examination of his friend, and stood up. He spoke for a minute to Fazzini; I think he was telling him to send a man down to Rocchetta for a doctor. Then he slipped off his golf jacket, took off his shirt, and began very methodically to tear it into bandages.

"Stenning," said Lenden painfully. The other stooped towards him, but did not stop his work. "I don't see how you come in on this."

"Flying for Airways now, old son," said Stenning. "I brought Miss Darle out here yesterday. In a Fifty."

Professional interest flickered for a moment. "Where did you put down? This is the hell of a place for landing."

"Racecourse at Nice," said Stenning. "You want to be careful there, if you're ever using it. They've gone and cut it all up with little drains. You want to put down at this end, right by the rails."

One of the Italians came up there with a little earthenware pot of water that he had got from some spring on the hill. Sheila dipped her handkerchief in it and wiped Lenden's face again, brushing back the long hair that curled down over his forehead. "That's awfully good of you," he said. "It's nice."

His eyes wandered to me. "What's up with your arm?"

I grinned at him. "It's only sprained. I came out here in your Breguet and piled her up on landing. I'm sorry about that."

"You've crashed my kite?"

I nodded. He thought about it for a minute, and then:
"When did you fly last?"

"In the war," I said.

"And you got out here on that Breguet?"

I nodded again. "She got off the ground quite easily. That's the part I had the wind up of, but once that was over I'd only got to sit still till we got here."

He stared at me with wrinkled brows. "Born to be hanged," he muttered weakly. "That's what it is."

He had to stop talking then, because Stenning got busy with his dressings. I was no good in that business with only one hand, and so I stood aside and left it to the others. Then, while that was going on, I walked over the hill to where Manek had been shot.

There were a couple of Fascists beside the body; they said something to me, but I shook my head. He must have been killed instantly. I wondered if in Italy that would be a manslaughter against Stenning.*

When I got back to the little glade the dressing was done. Stenning was on his feet again, his bare hairy arms smeared with blood which he was trying absently to remove with a pad of grass. I walked a little way aside with him. "We'd better get a stretcher of some sort," I said. "He's all right to move?"

He stopped wiping his arms for a moment, and looked me in the eyes. "I wouldn't try it."

There was no wind that morning. On the hill-side it was very still; I could hear the two Italians talking down by Manek, fifty yards away. I can remember standing there and noticing a great scent of rosemary and pines in the warm summer of that day.

"He's dying?"

Stenning didn't answer for a minute, but stood there wiping his arm mechanically, studying the spots of blood upon his skin.

"Yes," he said heavily at last, "he's dying. I don't think

* In the end nothing was done about it at all, and they let him go back to England with me two days later.

he's got a hope in hell unless it's to keep still. And he knows it himself."

And then he told me what was wrong, and what he had done about it. And I agreed with him, and we went back together to the dying man in the glade. Sheila was leaning over and speaking to him, and she motioned me to him as we approached.

He was very much weaker then. I stooped down beside him so that he wouldn't have to raise his voice.

"I'm damn sorry to have let you in on this, Moran," he said: "you shouldn't have come out." And then he said: "You ought to have put me down at the station that night, like I asked you."

"Couldn't do that, old boy," I said quietly. "Not on a night like that."

He shifted a little on his back, and in an instant Stenning was stooping anxiously to help him move. "It's been a rum show," he muttered when he was comfortable. "You've got crashed, and I've got shot up. And nothing gained. The whole thing a ruddy failure." . . . There was a catch of disappointment in his voice. He was getting very weak.

I glanced anxiously at Sheila. Behind the range of his vision she shook her head.

"I don't know about that," I said. "We've got the plates you took of Portsmouth, you know. We took 'em off Manek."

For one moment, I thought he was going to sit up. "You say you've got the plates?"

"You lie still," I said, and reached out for that black case. One of the Italians handed it to me. "They're here, quite all right. The case hasn't been opened."

I put it into his hand so that he could feel it. He lay there fingering it for a moment, and then he handed it back to me.

"Open it up," he said.

I could not have met Sheila's eyes at that moment. I had all that I could do to keep a steady face myself. "D'you want me to expose these chaps?" I asked.

He inclined his head painfully. "There's a little spring catch . . on the end," he said. "A little button."

224

"I've got it now," I said, and lifted off the cover plate.

He was insistent. "Get the plates out, and give them to me one by one," he said.

There was a slide there held by a sort of locking-pin, and underneath the slide there was a thin metal plate covered in black velvet. That pulled out in the same way as the slide, and under it I saw the greenish yellow of the first plate.

I lifted it out of the case and put it in his hand. He laid it on his chest in the bright morning sunlight and played with it for a little, holding it up and turning it about. And presently he laid it down.

"Now the next," he said.

There were twelve plates in that box, each separated from the others by a velvet shield. I gave them to him one by one. He held each one for half a minute or so, turning them all ways to the light and never speaking at all, until we got to the tenth. And then:

"God damn it," he said. "The sun's going in."

The brilliant sunlight of that Italian morning beat down upon us in the glade, drenching the country with its golden glow and drawing the scent out of the rosemary on which he lay. "It's only a little cloud, old boy," I said. "There's lashings of light left to cook these plates."

"That's right," he said faintly. "It was an awfully quick film they used. We had a lot of trouble developing the practice ones."

I handed him the twelfth and last. "That's the lot," I said. "You've got them all there now. The box is empty."

He fingered the last plate for a little, and laid it with the others. "That's a bloody good job done," he sighed.

He was silent for a minute or so. I thought it was the end, but he roused himself again. "You're sure they're cooked all right?" he inquired. "It's getting so dark."

"They're done all right, old boy," I said. "You've made a proper job of it."

He sighed again. "Well, bust them up," he said.

So I laid them together on the grass beside him and cracked

them into very small pieces with the handle of my automatic. And the sound of the tinkling glass reassured him a bit, I think, because:

"Miss Darle," he whispered. "I want to speak to Miss Darle."

Sheila bent over him. "I'm here, Captain Lenden," she replied, and wiped his face very gently with the water.

"That's nice," he said, and then he began to speak to her about his wife. And what he said was no concern of ours, nor has it any place in this account. It didn't take very long, and at the end of it he said:

"You'll tell her that?"

Very gently Sheila brushed the hair back from his forehead. "Why, yes, I'll tell her that. But there isn't any need, you know. She knows it all already."

He sighed. "I know she does. But I want you to tell her again. Just that it's all—all right."

He closed his eyes as if for sleep, but presently he opened them again and said "Moran". And I bent towards him.

"How did you come to crash my kite?"

"Doing a slow turn when I was coming in to land, old boy," I said. "Something went wrong with it, and we spun into the deck from about three hundred."

His voice had grown very faint. "You want to watch those slow turns on the Breguet," he said. I had to put my ear practically to his lips to catch the words.

There was silence, and then he said: "You don't want to use the rudder at all . . . hardly. Just the bank. And keep her nose stuffed down a bit and she'll go round . . . nicely."

About five minutes after that he died.

APPENDIX

So to the end. I have little more to add to this account, except two letters, which I think can hardly be omitted.

Six weeks after my return from Italy a raid was carried out upon Soviet House. A great mass of correspondence was examined and a selection of this material, dealing with matters of general interest, was made available to the public in a White Paper. Of the remainder, two letters were found to bear directly on the death of Maurice Lenden, and were brought to the notice of Lord Arner in connection with my own Statement. It is to be regretted that it has not proved possible to publish these interesting documents in their entirety.

The first letter is dated April 20th, 1927, and is signed, Ast. Strokoff. It is addressed from 132, Twenty-Seventh Avenue, New York, and a portion of it reads:

. . . In regard to the letters mentioned in your cable as being of especial importance, I have good reason to believe that everything was destroyed by Comrades Soller and Manek. I left the house and crossed the frontier with the others earlier in the night, so that I can say nothing definite about this. I shall be sending with Comrade Ogden a sworn statement upon the death of Manek, and I suggest that you should prepare a campaign of questions about this in the English Parliament as soon as he arrives. Comrade Jack Atterley, M.P. would be a good man to take this up, and you should write an article about it for the Worker. *The facts are that Comrade Manek was foully murdered in cold blood by the man Stenning, who shot him repeatedly through the body while he was held prisoner by the Fascisti. I am urging Comrade Ventoli to press this matter in Italy, but it is necessary to work more carefully in that country*

than in England, owing to the injustice of their despotic government. . . .

.The extract from the second letter is quite short. It is dated from Moscow, April 22nd, 1927, and is signed by Sanarowa, Minister of Internal Preparation. As a memorial, I think it may not be altogether unworthy of the man:

. . . As for the airman, Maurice Lenden, this man proved difficult and uncertain in temper from the first, and by no means devoted to the Soviet doctrine. In the end he proved weak and treacherous beyond all belief, and has been the occasion of a considerable set-back to our activities in Europe. It is recommended that no further confidence be placed in renegades of this description. . . .